PROVIDENCE

The Weird of Hali

Novels by John Michael Greer

The Weird of Hali:

I – Innsmouth

II – Kingsport

III – Chorazin

IV – Dreamlands

V – Providence

VI – Red Hook

VII – Arkham

Others:

The Fires of Shalsha

Star's Reach

Twilight's Last Gleaming

Retrotopia

The Shoggoth Concerto

The Nyogtha Variations

A Voyage to Hyperborea

The Seal of Yueh Lao

Journey Star

The Witch of Criswell

PROVIDENCE

The Weird of Hali

Book Five

John Michael Greer

Published in 2023 by
Sphinx Books
London

British Library Cataloguing in Publication Data

A C.I.P. for this book is available from the British Library

ISBN-13: 978-1-91257-395-0

Typeset by Medlar Publishing Solutions Pvt Ltd, India

www.aeonbooks.co.uk/sphinx

Prim houses slumber on the ancient height
Where dancers once defied the Pilgrims' ire,
Leaping and coupling 'round Walpurga's fire,
Hailing the coming of the vernal night.
They called it Merry Mount in days long gone,
Before the laws of frightened men prevailed,
The maypole toppled and the music failed.
The name is whispered now, the dance is done.
The hill remains. Beneath it, in a gloom
Unbroken by the years, untouched by light,
Strange presences endure the earth's cold night.
They shall not sleep forever in their tomb:
For what danced, joyous, under olden skies
Shall waken, and in dreadful wrath shall rise.

                    —"Merry Mount" by Justin Geoffrey

CONTENTS

CHAPTER 1

THE WIND FROM THE SEA

"This is so lovely," said Laura Merrill.

The parlor in which she stood might not, to another's glance, have merited the praise. Plain plastered walls and ceiling; a hardwood floor with more than a century's worth of scars and stains not entirely obscured by sandpaper and wax polish; a sturdy but well-worn sofa along one wall, two well-stocked bookshelves on another, and a pair of armchairs flanking the cast iron Franklin stove on the third; a braided rag rug on the floor, of a style more usually found in the hill country of western New York; two framed lithographs above the sofa showing sailing vessels, the brig *Hetty* and the barque *Sumatra Queen*; a big bow window on the fourth wall, looking out onto a typical New England streetscape gilded with the light of a summer afternoon: it could have been any of a hundred Victorian-era houses in witch-haunted Arkham.

Her husband Owen didn't argue, though. "And ours," he said, matching her smile with one of his own. Then: "You should probably sit down."

"I know." Her smile faltered. "That's going to take some getting used to."

She went to the sofa and sat, the movement still too fluid for human legs to imitate but not quite so graceful or easy as it had been a decade before. She was as beautiful as when they'd first met, Owen thought, brown eyes and curling brown hair and olive skin tinged with the green of the Deep Ones, and the salt scent all the folk of Innsmouth had, ringing changes on a decade of memories. "Care for a beer?" he asked her.

"Please. I think I could use one. Just being here, where I can smell the sea on the wind—"

He smiled again, went down the hallway to the kitchen.

By the time he came back with a glass in each hand, footsteps pattered down the stair from above, and their children came trotting into the room a moment later. Asenath, eight, with violet eyes, her mother's brown curly hair, and the coltish look of her age, flung herself belly down on the rug and propped her chin in her hands, facing them. Barnabas, five, blue-eyed and sandy-haired as Owen, with the inevitable book under one arm, climbed into one of the armchairs and tucked his feet up beneath him. "Well?" Laura asked.

"This is the nicest house ever," Asenath told her. "When I get older I want to be an alchemist and have a laboratory in the attic. It ought to be full of retorts and alembics and a great big roaring athanor, and it's even got a chimney of its own."

Owen managed to stifle a laugh. "We'll see," Laura said. "Barney?"

Barnabas looked up from his book. "I like my room."

"I'm glad to hear that," said Laura.

The child pondered her for a moment. "I watched seagulls from the window," he said. "Three different kinds."

"Do you know what kinds they were?" Owen asked him.

"No" said Barnabas, and set aside his book. He slid to the floor, crossed to the bookshelf, pulled out a field guide, and paged through it. "Herring gull, black-backed gull, and laughing gull," he said, then returned to the armchair and his book. Laura gave Owen an amused glance; Owen smiled in return, raised his glass, and clinked it against hers, then drank.

As he lowered the glass, a knock sounded at the front door. Laura gave him a puzzled look and said, "I wonder who that could be."

He turned to his daughter and said, "Sennie, can you get that?"

"Sure thing," she said, scrambled to her feet and headed for the entry. The lock clattered, and then she said, "Oh, hi." Louder: "Mom, Dad, it's Mr. and Mrs. Shray."

Laura gave Owen a startled look and tried to stand up, but he put a hand on her shoulder and pressed her gently back down onto the sofa, saying, "Don't you dare."

"But—"

"They know. Relax."

He got up off the sofa, went to greet his guests. Larry Shray was short and stocky and Asian—his real name was Shray Lharep, though few people in Arkham knew that—and his wife Patty, Polish-American by origin, had straight brown hair and a plump smiling face. Both of them were carrying big stainless steel pans covered with plastic wrap, and Larry had his perched on a stout cardboard box lettered in an ornate and elegant southeast Asian script. "So this is the place," Larry said, looking around with a broad grin. "Sweet. Where should we put these?"

The pans went onto the kitchen table, the box into a hastily cleared space on the bottom shelf of the refrigerator. "It's so good to see you again, Laura," said Patty, as she came back into the parlor. "I hope moving wasn't too much of a strain."

"No, not at all," Laura said. "How's Evan?"

"In Buffalo for the summer," said Patty. "We wanted him to spend time with his Tcho-Tcho relatives and learn their traditions." She smiled. "He didn't take much convincing. He thinks Grandma Pakheng is the most wonderful old lady on the planet."

"I don't know that I'd argue with him," Owen allowed.

Larry laughed. "She asked me to find out how you were doing and bring her blessings, so I gather that the feeling's mutual."

Just then another knock sounded on the door. Laura gave Owen a startled look, but he turned to Asenath. "Sennie—"

"I'll get it." She headed for the entry, opened the door. "Hi!" In a raised voice: "Mom, Dad, it's Mr. Martense and Robin."

Owen turned back to Laura, to find her looking at him in bafflement. "Didn't they have housewarming parties in Innsmouth?" he asked.

She processed that. "People didn't move much," she said finally, "and when it happened, you just settled in."

"In Arkham they do things a little differently." With a smile: "Don't you worry about a thing. There'll be plenty of food and drink, courtesy of our guests." He got to his feet again. "So you probably ought to finish that beer."

* * *

Justin Martense was better muscled than he'd been when they'd first met eight years earlier, life on a working farm had seen to that, but he still had the barley-colored hair and the mismatched eyes, one ice-blue, the other dark brown, he'd inherited along with his ancestors' strange destiny. His son Robin, not quite eight, had managed to miss out on the family eyes. His were pale, and his hair not so much blond as color-less; his face, thin and high-cheekboned, looked only a little like Justin's. He greeted everyone and then flopped on the rug next to Asenath, and the two of them were deep in conversation within moments.

"I'll have you know," said Justin, when he came back into the parlor from the kitchen, "that Aunt Josephine sent four dozen butter rolls, meatballs in gravy, *and* her special au gratin potatoes, along with her love. Arthur and Rose Wheeler send their love also, and a couple of other things that are still outside—I'll be right back." He headed for the door just as another knock sounded.

Asenath sprang up and went to get it. "Hi! Mom, Dad, it's Dr. Akeley."

Professor Miriam Akeley was silver-haired and thin as a heron, with a big shoulderbag slung from one elbow. Introductions followed—she hadn't met Justin or Robin before, though Patty and Larry were old friends—and she settled onto the couch as Justin headed back out. "I hope you're doing well," she said to Laura.

"More or less. Standing isn't as easy as it used to be, but that's no surprise. And you?"

"Better than I have any right to be," said Miriam. "Before the food and drink come out, I wanted to give the two of you this." She opened her shoulderbag, pulled out a manila envelope, and handed it to Laura, who opened it. Inside was a stack of maybe two hundred sheets of paper. Laura turned the pages one at a time with an expression of increasing astonishment.

Finally, without a word, she handed the stack of papers to Owen, who paged through the first dozen or so sheets and said, "This has to be the most complete version of the *Pnakotic Manuscript* I've ever seen."

"It ought to be," said Miriam. "It's a translation of the original in the temple at Ulthar, and I discussed all the uncertain points with the patriarch Atal."

By the time she had finished saying those words, Owen and Laura were both staring at her. "This is unbelievably precious," said Laura then. Turning: "Patty, Larry, you'll want to have a look at this."

While they were leafing through it, murmuring quietly to one another, Justin came back in with a box and a bundle teetering unsteadily in his arms. "This," he said, presenting the bundle to Laura, "is from Rose Wheeler, and this—" He handed Owen the box. "—is from Arthur."

The bundle proved to be a handmade quilt, bed-sized, in a dozen shades of blue and gray and green that rippled like waves. The box disgorged a great deal of shredded paper, and then a statue of the Great Old One Cthulhu, nearly two feet tall, exquisitely carved from driftwood still scented with the sea. Both were passed around and praised, and even Barnabas extracted himself from his book long enough to come over, give the statue of Cthulhu a long solemn look, and say, "I like that," before returning to the armchair.

When everyone had admired the quilt and the statue, and everyone but the children and Justin had pondered the Pnakotic Manuscript—"way over my head," Justin said with a quick lopsided grin—Owen bundled up the gifts and took them to the master bedroom off the hallway: the dining room originally, but Laura couldn't climb stairs without pain. Returning, he said, "I think it's probably time to break out the food and drink."

"Is this the lot of us?" Patty asked.

"I sent out some other invites," said Owen, "but I don't know if they'll show. It's a busy time for a lot of people."

Justin gave him a questioning look. "Jenny?"

Owen nodded, and Justin pasted on a smile and headed for the kitchen. Robin followed; Barnabas slid down from the armchair, put his book away, and trotted after, just ahead of the general exodus. Owen waited, standing in the doorway.

Asenath scrambled to her feet, but stayed behind and went to Miriam Akeley. "Dr. Akeley," she said, "they're all still fine, and starting to eat solid food."

"Your charges?"

Asenath nodded, beaming.

"I'm impressed," said Miriam. "Not surprised, mind you, but impressed." Asenath turned as pink as her olive complexion would permit. "Later on, I'll want to see them," Miriam went on, "and we'll need to talk about where they're going to go, now that they're ready to be weaned."

The girl swallowed visibly, but nodded.

Miriam got up and turned to Laura. "Can I get you something?"

"Oh, I'll get Mom's food," Asenath said. "I know what she likes."

"Go easy on the chob yizang, dear," Laura told her.

"It's good for you, Mom," Asenath said, and turned toward the kitchen.

Just then another knock sounded on the door. Asenath reversed course and trotted to the entry. The door opened and closed, and voices sounded, low. Then Asenath reappeared, beaming even more broadly than before. "Mom, Dad, it's Aunt Jenny."

"Hi, Miriam. Hi, Owen," said the woman who followed her into the parlor: thin and plain, with a mop of mouse-colored hair. "Hi, Laura. Don't you dare get up."

"I can still stand," Laura protested.

"Let's keep it that way," said Jenny Chaudronnier. She settled onto the couch as Miriam and Asenath headed for the kitchen. "Charlotte and Alain send their regrets—they've got way too much to do before we head for Boston and the ship to France first thing tomorrow, and Geoffrey's still being colicky." She looked up at Owen. "Ready?"

"No," Owen said with a grin. "But that's never stopped me before."

That got an unwilling smile from Jenny. "True enough. I hope you don't mind if I don't stay long. I've got some preparations to make, too, but I wanted to see the new place and say hi to everyone, and we've got some things to talk about."

"Let me get some food," said Owen, "and you'll have my undivided attention." Just then, another knock sounded on the door.

* * *

Owen's study was on the second floor near the stair, close enough that he and Jenny could hear the voices of the guests in the crowded parlor below, but its windows looked out over the garden in back. The fences between the separate yards had all been taken out, since every house in the block—rundown rental housing until that spring—had been quietly purchased by Innsmouth folk, and the Knights of Pythias Hall at the far end, sold off long ago by that elderly and dignified fraternal society, was being refitted for the purposes of a very different order. Evening light splashed over bare soil and stepping stones, and here and there vegetables, herbs, and flowers sprouted, put in by families that had moved in before the Merrills.

"Laura looks as happy as I've ever seen her," Jenny said.

Owen nodded. "Dunwich could never really be home—not that far from the ocean. We've got a lot of friends there, and we'll go back to visit as often as we can, but the wind from the sea matters to her." He shook his head. "We'd have gone back to Innsmouth if there'd been any point to it. As it is—" He shrugged.

"I haven't been there," Jenny said. "How bad is it?"

"A mess. The other side did a lot of damage after Laura's people fled, and there's been ten years of storms and rising seas since then. Most of what used to be standing has fallen in. Laura and I went up there last autumn."

"That must have been hard for her."

"For both of us," said Owen. Then: "Any word yet from Europe?"

"Not to speak of." She turned to face him. "One of my cousins from Vyones went to Stregoicavar in May—she just got back a week ago, after some long talks with the lodge elders. They've still got a few documents from the time when Ward went there."

"That's impressive," Owen said, "all things considered."

"Oh, they lost a huge amount. The lodge hall got burned down during the Second World War, and they spent the entire Communist era meeting in living rooms and the like, staying one step ahead of the secret police the whole time. Still, they've got a bunch of old records. Some things were saved from Castle Ferenczy before it was blown up, and I've been in touch with friends in Prague who think they can get me a lead on some of Josef Nadeh's papers. So—" She shrugged. "If Ward sent a copy of the Angell collection to Europe, and copies still exist, I have at least as good a chance of finding them as anybody."

"And if there's a copy in Providence—well, I'll do my best."

"The town's been scoured for it more than once, but it's worth a try."

He nodded. It had taken the two of them years to connect the scattered clues—to link Dr. George Gammell Angell, the eminent Brown University philologist who'd died in 1927, with Charles Dexter Ward, a young man from a wealthy Providence family who'd earned a reputation for eccentricity before he vanished from a mental institution in 1928 and was never seen again. The two had known each other socially, that was easy enough to discover, but to find out that the younger man had spent long evenings consulting with the elder all through 1926 was another matter. That only came out by way of a letter from Angell to a colleague of his at Miskatonic University, Dr. Albert Wilmarth, and it had taken months of patient digging through boxes of old documents that the Wilmarth estate had donated to Orne Library to unearth a cryptic diary entry that told them the thing they most needed to know:

July 18, 1926
Arrived Providence 6:18 p.m. Met GGA and CDW for dinner—talked about Kh. legends, N'con, etc. GGA much better informed about all this than I'd realized. Warned him about Yellow Sign. Has collection of Aklo spells unlike anything in N'con—says he got them in an underground place, but wouldn't say where. Says they could summon Kh. from R. Warned him

> to be careful. CDW to get his papers if any-
> thing happens. Tried to talk him into burn-
> ing them, and he laughed. Hope he doesn't
> regret it.

Owen and Jenny had looked up at the same moment from the yellowing pages of the diary, and given each other wide-eyed glances. If those papers had survived ...

"You've made all the arrangements?" Jenny said then. Outside, gulls wheeled over the garden, and lights flickered on in windows here and there.

Owen nodded. "It was kind of hectic, in the middle of moving, but yes."

"If you need to postpone the trip—"

A firm shake of his head denied it. "Not a chance. Laura and the kids will be fine—this whole block is full of Innsmouth folk now, the next block's mostly Starry Wisdom people from Dunwich and Chorazin, and of course we've got plenty of friends in Kingsport." With a sudden grin: "Unless the Pnakotic Manuscript has everything we need. Have you seen Miriam's new translation?"

"I got my copy a few days ago," said Jenny. "It's got some astonishing things in it, but not that. On the other hand, if you ever want to summon the dark young of Shub-Ne'hurrath or make the Hounds of Tindalos turn aside from their prey, that's an option."

"Seriously?"

"Seriously. Do you know what Miriam's working on next? A complete edition and translation of the *Seven Cryptical Books of Hsan*, with the patriarch Atal's commentary, and all the passages from the seventh book that have been lost in the waking world." She shook her head. "Turn a scholar loose in the Dreamlands, I suppose that's what you can expect."

"I don't know of anything in the *Seven Books* that bears on Great Cthulhu," said Owen.

"Nor I. She might surprise us, but the Angell papers really are our best bet."

"I know," Owen said.

Out beyond the study windows, the evening turned gray, and great clouds billowed up over the Atlantic ten miles off. One of the clouds just then reminded Owen of the wooden statue he'd taken into the master bedroom: the great bulbous arc of the head, the multiple eyes, the tentacles streaming down below.

"I know," he repeated. "If we're going to wake the Dreaming Lord, that's the key."

* * *

By the time night wrapped close around the house, the party had settled down to two children and four adults—the other adult guests had gone their assorted ways, and Barnabas, having systematically cleared every dish from the parlor, gotten them into the sink with the aid of a footstool, and given an oddly formal hug and kiss to his parents, headed upstairs with his book under his arm. Laura and Miriam sat on the sofa, discussing the Pnakotic Manuscript; Owen and Justin settled into the armchairs, and talked about the doings of mutual friends in upstate New York; and Asenath and Robin sat on the carpet, playing Chinese checkers.

All at once Asenath looked at the clock, jumped up, said, "I'll be right back," and headed for the kitchen, returning a moment later with a glass of milk, an eyedropper, and a banana. Miriam said, "When you've fed them, Sennie, you should probably bring them down here."

Asenath swallowed visibly, nodded, and hurried up the stairs.

Justin gave Owen a questioning look, and Owen laughed. "Kyrrmis," he said. "You know about the breeding project, right?"

"Not much more than the fact that it exists," Justin admitted.

"We found three more in Maine this February," Miriam said. "Two in good shape, and a third, female, very pregnant, and very sick. She was carrying triplets, which is as rare for kyrrmis as it is for humans, and ..." She shrugged. "The short version is that we lost her during the birth, and nobody thought we were going to be able to save any of the pups, but Asenath volunteered to try to raise them. She's helped with them before."

"I should probably mention that Miriam is—would 'head of the kyrrmi committee' be too formal?" said Owen.

"Quite a bit too formal," Miriam replied. "There's maybe two dozen of us who breed them these days, and I've had one longer than anyone else, that's all."

"If you want the last word in persistence," Laura said then, "you want an eight-year-old. Sennie literally got up every hour all night to feed them for the first three months after they were born. I honestly think she kept them alive through sheer stubbornness."

"I get that," said Justin, with his lopsided smile.

A long moment of silence fell, and then Robin, who had been looking increasingly uncomfortable, turned to his father and said, "Dad, it's getting kind of tough."

Justin glanced at Owen, who nodded and said, "Sure." Justin nodded to his son, who let out a long ragged breath and visibly relaxed. As he did so, his arms and legs split and splayed outward; what had appeared to be nondescript clothing dissolved into unhuman shapes, and within moments he had turned into a softly writhing mass of ropy tentacles from which pale eyes emerged and vanished at intervals.

"You're getting very good at holding a human shape, Robin," Owen observed.

Something that was not a mouth managed a recognizable smile. "Thanks, Mr. Merrill."

"His mother is the Black Goat of the Woods," Justin said to Miriam, "and—well, sometimes the children of the Great Old Ones turn out this way."

"So I've read," said Miriam, who appeared entirely unfazed by the spectacle.

Time passed and conversations twined around themselves, and finally footsteps sounded on the stair. A moment later Asenath came back into the parlor. She glanced at the writhing shape Robin had become, but seemed no more startled than Miriam had been. In the flat cardboard box she carried, curled up on a blue towel, were three brown-furred animals who looked a little like small rats. A second glance showed flat faces like a monkey's; large forward-facing eyes; paws with opposed thumbs, like little pink hands; odd proportions, not quite like rats but not quite like anything else. One had visible canines and a first slight trace of a beard; all three were dozing, and their bellies rose and fell with their breath.

Everyone clustered around the box as Asenath brought it to the couch and set it between her mother and Miriam. "You've done an amazing job, Sennie," Miriam said. "Which is the poor little one we didn't think would live out the night? I honestly can't tell."

Asenath gently touched one of the creatures who lay curled up in a corner, a little smaller than the others. "This one. She's really done well."

"She has indeed," said Miriam. She glanced at Owen and Laura, then back to Asenath. "The kyrrmi committee, as your father termed it, had a discussion about these three. You know that kyrrmis have to go to witches and initiates who need familiars." Asenath closed her eyes and nodded. "But we wouldn't have even one of these to give out if you hadn't worked so hard to keep them with us, and so we've all agreed that you can choose one of them for your own."

Asenath's eyes snapped wide open, and she burst into tears and flung her arms around Miriam, mumbling something incomprehensible. A moment later, though, she drew back, and turned to Owen and Laura. "Mom, Dad," she asked with wavering voice, "May I?"

"We've already discussed it with Dr. Akeley, dear," said Laura, "and yes, you may."

Asenath burst into tears again and gave each of her parents a hug, then turned to the box. After a long moment, she lifted the smallest of the three out of the corner where it slept, and cradled it against her shoulder. It blinked sleepily up at her and let out a soft chirring sound. "This one," she said. "I'll call her Rachel."

"We'll arrange for the others to go to their homes in a few days," Miriam said then. "The initiates who are next on the list both live here in Arkham, so Rachel will be able to visit her brother and sister often—you know how important that is to them."

Asenath made agreeable noises and settled down on the rug again, still cradling the little creature, while Robin talked to her in a quiet voice and stroked the kyrrmi's back with one tentacle. After a while, Asenath got the kyrrmi settled in her lap, where it immediately fell asleep, and they resumed their game of Chinese checkers.

* * *

Later still, Justin said his farewells, woke his drowsing son, and said, "Human form for a bit, Robin. Just 'til we're in the car." The mass of tentacles duly drew together into the shape of an eight-year-old boy, who managed a sleepy good-bye to everyone before Justin scooped him up in one arm and carried him out the door. Asenath thanked Miriam again and burst into yet another round of tears halfway through, then gave her parents goodnight hugs and kisses and headed up the stairs with her box of kyrrmis. That left Owen, Laura, and Miriam, and one more round of drinks before the night wound down.

"I'm not sure if it's even appropriate to mention this," Miriam said, "but have you thought about whether Asenath might like to become a witch?"

"Oh, we've already settled that," said Laura. "She's going to get the training we give children in the Esoteric Order of Dagon, of course, and she'll receive the initiations in due time if she earns them, as I'm sure she will—but yes. She's been fascinated by witchcraft since she was small, and Martha Price has agreed to take her as an apprentice."

"That's good to hear," said Miriam. "Martha—is that Abigail Price's granddaughter?"

"Yes," said Owen. "Did you know Abby Price?"

"Only briefly," Miriam admitted. "She taught Jenny, of course, and Jenny introduced us about six months before Abigail passed away. I wish I'd had more of a chance to get to know her. A very interesting person."

"True enough," said Owen. "Martha studied with her for the last fifteen years she was alive, and we've arranged for Sennie to study with another witch over in upstate New York, a woman I know named Betty Hale, when she's finished her apprenticeship and it's time for her to learn from someone else."

"I'm very glad to hear that," said Miriam. "The kyrrmi committee, as you called it, has been talking quite a bit for the last year or so about the possibilities once witches and their familiars can be trained together."

"I think she'll go very far," Laura said.

"And Barney's doing well?" Miriam asked then. "I know you were a little concerned."

"A little," Laura admitted, "but we've figured out what's going on."

"I have no idea what they call it now," Owen added. "When I was in school it was called Aspergers syndrome." Miriam gave him a startled look, and he smiled. "He'll do fine. He's so smart he's scary. Did you happen to notice the book he was reading?"

"No," she admitted.

"Bulfinch's *Mythology*."

Miriam's mouth dropped open. "He's five years old!"

"I know," said Owen. "We've been talking it over, story by story, as he reads it, and he understands most of it. Like I said, scary."

"He just needs a little more structure than Sennie," Laura said, "and a little more help figuring out how to deal with people. He's probably going to be quite the scholar by the time he's grown up."

"We could use more of those," Miriam admitted. "I hope Miskatonic will still be around when he's ready for college."

That called up a moment of silence. "How bad is it?" Owen asked.

"We've got enough funding to keep going through fall semester," Miriam admitted, "and probably spring, but I'm not sure how far beyond that we can go. There's not much income these days from the endowment fund, you know as well as I do what kind of shambles the state budget is like, and the students are already paying more than they can afford. We're trying to figure out what we can do, but it really doesn't look good for the long term."

"I'm sorry," said Laura.

Miriam shrugged. "It's not as though we didn't see it coming—and at that, we're better off than a lot of universities these days." She finished her wine, set the glass down. "Good heavens, I had no idea it had gotten this late. Thank you, both of you, for a very pleasant evening." They said their goodbyes, and Owen saw her to the door.

CHAPTER 2

THE ROAD TO PROVIDENCE

Four days later Owen kissed Laura and the children, shouldered an old orange and black Miskatonic University duffel bag, and headed out into the morning. The gambrel roofs of the old town crouched beneath scattered clouds. Off in the middle distance, across the river, the great cyclopean masses of the university campus rose up stark against distant hills. Somewhere not far away, a car's engine struggled to life, uncannily loud, and then choked and sputtered into silence.

Arkham had changed drastically since he'd last lived there, and the time he'd spent in the old downtown district while choosing a house and moving into it had only begun to take the edge off the unfamiliarity. A decade back he'd been a grad student at Miskatonic, before the age-old war between the Great Old Ones and their enemies had swept him away from his familiar world forever. Back then, the few sparks of life Arkham still had were in the university district north of the river, and everything further south had been a case study in urban blight.

Now the tides of change seemed to be flowing the other way. As Owen headed down the long slope of Peabody Avenue toward the river, he passed one old house after another that had curtains in the windows for the first time in many years, and a café and two small shops newly open for business in otherwise empty commercial buildings. The handful of old businesses that had managed to cling to life through the town's long decline, for that matter, looked as though things had turned up for them, too. The venerable First National grocery at the corner of Walnut and College Streets had gotten someone to pressure-wash the brick walls and the old red sign, and the Rexall drugstore on Lich Street, which sold as many colored candles and curious oils as prescription medicines, had clean white siding and a board announcing new hours that were noticeably more expansive than the old ones had been.

It was when he'd crossed the steel bridge across the Miskatonic and the railroad tracks beyond them that the other side of the balance came into view. Ten years back, that end of town had been full of old houses cut up into apartments or enlarged with big ugly additions, with little strip malls and hole-in-the-wall stores here and there selling liquor, takeout food, and the like. Much of the rental housing was empty now, and so were the strip malls and shop spaces. Years of economic crisis and budget shortfalls had left deep marks on the university quarter. Lovecraft Park still had neatly mowed grass, the bronze statue of H.P. Lovecraft himself gazed vaguely off toward the Blasted Heath reservoir west of town as he'd done a decade before, and here and there a house still had residents, but the broader picture was one of spreading decrepitude.

Over it all rose the huge buildings of the Miskatonic campus—the new campus, strictly speaking, for the original campus was south of the river in the old downtown, around a long-neglected quadrangle. The postwar boom of the last century had given the university massive new buildings in what were then the northern outskirts of town, between the great whaleback curve of Meadow Hill and the lower hills further east. Owen hadn't yet been born when the buildings rose, and they'd passed their prime long before he'd taken the bus from Indiana to Massachusetts and seen them for the first time, but he still remembered them as they'd been a decade back, more or less clean and well-maintained. The rundown look and the scattering of boarded-up windows he could see as he paced up Peabody Avenue shocked him.

Still, the campus wasn't his goal. He crossed Curwen Street—the light wasn't working, but there was next to no traffic—and then veered left to Dyer Street and the bus station. That at least hadn't changed much. The little lobby still had a few schedules posted, and the big shelter outside where the buses pulled up still had the uncomfortable metal benches he remembered. He'd already made sure of the schedule that mattered, but he glanced at it again as he passed the lobby: a plain sheet of paper with a black and white logo along the top and a list of times and stops spilling down the Atlantic coast from Arkham to Boston and beyond. That taken care of, he found an empty bench, settled on one end with his duffel beside him, pulled a battered H.P. Lovecraft paperback from one of the duffel's outer pockets, and started to read.

A few county buses pulled up as he sat there, swallowed and disgorged passengers, and headed off to the far corners of Essex County. A sign over one end of the shelter still announced MBTA buses to the light rail station in Salem, but that was a relic of a bygone day—the light rail had to shut down due to budget cuts two years before, and the big white MBTA buses stopped running that far north shortly thereafter. Those who wanted to leave Essex County had to rely on other options now.

The option that mattered to Owen rolled into the station maybe twenty minutes after he got there: an elderly bus that must have been sold off by some urban transit system many years back. It had SARGENT BUS COMPANY on the sides in green paint, and the handlettered sign over the front window read PROVIDENCE VIA BOSTON. Owen was on his feet, shouldering his duffel, before it pulled up to the curb. Half a dozen other passengers got up with him: an elderly black couple, a blonde woman in her thirties with two children in tow, and a young man with olive skin, dark hair, and a face like an Aztec statue, who looked at the paperback in Owen's hand, grinned, and said, "Lovecraft? Cool." Owen gave him an amused glance and nodded.

A moment later the door hissed open. Owen waited his turn and climbed the steps. The driver, old Edith Sargent, nodded to him. She was also the owner; the Sargent Bus Company these days consisted of her, one part-time mechanic, and one bus, running its lonely route along the coast from Newburyport to Providence and back for time out of mind. The company existed primarily for the benefit of the Esoteric Order of Dagon and its members, though it took plenty of other fares these days.

He said, "Hi, Edith," and got a smile in response, then paid the fare for Providence, tossed his duffel into the makeshift luggage rack up above, and sat. The other passengers found unoccupied seats as the bus coughed to life and pulled away toward the street.

* * *

The route headed south out of town on Old Kingsport Road to Kingsport, from there to Beverly, and then followed the old highway through Salem to Boston—I-93 would have been quicker, but a couple of poorly maintained overpasses had fallen down a few years back and neither the state nor the federal government seemed to be able to find the money to fix them. Miles upon miles of rundown suburbs rolled past the window next to Owen, spotted with derelict houses and empty strip malls. More passengers boarded in Lynn and Revere, and then the bus rattled its way into downtown Boston. It stopped outside the battered hulk of South Station, let out a few passengers, and picked up almost twenty more. By the time the last of these boarded and paid their fares, the seat next to Owen's was one of the few that wasn't occupied.

One of the newcomers stopped by the seat and asked Owen, "May I?"

He glanced up at an attractive black woman in her twenties, maybe, in an elegant blue dress, with a child in a hoodie and sweat pants following her, head bowed and hands in pockets. "Sure," said Owen. "I can move to another seat if your child needs one."

"Don't worry about it," she said, sitting down. "Pierre can sit in my lap." She lifted the child up, and he sat in an odd slumped position, head bowed, so that Owen still couldn't see his face. "Thank you," she said then. "I—"

Her voice stopped suddenly. Owen glanced at her, noticed that she was staring at the book in his lap: *The Case of Charles Dexter Ward and Other Stories*. She blinked, shook her head, gave him an apologetic smile, and looked away. Owen considered her for a moment longer, then turned his attention back to the book as the bus lurched into motion again.

From there the southern suburbs of Boston stretched out interminably, a blanket of half-empty malls and battered subdivisions through which the verdant Massachusetts countryside of an earlier day broke through only in occasional patches. As the bus passed a sign pointing the way to Quincy, off to the east, Owen nodded slowly, remembering a scrap of American history that got left out of most textbooks. Merry Mount had been near Quincy, he remembered: Merry Mount, where Thomas Morton defied the Puritans, lived amicably with the native people, and celebrated the festivals of the Great Old Ones on American soil. After the settlement was destroyed, he thought he recalled, some of the survivors had escaped south to Rhode Island. Had any of them taken the same route the bus was following? It was a pleasant thought.

And Joseph Curwen, the famous alchemist of colonial times who'd fled to Providence from Salem at the beginning of the witch panic—had he taken some similar road? Owen imagined him hurrying south on horseback through the forests and scattered farms of colonial Massachusetts, glancing back from time to time at the packhorse carrying the forbidden books he'd found in his European travels. Those books had come down to Charles Dexter Ward, Owen knew, together with certain stranger legacies. Would any of them turn up in the course of Owen's own search? He smiled at the thought, but knew the possibility was there.

Brookline, Dedham, and Norwood slid past. Thereafter the trees of an assortment of state forests and green belts lined the highway at intervals and screened out the twenty-first century for a time, until North Attleboro marked the outskirts of the built-up area around Providence. That had a different flavor to it. The booms and busts of the tech industry that had reshaped so much of the Boston area so drastically had passed the Providence area by, leaving a less raucous architecture largely in possession of the ground.

Finally the bus wound through narrow streets where a clutch of glass and concrete skyscrapers had hatched and burgeoned in some previous decade, and stopped at an open-air transit mall in the middle of downtown. Tall buildings faced the mall across the street on one side, and the trees of a narrow city park rose up on the other. "Providence," Edith Sargent called out needlessly. Owen, who was in no hurry, sat back and finished reading his book while most of the other passengers piled off. Finally, when the aisle was clear, the woman sitting next to him helped her child down, then stood and headed for the exit. Owen unfolded himself from his seat, got his duffel down from the rack above, and followed.

Outside skyscrapers loomed overhead, blotting out masses of sky, and bronze statues gazed down blankly from a Civil War monument. The woman who'd sat next to him glanced at the office buildings and the skyline, shook her head, sighed, and headed to the edge of the street behind the bus to wave over a taxi. Her child walked alongside her with a curious shuffling gait, hands still in pockets, head still bowed. A few moments later they'd climbed into a cab, and the cabbie drove away.

Owen went the other direction, toward the Civil War monument and beyond it. A woman in unkempt clothing perched at the foot of the monument, feeding tidbits to three lean and ragged cats. As Owen passed her, the woman looked up from beneath uncombed taffy-colored hair, and nodded to him, as though in greeting.

"Hi," he said.

The woman smiled, said nothing, turned back to the cats. Owen walked on. It must have been a trick of the light, he decided, that made her eyes look like cat's: tawny, with vertical pupils gapped slightly open.

At the nearest sidewalk he crossed toward the skyscrapers and walked a few blocks south, then turned left. Though he'd never been to Providence before, he knew exactly where he was going: a certain section of sidewalk in front of a certain well-aged office building. Halfway between two spindly trees, he stopped and waited.

Not two minutes later, a scruffily dressed middle-aged man with thick glasses and thinning black hair walked up to him and asked, "Heard any news from Susran?"

"Not since the birds flew away," Owen replied.

The man grinned. "Owen Merrill, isn't it? Sam Mazzini." They shook hands, and Sam indicated the duffel. "You need a hand with that?"

"No, I'm fine."

Sam nodded, gestured off the way Owen had come. "I hope the trip down was okay."

"Nothing to complain about," said Owen.

"Glad to hear it." With a shake of his head. "I miss the trains. Used to be you could get to Boston in an hour and New York in three. One of those things."

They crossed the street, wove their way under the shadow of tall brick buildings. Traffic seemed sparse to Owen, and not all the buildings had lights in them. After a while they crossed a freeway on an old concrete overpass; the road surface below was visibly cracked and patched, and not many cars picked their way along it.

"You're with the new Arkham church now, aren't you?" Sam asked then. "I probably don't need to tell you how excited most of us here were when we heard about that. Two new churches, for the first time in—how long has it been? A hundred years, give or take?"

"About that." They both fell silent while a businessman in a suit hurried by, eyes fixated on the screen of his smartphone. "We're pretty excited in Arkham, too," said Owen once they were alone on the sidewalk again. "The old East Church downtown cost us only about half of what we'd set aside, so we've got the sanctuary set up and consecrated, all the sacred books in the library, and everything. We've even found an organist." With a quick glance at his guide: "We've had converts come in, too. I don't know what the people down here think of that."

Sam met his glance. "Oh, there's been some bickering about that, sure. Some of the elders don't trust anybody who's not a birthright member, but most of us are okay with conversion— and we've got some really good people that way lately. You were a convert, weren't you?"

"Ten years ago."

"What degree?"

"Now? Third."

Sam let out a low whistle. "Third in ten years, that's pretty good. You must have worked your butt off. Me, I'm fifth these days, but I got started when I was a kid, and my family prayed to the Great Old Ones back in the old country. A lot of folks around Naples do that, you know."

"I didn't," Owen admitted.

The sidewalks filled up with people, so they let the conversation lapse. Ahead stretched the long gentle slope of an avenue, lined on both sides with the clapboard walls and sagging Doric porches of an earlier day. Garish signs told of cafés, nightspots, little businesses of a dozen different kinds, and where doors stood open, the music that spilled out onto the sidewalk ran the gamut from classical to hip-hop.

Finally they reached a windswept open square, paved in asphalt uneven enough that Owen was sure cobblestones lay beneath it. On the far end, a stone wall rose up six feet or so, topped with a bleak chainlink fence. Beyond it was nothing: a flat open space, as far as Owen could tell, where a building of quite some size must have stood many decades ago.

"Recognize it?" Sam asked him.

"The Mother Church?" Owen guessed.

Sam grinned. "Got it in one. Yeah, that's where old Dr. Enoch Bowen started it all. Our church these days is just two blocks away, and it's on the same moon path. The place you'll be staying is even closer. Come on." He gestured, and Owen followed.

* * *

The Starry Wisdom church kept rooms for visitors on the upper floor of an old clapboard building on a narrow alley a block and a half from the site of the Mother Church. It was a cozy and fascinating place, a little corner of the city where the nineteenth century still lingered, and where stray cats squabbled and licked themselves themselves atop a ramshackle outbuilding. Owen's tiny bedroom, even smaller bathroom, and a larger space that served as sitting room, dining room, and kitchen all in one, were on the southeastern corner of the building; most of the windows looked across the alley at a taller building next door, but the main room's eastern windows peered over roofs toward the lower town's hulking skyscrapers. On the horizon, some two miles away, rose the stark mass of College Hill, bristling with roofs and steeples whose outlines stood out unyielding against the pale blue of the sky.

"What do you think?" said Sam Mazzini, as Owen considered the place.

"Very nice," Owen replied, and meant it. His books would fit neatly on a little bookshelf next to the quilt-topped bed, and he'd spotted the teakettle already in place on the tiny two-burner stove. After ten years in the little mountain village of Dunwich, the cityscape beyond the windows seemed to whisper of spectral, unreachable worlds.

"Great. Now you'll need a bit to get unpacked and settled in, I bet. Charlene—that's my wife—she made me promise to bring you for dinner tonight, if you're okay with that—"

"Please," said Owen, "and thank you."

"Sure thing. Before then, the elders want to meet you, of course. So, half an hour, maybe?" Owen said something agreeable, and a few moments later the door clicked shut and Sam clomped down the old wooden stair beyond it.

It took Owen only a few minutes to get his clothes and other belongings put away, the books he'd carried with him settled on the bookshelf, the little CD player—battery-powered, since electricity wasn't too reliable any more—and a dozen or so disks stacked next to it. More time went into putting the last things from his duffel where they belonged. Atop the bedroom dresser he spread a green linen cloth, and onto that went two short candlesticks holding votive candles, two brass bowls for herbs, and a little statue of white stone, not quite six inches tall, that portrayed a woman-breasted cat.

Those weren't part of the Starry Wisdom, and Owen wasn't sure what the Providence elders would think of them. Among the folk of drowned Poseidonis, Jenny's people, each person prayed to one of the Great Old Ones, and there was a way of casting the omens to find that one among the old gods of nature each person should invoke. The elders of the Starry Wisdom and the priestesses of the Esoteric Order of Dagon still weren't quite sure what to make of it, but Owen and Laura had cast the omens for themselves and their children and taken up the old Poseidonian prayers alongside their other spiritual practices.

For more centuries than anyone cared to count, the various orders and churches and family lineages that worshipped the Great Old Ones kept their own teachings and practices to themselves, interpreting the sacred books in their own ways, helping one another at need but remaining aloof otherwise. That was changing now. Some people, Owen and Laura among them, had been initiated into more than one tradition, and scraps of lore from varied sources were being woven together in Arkham and elsewhere. Plenty of oldtimers shook their heads and murmured their doubts, but the Watcher who lurked above the sanctuary of each Starry Wisdom church had looked on the changes with its three-lobed eye and found them good.

Just one of those things, Owen told himself. If they get upset, I'll deal. He got the little shrine set out properly, nodded once, and then changed out of his traveling clothes. Those would have been fine if he'd been meeting the elders of a little rural church like the ones he'd attended in Dunwich or Chorazin, or a newly founded church like the ones in Arkham or Lefferts Corners, but Providence was the oldest of all the Starry Wisdom churches, and you had to go to Boston or New York to find a larger congregation. That called for a jacket and tie, and the little enameled tie-pin old Emily Sawyer in Dunwich had given him as an initiation gift: the ankh-symbol of ancient Egypt, the emblem of the Starry Wisdom.

He had time to run a comb through his sandy hair and get his short beard to behave before Sam Mazzini knocked on the door again. He'd found a jacket and tie, too, but Owen suspected he'd still look scruffy in a tux. "All set? Great. Let me take you over to the church."

Out in the alley, afternoon was deepening toward evening. Sam led him to the alley's end, across a wide avenue, and then back into a maze of narrow brown alleys on the far side. Most of another block brought them to the back of an old brick church from the middle years of the nineteenth century, its buttressed walls rising up to a steep peaked roof, its steeple in front topped with a pyramidal roof in place of the old spire.

Three steps led down to a sturdy door with a peephole in it at eye level. Sam knocked on it in a curious rhythm; after a moment, it swung inward and a thin, slightly stooped elderly man wearing thick round glasses peered out at them. "Good evening, Sam," he said. "And this is?"

"Owen Merrill."

"Ah, yes, Mr. Merrill. Welcome to Providence." They shook hands. "If you'll both come with me." He motioned them in, locked the door behind him.

The dimly lit hallway inside ran a short distance and then ended at another door, which the old man unlocked and then locked behind them. Beyond that was a longer hallway, no better lit. A door halfway down led to the church's fellowship hall; another door stood half open at the hallway's end, and golden light streamed out through the gap.

"Alexandra, Phaedra, Peter," said the old man as he pushed the door at the end all the way open. "Our guest is here."

* * *

Inside was an office with two big wooden desks on one wall and a row of bookshelves on the wall facing it. Between them was a circle of overstuffed chairs covered in pale brown leather. An old and ornate light fixture above, all aged metal and golden-yellow translucent glass, provided the illumination. Two old women and an equally elderly man sat there, all of them white-haired and dressed in the formal fashions of an earlier day.

"Mr. Merrill," said the man who'd met them, "this is Mrs. Alexandra Bowen, of whom I'm sure you've heard. This is Miss Phaedra Dexter, and this is Peter O'Halloran. And I should introduce myself, of course. Albert Pearse."

Hands got shaken, and Pearse waved Owen to a seat, then turned and said, "Thank you, Sam. It won't be long." Sam nodded and, without a word, left and shut the door behind him.

Owen glanced from face to face, tried to take the measure of the church elders. Bowen, tall and rawboned, had her hair tied back in a bun; her deep brown eyes regarded him from behind rimless glasses. Dexter looked almost diaphanous by contrast, a little fragile woman with large watery eyes and flyaway white hair, while O'Halloran, square-jawed and strongly built, looked like the big wholesome Irishman at least one of his ancestors had been.

"I trust your trip down from Arkham wasn't too difficult," said Pearse then, settling on one of the empty chairs.

"Not at all," Owen replied.

A moment of silence passed, and then Bowen spoke. "The elders in Arkham speak highly of you." Her voice was dry, sharp-edged. "You're a convert, I believe?"

"Ten years ago," said Owen. "I know I still have a lot to learn."

She favored him with a nod. "I trust you'll be attending services here."

"That's my intention." Owen ventured a smile. It wasn't returned.

"The research you're doing," said O'Halloran then. "Can you tell us a little about it?"

"A favor for Jenny Chaudronnier," said Owen. "She wants to find certain documents that might have been owned by a scholar who lived here early last century—a Dr. George Angell. They touch on some details of a very old branch of the lore. She's in France this summer, and she asked me to see if I could locate them, or get any leads on where they might be."

"Oh, we've heard of Miss Chaudronnier, of course," said Phaedra Dexter, with a bright little smile. "I imagine you've done research for her before."

"Fairly often, actually."

"It must be quite something to work with a genuine sorceress."

Owen nodded in response, unsure how much to say.

Another silence passed. "Of course," said Bowen then, "we would be happy to give you any help you require. Was this Dr. Angell a member of our church?"

"Not as far as I know," Owen said. "A professor at Brown University, and a scholar of ancient languages—if he had connections to the Starry Wisdom or any of the other orders, the records I've seen so far don't mention that."

That seemed to exhaust Alexandra Bowen's interest in the subject. "Very well," she said, and turned to Pearse. "Albert, you'll see to it that he gets the necessary introductions, won't you? And send a message to Arkham to let them know he's here."

"I'll do that," said Pearse.

"Thank you," Owen said, "all of you. I appreciate your willingness to have me here."

Bowen nodded again. "You're most welcome, Mr. Merrill."

It was as clear a dismissal as he'd ever been given, and he got to his feet. Pearse stood also, went to the door, showed him through it, gave him a smile, and then went with him along the hallway to open the two locked doors. A minute or so later Owen was standing in the alley behind the church as the lock on the outer door clicked shut behind him.

"Out of the lion's den," Sam Mazzini said, boosting himself off a low stone footing that easily doubled as a bench. "I hope you didn't get bit."

"Not particularly," said Owen.

"Okay, good. If you like, we can head on over to my place right now. Charlene really wants to meet you—she's got family out west, and heard all kinds of stories about that business in Chorazin. We can drink a couple of brews, and then have dinner, okay?"

"Sounds like a plan," said Owen.

"Great." Sam led the way along another set of winding alleys, talking about his wife and their children. Owen smiled and nodded, and tried to set aside the feeling that he'd been weighed by the Providence elders and found wanting.

* * *

Owen was waiting outside the John Hay Library the next morning before its doors opened. He had an old Miskatonic backpack slung from one muscular shoulder, courtesy of a charity shop in Arkham. Stocked with two spiral notebooks and as many pens, it reminded him forcibly of his student days. The morning was clear and warm, and the Brown University buildings were in better condition than Miskatonic's, though Owen could see the telltale signs of deferred maintenance. Once the library doors swung wide, he found his way to the stark white-walled Special Collections reading room. There he requested the first box of papers from the estate of George Gammell Angell, and sat down to wait at the table furthest from the desk.

Fifteen minutes later he was sorting through some of the papers that had been in the old professor's home the day he died: drafts of scholarly articles, correspondence with friends and colleagues, bills from the grocer's, the coal company, and a plumber who'd fixed a leaky sink, and more. The great-nephew who'd been his executor had been thorough rather than selective, Owen gathered. Still, he read through it all. The chance that any one document, or any one box of documents, would tell him what he needed to know was so small he didn't bother worrying about it; it would be the slow correlation of tiny scraps of knowledge, if anything, that would lead to the rituals that might awaken Great Cthulhu from his aeonian dreams.

He spent the entire day reading his way through two boxes of papers, taking notes in pencil, and giving up only at five, when the special collections room closed. He found nothing that seemed to matter much, and the only two odd things that happened all that day had, as far as he could tell, nothing to do with his quest. The first was simple enough: twice over the course of the day, he felt an odd feeling, as though someone was looking at him from behind. A quick backward glance each time showed no one there, and after the second time, Owen put it down to nerves, and dismissed it from his mind.

The second odd thing was just as simple: the woman who'd sat next to him on the bus from Boston to Providence showed up two hours after he did, put in a request, and then had a conversation in hushed voices with the young man behind the desk, which involved a number of glances toward Owen. They seemed to settle something between them; after another fifteen minutes or so she got a box of documents, sat down at the same table as Owen, and began reading them. She kept studying, as he did, until the department closed.

She was there again the next day, and the next, and the one after that. More than once, when she got a box of documents from the archives, Owen recognized it as part of the Angell collection he'd already examined; more than once, when he got a new box to begin reading, he recalled seeing some of the papers from it on the table across from him. That got his hackles up. It seemed improbable that the two of them would be searching the same documents at the same time by chance, and the likely alternative was one he didn't want to think about—

The Radiance.

The too familiar name chilled him. He made himself continue reading, looking for scraps of information that might point him toward his goal.

Each evening he left the library and walked down College Street to the bridge over the river, and then wove his way through the downtown district. As often as not he passed the woman with the strange eyes he'd seen on his arrival, sitting in a disused doorway or a bit of sidewalk with a clowder of cats around her. Now and again crowds gathered along the river—some sort of occasional festival called WaterFire took place there every so often, he gathered from stray comments and posters, and now and then when evening came and he glanced out his window toward the east, he caught sight of a few stray points of fire rising from the river's track and heard amplified music echoing off distant buildings.

Now and then, when an onshore wind and a high tide whispered conspiracies to each other, he had to wade through a few inches of brackish water where the sidewalks dipped too low. That was common on every coast as the seas rose implacably, and Providence was fortunate; it had never gone in for subways, and so lacked the flooded underground labyrinths that were causing so many problems in Boston and New York. Sometimes he felt the moon paths, the ancient alignments that carried the life force through the bones of the land, straining against the hard abstract lines of city streets. Sometimes, too, the skyscrapers he passed looked oddly insubstantial—or was it simply that he sensed the presence of other days, before their rise or after their fall?

There were days when he could almost glimpse the forested hills surrounding the inlet where the Narragansett people raised their wigwams, showing through the buildings of his own time. There were other days when he glimpsed the colonial Providence Joseph Curwen had known, the bustling town of the 1920s in which Charles Dexter Ward had lived out his short strange life, or other less familiar images he guessed probably came from the future. Owen was used to such glimpses. One night ten years back, amid gunfire and sorcery, he'd encountered Yog-Sothoth and glimpsed the universe briefly through the eyes of that Great Old One, the Gate and the Guardian of the Gate. Since then, time had never quite flowed smoothly for him.

On the far side of downtown he crossed the gray and crumbling barrier of Interstate 95 on the Washington Street overpass, and headed back up the long gradual slopes onto Federal Hill, leaving the broad avenues for the narrow brown alleys as soon as he could. Through the unmarked door, up the long stair, and into his apartment: it soon became a familiar routine.

His evenings had other entertainments. The elders aside, most of the church members were a sociable lot, with no trace of the famous New England standoffishness; a good many were descended from more recent immigrants, and some, like the Mazzinis, still had family on the other side of the Atlantic. Owen dined twice at the Mazzinis that first week and once with Tom Castro, a big brown-skinned man with grizzled hair, who had three grandparents from the Cape Verde islands and a fourth from Dunwich, one of the rare Whateleys who'd gotten a case of wanderlust and ended up in the merchant marine. Owen's ten years in Dunwich were enough for Tom to consider him practically family, and they spent a very pleasant evening talking about Dunwich and the new church in Arkham.

Other evenings he spent at Sancipriani's, a sprawling restaurant full of great oaken tables two doors down from where he stayed. Every Starry Wisdom community Owen knew of had such a place, but Sancipriani's was on a grander scale, with enough room inside to fit Dunwich's Standing Stone restaurant four or five times over. The rooms in front were for outsiders, who ate there tolerably often and provided a useful source of cash for the church and its members; in back, facing the alley and entered via an unmarked door, was a long rambling room with plenty of nooks and shadows for the worshippers of the Great Old Ones, where Owen bowed his head and heard strange benedictions said over the best *timballe* and pizza Margherita on the east coast.

Most nights, before the wine started to flow too freely, he said his good evenings and headed back to his apartment, made himself a cup of tea, put on a CD of Delta blues or Appalachian folk music, and then tried to make sense of whatever scraps of information he'd been able to gather in the course of the day's research. Far more often than not, he sat there staring at nothing in particular, trying to force meaning out of data that simply wouldn't yield it. Then came prayers at the little shrine he'd set up, followed by sleep, before the first light of morning roused him to prayers and meditations, his morning workout, a quick bite to eat, and the streets that led back to the John Hay Library. More than a week passed that way before his researches brought him something other than the ordinary relics of a scholarly life.

CHAPTER 3

THE CALL OF CTHULHU

The only interruptions to his routine during those first days in Providence were a visit to the little co-op grocery that Sam Mazzini managed, to lay in a stock of food for breakfast, and the services at the Starry Wisdom church on Sunday morning and Wednesday evening, where he sat in the section of the pews set apart for initiates of the third degree. That had its own familiar rhythms; there were words to speak aloud and words to repeat in the silence of the mind, patterns to make with intertwined fingers and others to picture in the mind's eye, while the voor, the subtle life-force that flowed through the moon paths of the land and the hidden channels of the body, danced and flowed and cast strange shadows in the corners of the worship hall.

The hall itself was big and bleak, with the windows carefully sealed against daylight and a row of light fixtures hanging from chains from the ceiling high above. An ornate ankh stood high on the eastern wall above the pulpit, but the walls were otherwise so bare that the bank of circuit breakers near Owen's seat, which controlled the lights for the main and upper floors of the church, stood out like an ornament. The four elders sat in big dark chairs beneath the ankh, facing the rest of the congregation. That wasn't something he'd seen in any other Starry Wisdom church, but he didn't feel comfortable enough to ask about it.

Coffee downstairs in the fellowship hall after the services, on the other hand, could have been anywhere, with the same menu of gossip, coffee and tea, and homebaked cookies as in Dunwich or Chorazin. Normally the elders went elsewhere— the room where they'd met him, Owen guessed—but one Wednesday evening, Phaedra Dexter sat down across from Owen and asked him a few bland questions about the church in Arkham, then said, "You mustn't pay any mind to the people here who aren't comfortable with converts, Mr. Merrill. Why, my father was a convert, and his father was something rather more upsetting still. Do you know who he was?"

Owen admitted his ignorance, and she smiled and went on. "The very Dr. Ambrose Dexter who took the Shining Trapezohedron from that writer's apartment and threw it into Narragansett Bay. So you see, we all have things to atone for." She made a little more conversation and then got up and headed off somewhere else, leaving Owen to his thoughts.

The Shining Trapezohedron! It had been the most sacred relic of the Church of the Starry Wisdom: found by old Enoch Bowen in the crypts of a forgotten temple of old Heliopolis, set up in the sanctuary of the Mother Church, and left there— for it could not be moved without terrible danger, once its full powers were awakened—when mob violence backed by religious bigotry forced the church into hiding. Owen knew the rest of its history well, for H.P. Lovecraft's friend and fellow-author Robert Blake had been involved, and Lovecraft himself had turned the whole affair into a short story a few years after Blake's sudden and terrible death. The subject occupied his thoughts so completely for the next quarter hour or so that weeks passed before it occurred to him that nobody in Providence had expressed the least discomfort with his convert status.

He wrote two letters to Laura and sent them by way of the Starry Wisdom's private postal system, which involved placing letters in a certain underground vault and leaving as quickly as possible. What payment the couriers received for their labor Owen didn't know, and now and then suspected he'd rather not find out. Two replies came back promptly, assuring him that Asenath and Barnabas were fine and so was she, and filling him in on the progress of the Esoteric Order of Dagon chapter in Arkham. That filled the days until his search among Angell's papers brought him a first glimpse of what he sought.

That day had gone like the ones before it, and the clock on the wall showed the afternoon half gone when it happened. He was well into the Angell collection, sorting through a box of papers on Babylonian linguistics, when he glanced across the table at the black woman whose quest seemed to parallel his own. Just then she took something out of her box. It wasn't paper; it was a flat piece of baked clay less than an inch thick, and something like five inches by six in area. A moment passed before he recognized it, and froze.

He managed to look away before she noticed that he was watching her. It took an effort to keep slogging through one page after another on Aklo loan-words in Babylonian religious texts, though, when something linked so tautly to his quest sat across the table from him. He hazarded another glance a few minutes later, saw the clay object again on the desk next to a stack of paper covered in handwriting in an early twentieth century hand.

There could be no doubt, then. He made himself keep reading.

* * *

He found nothing of use in the box he'd gotten until he reached the very bottom. There, when he'd taken out the last of a stack of page proofs for an article meant for the *Zeitschrift für Assyriologie*, one sheet of paper remained, half the size of the others. Owen lifted it out. It was a brief handwritten note on the hotel stationery of an earlier time:

Hôtel d'Ys
12, rue de Vavin, Paris

11 January 1924.

My dear Dr. Angell,

Many thanks for your assistance with the words of the Aklo Sabaoth! I guessed the text had been garbled; to have that confirmed, and the words corrected, is welcome indeed.

The research goes well. I look forward to telling you all the details when circumstances let you visit.

Lydia sends her very best wishes, as do I,

Your sincere friend,
Charles Dexter Ward

Owen frowned, read the note again, and then carefully copied it word for word. It didn't tell him much he hadn't already learned, except that whatever research Ward had done in Europe touched on some of the most dangerous passages of the *Necronomicon*. The Aklo Sabaoth—that was not an incantation to be uttered lightly, or even read silently without tracing the Elder Sign in the eight directions first. He wondered casually who Lydia might have been, then repacked the box and took it back up to the counter.

As he got there, the black woman finished returning the papers and the clay bas-relief to the box she'd been sorting through, stood up, and approached the counter as well.

He decided to take a risk, put a bland smile on his face, and glanced at the label on her box. "Is that part of the Angell collection too? We should probably just swap boxes."

That got him a sudden wary look, and then an instant later, a carefully measured smile. "Probably," she said; her voice had a faint French accent. "Anything interesting in yours?"

"Mostly Babylonian linguistics," he replied.

She chuckled. "Not my cup of tea. This one's mostly research on a religious cult."

Owen nodded, and just then the librarian came over. A few minutes later, Owen had the box on the table, and carefully took out the contents, one at a time.

The bas-relief had its own little foam-lined box. Owen opened it, and considered the image in clay within. At the bottom, an archaic script Owen recognized at a glance spelled out words every worshipper of the Great Old Ones knew by heart—*Ph'nglui mglw'nafh Cthulhu R'lyeh wgah'nagl fhtagn*, "In his house at R'lyeh dead Cthulhu waits dreaming." Above, against a background that suggested Cyclopean architecture, was the image of the Dreaming Lord himself: the great bulbous head with its many eyes and cascading tentacles, the sweeping wings, the mighty clawed limbs. He nodded slowly. H.P. Lovecraft had described the bas-relief well enough in his story "The Call of Cthulhu"—the horror writer had borrowed constantly from occult lore, and incorporated actual events whenever possible to give his tales an air of reality.

He set the clay bas-relief aside, began reading the papers that filled most of the box. First came stacks of press clippings, each reporting some strange event between the first of March and the second of April in 1925. An ethnologist studying an isolated First Nations village on the coast of British Columbia wrote of nightly rituals that no previous scholar had heard of and his native informants would not explain; a British official in India repeated strange rumors among the hill tribes of Tamil Nadu, about the awakening of a sleeping god; a famous psychologist in Zurich heard identical dreams described by a dozen different patients, and struggled without success to fit them into his theories about archetypes and the collective unconscious; a police report from Buenos Aires told of thirteen people in strange robes found seated in a circle around an altar in a basement room, all of them dead with expressions of stark terror on their faces. There were hundreds of other clippings, ranging from ordinary cases of panic, mania, and eccentricity all the way to hair-raising tales of sorcery and improbable events.

Owen nodded slowly. The attempt to awaken Cthulhu in the spring of 1925 was still a matter of stories and bright memories among the initiates of the Starry Wisdom and a dozen other groups that revered the Great Old Ones. Though it failed—the stars hadn't come right yet, or some other factor had interfered—it had been the first time in centuries that initiates of so many traditions had joined in a single working. Had they come close to success? Only the Great Old Ones knew.

He finished with the press clippings, went on to the first of the two manuscripts. It began with the words CTHULHU CULT, printed out in capitals, and had two sections, one headed "1925—Dream and Dream Work of H.A. Wilcox, 7 Thomas St., Providence, R.I.," and the other "Narrative of Inspector John R. Legrasse, 121 Bienville St., New Orleans, La., at 1908 A.A.S. Mtg.—Notes on Same, and Prof. Webb's Acct." He skimmed both sections. H.P. Lovecraft had summarized them tolerably well in his story: the dreams of the young Providence artist, the police raid on a ritual in the Mississippi delta (though of course Lovecraft hadn't been able to resist putting in the old and ugly blood libel about human sacrifice), and the meeting of a defunct archeological society, where traditions from the Louisiana bayous had been compared with those from a nearly extinct people on the west coast of Greenland and found to be identical.

The second manuscript was an account by a Norwegian ship's officer, Gustaf Johansen, of his encounter with a spectral island in the middle of the Pacific and the vast phantasm that he and the sailors with him had seen in their brief stay there. Lovecraft had rewritten Johansen's story considerably, making it far more lurid than the honest seaman's account it had originally been, but nothing in Johansen's own account told Owen anything he didn't already know. He finished, packed everything back into the box, stood up, and happened to glance at the woman whose research seemed to be running parallel to his.

She was staring at a piece of paper on the table, and tears gleamed on her cheeks. Owen glanced at the paper and recognized it at once: the letter from Charles Dexter Ward.

* * *

That evening, on the way home, he was startled to see the words ENOCH BOWEN in large type on something on a campus bulletin board. Outside of the Starry Wisdom Church, Owen gathered, the name of its founder wasn't anything like a household word in Providence, so he went to look. The poster announced a new exhibit at the Haffenreffer Museum, Brown's museum of anthropology, covering Bowen's career as one of America's pioneer Egyptologists. There was the man's face, copied from an oil portrait, and a string of Egyptian hieroglyphs carved in stone, surrounded by an oval. Owen didn't happen to be literate in ancient Egyptian, but he'd seen that set of hieroglyphs often enough to recognize them: the name-cartouche of Nephren-Ka, the last pharaoh of the Third Dynasty, whose temple at Heliopolis Bowen had discovered and excavated. The exhibit was scheduled to open in three days. Intrigued, Owen wrote down the details in one of his notebooks before walking on.

Once he'd gotten back to the little apartment, stowed his pack in the tiny closet, and washed his hands and face, he headed over to Sancipriani's to see about an early dinner. The back room wasn't anything like as crowded as usual, but Tom Castro was sitting near one end of a massive oak table. He was talking with someone Owen didn't recognize, a woman with short gray hair and the kind of clothing he was used to seeing on construction workers.

"Owen!" Tom waved him over. "You haven't met Ellen yet, have you?"

He joined them, made the appropriate noises. Ellen Chernak, it turned out, was a seventh-degree initiate in the

Starry Wisdom. That startled Owen, for every other Starry Wisdom church he knew about brought initiates of that level into the council of elders as a matter of course, if they hadn't gotten there already at the fifth or sixth degree. He reminded himself that he didn't know how the larger congregations did things, and decided not to ask about it.

"Me?" Ellen said, answering a different question. "I do carpentry, for outsiders as often as not. You wouldn't guess that my ancestors were founding members of the church, I bet." A genial shrug, then: "Tom says you're from the new church up Arkham way. How's that going?"

Julie Olmert, who was plump and dark-haired and waited tables in the back room most nights, came to get their orders, and made some friendly talk before heading into the kitchen. By the time she came back with wine and bread, Owen, Tom, and Ellen were deep in conversation about the Arkham church, and Julie listened for a few moments and then went away.

The entrees arrived just as the place began to fill up, and the conversation lapsed. As soon as Ellen's meal was done, she said something about getting an early start the next day and headed out into the evening. Tom bought another round of wine for Owen and himself, and started talking about the farms the church owned in the western part of Rhode Island. Owen listened and nodded, thinking about empty farms he'd seen near Arkham.

The door to the alley swung open again, letting in a familiar figure. "Oh, good," said Sam Mazzini. "I was hoping you'd be here, Owen. Hi, Tom. Mind if I join you?"

Tom waved him to an empty chair, and Owen said, "What's up?"

"Arkham's pretty close to Innsmouth, isn't it? Know anyone who was from there?"

Owen managed to keep his surprise off his face. "Yes, actually," he said. "My wife Laura was born there. You know what happened to Innsmouth, right?" When Sam nodded: "The people scattered, of course, but most of them are back on the north coast these days, and we've got quite a few of them in Arkham. Why?"

"The kids were asking about it, I don't know why. Hey, are you free Sunday for dinner?"

"Sure." They settled the details, and Sam said, "You won't believe what I saw today. Brown University's opening a museum exhibit on old Enoch Bowen Saturday—they've got posters all over the place."

"Yeah," said Owen. "I saw one on the Brown campus. Are you going?"

"Oh, I don't know," said Sam. "We'll see." He seemed uncomfortable with the thought.

The conversation veered elsewhere, then, and Owen stayed later than usual and drank more wine than he'd intended. He wasn't quite weaving when he left Sancipriani's, but it took a certain amount of concentration to avoid that and make it up the long flight of stairs to his door.

When he unlocked the door and went inside, he spotted a piece of paper lying on the floor—someone, he guessed, must have pushed it under the door. He picked it up. Someone had typed a short message on it, using an old-fashioned typewriter with a broken letter O:

    don't be too certain of your welcome here

He stared at it for a moment, frowning, and then went around the little apartment, made sure that nothing else had been disturbed. Everything was as he'd left it. Even so, the message left him feeling uncomfortable enough that he bolted the door and traced a protective symbol over it before making a cup of tea and settling down to the last of his evening routine.

* * *

Owen might have forgotten the note if things had continued as before. Over the days that followed, though, as though the thing had been a prophecy, an odd constraint seemed to slip into his relationships with the Providence congregation. It wasn't anything he could put his finger on at first—people seeming distracted or on edge, conversations running down a little more quickly into silence—and it didn't happen with everyone at once, but each day the distance seemed to widen just a little. It left Owen puzzled, though he tried to convince himself that it was nerves on his part, or maybe some trouble in the congregation that would soon pass.

Even so, the next three days went by without trouble, and with no shortage of Angell's papers to read and no answers for his unspoken questions about the young black woman who sat across from him and studied the same material with the same intensity he did. Saturday plodded past—the boxes he'd reached by then were mostly corrected page proofs for Angell's many articles on the comparative grammar of the Semitic languages, but he had to go through them all page by page to be sure there was nothing else.

On the third day, aroud two o'clock, he thought he'd finally found something: a large envelope that had been mailed to Angell by one C.D. Ward from an address in Pawtuxet. Inside was a sheet of paper that appeared to be a rubbing from an inscription, with a crack down the middle suggesting that the stone had been broken in two pieces. It was in the half-barbarous Latin of the Roman Empire's final years, but Owen had learned Latin years back to make sense of certain archaic tomes, and was able to puzzle out the meaning with a little effort:

*THE TOMB OF M. AMBROSIUS SYLVESTRIS CALLED
MERLINUS IN THE HILL BY THE RIVER TIFIUS NEAR THE
FORTRESS OF THE DEMETAE DELVE UNDER THE
STONE WITH TWO DRAGONS YOU WILL FIND THE
CRYSTAL CAVE WHERE HE WAITS FOR THE HOUR
FORETOLD*

Owen read it twice in bafflement, then shook his head; he recalled the famous and fraudulent medieval tombstone of King Arthur at Glastonbury, and wondered if Ward had been bamboozled by something of the kind. Still, he dutifully copied down the inscription; it prodded a fragment of memory— something out of a Lovecraft story, maybe?—but whatever it was refused to surface. Nothing else of interest turned up, and when the clock showed five minutes to five, he took the box back to the librarian and went out into the open air with a sigh of relief.

Manning Hall, the building that housed the Haffenreffer Museum, was across a street, a wrought iron fence, and a broad lawn from the John Hay Library. The Enoch Bowen exhibit didn't have its opening event until six o'clock, though, so Owen had an hour to kill. He wove through campus to the commercial district along Thayer Street just east of it, found a local burger place with a sign out front saying HOWARD'S, and went inside. As he'd half expected, a big painting of H.P. Lovecraft in garish colors adorned the wall behind the cash register, glow-in-the-dark plastic octopuses dangled from the light fixtures, and the house specialties were named after the Great Old Ones. Amused, Owen ordered a Cthulhu burger with fries and a porter from a local brewery. The burger turned out to be a battered and fried fish filet slathered with guacamole, and the fries were forgettable, but the beer was quite tolerable and Owen made a mental note of the brewery's name.

At six o'clock sharp he was back at the Greek facade of Manning Hall. Inside, he joined thirty or forty others in a space where folding chairs faced a podium, and reproductions of old daguerrotypes blown up to mural size hung from temporary partitions: Enoch Bowen, mostly, posing beside Egyptian ruins, seated in a book-lined study, or standing among men and women Owen recognized as founding members of the original Church of the Starry Wisdom. A quarter hour late, the director of the Haffenreffer Museum went to the podium and made appropriate noises, and then a professor emeritus from the university, a stocky and smiling old man who leaned on a cane of twisted wood, spent half an hour or so discussing Enoch Bowen's place in the history of nineteenth-century thought. Owen applauded with the rest, and followed the modest crowd into the exhibit itself.

The museum had managed to gather together an impressive collection of artifacts and memorabilia from Bowen's day: tools his workmen had used to dig into the ruins of Heliopolis, letters he'd sent home to colleagues at Brown, a section of an inscribed wall with the cartouche of the pharaoh Nephren-Ka surrounded by the ornate hieroglyphs of Old Kingdom Egypt, ritual vessels of malachite and jet, and much more. Owen stopped for a few moments in front of an exquisite foot-high stone statue of the Blind Ape of Truth, recalling the night he'd received the second degree initiation of the Starry Wisdom in Dunwich and recited certain words before an early twentieth century copy of a similar statue. In the Starry Wisdom teachings, the Blind Ape of Truth taught the lesson that the universe neither knew nor cared about the countless lives it spawned and swallowed up again, and would not go out of its way to fulfill humanity's wishes, no matter how dazzling or desperate those might be. It was, Owen thought, a useful reminder.

A little further on, three old daguerrotypes, a panel of text, and a panel of Egyptian hieroglyphs with interlinear translation made him stop for a long moment. The photos showed a curious metal box with seven sides, no two of which were the same breadth, and seven corners, no two of which made the same angle. The flat lid and the sides had bas-reliefs showing rugose alien shapes rising up on great outspread wings. The text on the panel called it a reliquary, which was technically correct, and speculated about the un-Egyptian carvings on it. Any initiate of the Starry Wisdom could have explained to the curators who had made the golden box and what they had placed within it, but Owen doubted the curators really wanted to learn about the crinoid things of Antarctica or the strange gem that had come to them from Yuggoth in the cold and distant outskirts of the solar system. The message of the hieroglyphs, though, was new to Owen:

```
Nephren-Ka, Lord of the Two Lands, to the
god [unknown]hotep offers this jewel named
'Great of Magic in Heliopolis.' Beware!
Beware! Let it not behold the face of Ra,
or the one who watches will depart. Let it
not be in darkness, let it not be covered,
or the one who watches will come forth. Let
the one who uses it never depart from Maat,
or the one who watches will avenge.
```

Owen nodded slowly. The hieroglyphs, the small print said, had been copied by Bowen from the walls of the crypt where he'd found the Trapezohedron. Owen thought he could guess the meaning of the hieroglyph marked "unknown," which looked rather like a three-lobed eye. Ra was the sun, of course, and Maat was the inscrutable order of the universe. As for the rest, the crystals the Starry Wisdom had learned to use after the loss of the Shining Trapezohedron had the same requirements: they had to be kept in low indirect light at all times, and the higher initiates who worked with them had to follow certain strict rules or risk a peculiarly ghastly fate.

He repeated the translation silently to himself several times to fix it in his memory, and went on to other displays. One of these, near the exit, showed relics of some of Bowen's other scholarly interests—scrolls of magical incantations in Aramaic and *koinē* Greek, ritual implements from the mountains of China, a Roman altar from Caermaen in Wales with a dedication to Nodens, a curious tablet of black stone covered with strange spirals and whorls, and the like. One item made him stop and consider it closely: an alabaster statue of a seated cat with a woman's breasts, carved in an abstract unfamiliar style but otherwise similar to the one on Owen's dresser in the little apartment on Federal Hill. Angular characters that looked a little like Viking runes marked the foot of the statue, but they weren't runes; he'd learned the script of ancient Hyperborea, the land that modern atlases called Greenland, just well enough to pick out the name of the cat-goddess Phauz, one of the many daughters of the Black Goat.

* * *

He studied the little statue for a while, then turned toward the next display. At that same instant another of the attendees turned to face him: a man about his own age in a nondescript jacket and slacks, with brown hair in a military buzzcut, an angular clean-shaven face, harsh blue eyes. Owen glanced at him in passing, wondering why his face seemed familiar, and the man gave him an equally casual glance and then a second, quick, with narrowed eyes.

That was enough to send Owen out of the exhibit at once. He took care not to appear to hurry, and to show no sign that he'd noticed the glance, but he was through the doors and onto the portico in moments. A quick glance across the broad lawn showed no one watching; he headed down the stair fast and slipped into the narrow gap between the museum and the next building over, ducking behind an ornamental shrub, to see if anyone would follow.

That was when he remembered where he'd seen the face before. Memory surged: a night seared by lightning, the great stark mass of Elk Hill rising up against luminous green clouds, the same man facing him with narrowed eyes, a pistol in his grip and a Radiance negation team under his command. Dyson, Owen recalled: that was what Rowena Slater had called him, a few minutes before she'd died. The memory chilled him, and the implications chilled him even more.

A few people came out of Manning Hall then and walked across the green, but Dyson wasn't one of them. With a quick glance, Owen slipped away into the deepening gloom.

He made a wide circuit around the lawn, then headed for the river by the most evasive route he could think of.

The skyscrapers of downtown Providence loomed high up toward half-seen stars as Owen threaded his way among them. He saw few people there, though the woman with the strange eyes was half curled up in a doorway with cats surrounding her; she watched him in silence as he hurried by. Federal Hill was less empty, with restaurants and nightspots busy with the evening trade and light and music splashing out onto the sidewalks. Even so, he was glad to get back to the little apartment without further incident.

There were no typewritten notes on the floor, fortunately, and the view from the windows showed a Federal Hill nightscape unchanged from previous evenings. Owen got the teakettle heating, copied the text from the crypt from memory into one of his notebooks, and then sat at one of the two chairs by the little kitchen table, staring out at the night. It occurred to him, for the first time since he'd left Providence, just how far he was from the people he knew he could trust.

Dyson had been surprised to see him, Owen was sure of that. The man's doubletake had been too quick and natural to be pretense. That offered some comfort, but not much. Whatever had brought Dyson to Providence, a mention of Owen's presence there to his superiors might be answered by new orders to capture or kill a known enemy of the Radiance.

When the kettle boiled, he got up, set a cup of tea steeping, and then got paper and a pen and started writing a letter to Laura. He started with familiar words of love and good wishes, then described his encounter with Dyson, and then—

He could think of nothing else to say. Minutes passed; he faced the paper, sipped at his tea, and not another word surfaced. After a time he put the half-finished letter in a dresser drawer for later, got one of his books, and tried to make himself read it until drooping eyelids called him to evening prayers and bed.

The following day was a Sunday, so the Starry Wisdom service kept him busy until after noon. Phaedra Dexter seemed to be looking in his direction rather more often than chance would explain, but nothing unusual happened other than that, and afterwards he went to the Mazzinis' for an early dinner and a long evening. Charlene Mazzini had a thin expressive face and long black hair tied back in a ponytail; in her working hours she ran the library of the Starry Wisdom parochial school and taught reading to the first three grades. While she and Sam bustled about in the kitchen assembling *pasta e fagioli*, their three children begged Owen for any stories he knew about the Deep Ones. That startled him, but he managed to recall a couple of tales he'd heard from Laura, and those kept them rapt and listening until it was time to wash up for dinner.

Over the meal, he asked about that, and Charlene dimpled. "It's that book we got for the library from old Mrs. Tagliatti's estate," she said, "the one with the really nice ink drawings of the child and the octopus and everything." She turned to the children. "What was it called? For the life of me I can't remember the name of it."

"*A Princess of Y'ha-nthlei!*" they chorused.

Owen gave them a startled look.

"You've heard of it?" Sam said, topping up the wine.

"Well, yes," he admitted. "My wife wrote it, actually."

That got him astonished looks from all around, and he ended up promising the younger Mazzinis that if Laura ever came down to Providence or they went to Arkham he'd be sure to introduce them. Thereafter the talk strayed into other channels, but when Owen returned to his apartment he sat up for a while sipping tea, and then got out the half-finished letter. All at once he knew what he could write to Laura, and told her about the Mazzini children and their delight in *A Princess of Y'ha-nthlei* and the stories of old Innsmouth. He finished with a warning that he might have to go to ground if the Radiant negation team came for him, sent her his love and blessings, and signed.

CHAPTER 4

A SILENCE ON THE BREEZE

The next morning, after putting the letter in the underground vault and hurrying away, he was back at the John Hay Library. For a change, the woman whose quest seemed to parallel his didn't show. He got the next box of papers from the Angell collection, and settled down to a day of study. The papers in the box seemed promising at first—letters to Angell, mostly, and the thought that something from Charles Dexter Ward might be in among them had his pulse racing.

Three hours later, he set the last of the letters aside with a shake of his head, having found nothing of interest. Rough drafts of a few scholarly papers followed, but nothing more useful, and he trudged back to the little apartment on Federal Hill once the reading room closed, trying not to wonder if he was wasting his time. The crowd at Sancipriani's was noticeably thinner than before, and the sense of constraint and distance he'd felt earlier had become much more evident.

The next day went the same way, and the day after as well, though that was a Wednesday and he left the library early to be ready for the evening service at the church. The following day Owen got the last of the Angell collection, settled into a chair, and gave the archival box a bleak look before opening it. There were other places to look if Angell's papers gave him no clues, he knew, but the nearly complete absence of letters from

Charles Dexter Ward left him unsettled. There had to have been much more correspondence between them, he knew, and wondered whether someone had hunted it down and hidden or destroyed it.

The box turned out to have nothing from Ward and nothing bearing directly on his quest, but one document caught his attention early on. It was a single sheet of paper that had somehow gotten into the middle of a correspondence with Cambridge University Press over the reprinting of *A Grammar of the Akkadian Language on Comparative Principles*. Owen glanced at it briefly, expecting to see some new quibble over contract terms, but it wasn't a letter.

At the top of the sheet, a line of what looked to Owen's eye like Babylonian cuneiform writing, neatly rendered in ink, was followed by *dumu-ne zalaga* in Angell's hand; below that was ἑταιρία φοτις in Greek letters—Owen managed to pick this out as *hetairia photis*, which meant something like "society of light." Below that were a few lines written in a cryptic style:

> *apud stele 223—see Altberg-Ehrenstein, p. 611*
> *f. c. 1138 BC Babylon by Shamash-Nazir*
> *reorg. 310 BC Seleuceia on Tig.*
> *Agathocles of Megara, first* ἑταιρίαρχος
> *Comp. with Irem tablet K459*

He stared at it, trying to remember where he'd encountered the words *dumu-ne zalaga* before. Then, all at once, recollection: a blustery autumn day on a beach facing the cold gray Atlantic, when he'd sat on a driftwood log and listened in silence as everything he knew about the history of the world was turned inside out.

Carefully, making sure none of the handful of people in the special collections room saw anything unusual, he opened his notebook and copied down every word. *Dumu-ne zalaga*—in ancient Sumerian, the language of scholarship in Babylonian times, that meant "children of light," just as *hetairia photis* meant "society of light." The other names the same organization had taken during its long existence had the same implication: we alone are the children of light, and all those who disagree with us are the slaves of darkness.

The Radiance. Owen shook his head, thinking of the man he'd seen at the museum, the implied risk that at least one of their negation teams was in Providence at that moment, the danger implied by that fact. The reference to a tablet from Irem made him wonder, too, for the Moon Temple of Irem had been the last of the seven temples of the Great Old Ones the Radiance had destroyed in the time of Alexander the Great. There Hali, the last high priest of the Moon Temple, died writhing in a pool of his own blood, after speaking the Weird that bore his name—at once prophecy and curse, a wild card no one knew how to play, for not even Nyarlathotep the Crawling Chaos knew what Hali's terrible final words had been.

After a time, Owen went back to Angell's papers and kept searching. The only other thing he found worth noticing, though, was scrawled on the margin of a letter from an editor at Cambridge University Press. It was just two lines of poetry:

> The maypole toppled and the music failed.
> The name is whispered now, the dance is done.

He recognized it after a moment as a bit of Justin Geoffrey's verse, and made a note of it. That evening, when he got back to the apartment, he went straight to the little shelf where he kept the books he'd brought from Arkham, and pulled one out, a slim hardback with art-deco patterns on the jacket and the title, *The People of the Monolith*, in ornate lettering. It took him only a few moments to find the poem he wanted.

> MERRY MOUNT
> Prim houses slumber on the ancient height
> Where dancers once defied the Pilgrims' ire,

Leaping and coupling 'round Walpurga's fire,
Hailing the coming of the vernal night.
They called it Merry Mount in days long gone,
Before the laws of frightened men prevailed,
The maypole toppled and the music failed.
The name is whispered now, the dance is done.
The hill remains. Beneath it, in a gloom
Unbroken by the years, untouched by light,
Strange presences endure the earth's cold
night.
They shall not wait forever in their tomb:
For what danced joyfully 'neath olden skies
Shall waken, and in dreadful wrath shall
rise.

He closed the book slowly, remembering other places where
the worshippers of the Great Old Ones had found a short-
lived sanctuary in the New World and then been driven off
or killed. Merry Mount had been neither the first nor the
bloodiest such place; eight years back at Chorazin he'd had
to deal with legacies from another, Roodsport in Maine, from
which only two people had escaped alive. In Geoffrey's lines,
though, he sensed more sharply than usual the immense trag-
edy of the New World, the way those who'd fled persecution
and oppression in Europe so readily became persecutors and
oppressors in their turn. Why Angell had copied the lines he
didn't know, but the last couplet circled through his mind for
days thereafter.

* * *

It was a few days later that he found out for certain that the
Radiance wasn't the only source of danger in Providence.

He was returning from the John Hay Library at evening as
usual. Though the Angell collection had given him little help,

the library's collections included plenty of other things that might be relevant, among them shelves upon shelves of occult magazines from the 1920s. He knew from prior research that Charles Dexter Ward had written articles on alchemy for *The Occult Review*, *Le Lotus Bleu*, and other journals of the same kind; there was also supposed to be an essay on the same subject by the famous New Orleans occultist Etienne-Laurent de Marigny that cited private correspondence with "a young scholar of Rhode Island" who pretty much had to be Charles Dexter Ward, though nobody he'd read had cited the article or even named the journal where it appeared. Whether any of those would contain anything bearing on the lost Angell papers, Owen had no idea, but he'd resolved to leave no stone unturned.

Three days sitting in the periodicals stacks, paging through volume after volume of old occult journals nobody ever bothered to add to research databases or even report in the long-lapsed *Reader's Guide to Periodical Literature*, brought him no closer to his goal. He'd found two of Ward's articles, and noted down the details for future reference—Miriam Akeley would want to know about them, he guessed, and for all he knew Jenny Chaudronnier would someday add alchemy to her already impressive knowledge of forbidden lore. Even so, getting up from the table and heading toward the library's ground floor felt like the commutation of a sentence.

The air outside was hot and humid, with a steady wind pushing clouds up from the south. Owen started down College Street in a pensive mood. By the time he neared the bridge over the Providence River the tide was coming in hard, and with the wind driving the same way, brackish water was bubbling up out of storm drains and sloshing across the cracked and potholed streets. The bridge itself was well above water, but the approaches on either side were awash, so he had to veer north to Steeple Street and cross there, at the confluence of the two rivers that divided Providence's northern side. A bronze statue of H.P. Lovecraft stood on the bridge, with a bronze cat wreathed about his ankles; Owen gave it an amused nod of greeting and walked on.

Once across, he veered south again and paced through the downtown district. Vending boxes for the local paper, the *Providence Journal*, had a headline yelling about the latest news from Greenland—there'd been another big meltwater surge, another thousand square miles or so of former ice sheet bobbing around the North Atlantic, and sea level up worldwide another inch or two. That was hardly news any more, and Owen kept walking.

Halfway through downtown, he happened to notice two people on the other side of the street, heading the same direction he was. They were just two of many pedestrians, and they looked perfectly nondescript, but their movements reminded him of Special Forces guys he'd known in Iraq, and something subtle seemed to knot and twist about them. It took Owen a moment to realize that it was a peculiar pattern of voor, and another to recall where it was he'd sensed it before.

By then the two of them had reached the corner and turned to cross to his side of the street, and he recognized one of them. Ten years had passed since he'd seen her lean tanned face, and her hair had gone from blonde to silver in the interval, but there could be no doubt who it was: April Castaigne, the commander of the Fellowship of the Yellow Sign.

The sudden appearance of a shoggoth right there in downtown Providence wouldn't have startled him more. The soldiers of the King in Yellow went where their master sent them, into the world's far corners and, if rumor was to be trusted, into other worlds as well. To see them twice in ten years in the same part of the world was all but unheard of. Still, there Castaigne was, waiting at a street corner for the light to change. Owen considered his options, decided he owed it to her and the Fellowship to warn them of Dyson's presence.

At that moment someone took hold of his arm.

He turned, fast. The woman with the strange eyes was standing beside him, where he was sure she hadn't been a moment before. Owen tried to say something, but she pressed a finger to her lips, and the words froze in his throat. A quick motion of her head told him to follow, and without any decision on his part, he went with her into a gap between two old brick buildings.

"You know who she is," the woman said. Her voice had a curious silken quality. "She isn't looking for you—but she must not find you."

Owen's voice returned to him then. "Why?"

"Whose will are you trying to thwart?"

The question left him stunned and silent. After a moment she smiled, and said, "Go."

He went. It was as simple as that: a compulsion seized him, kept him walking until he was halfway across an overpass with the cracked and half-abandoned freeway stretching out to either side. He blinked, then, shook himself, and after a moment kept walking toward Federal Hill, having nowhere else to go.

The woman with the strange eyes—

She wasn't human. That much he was sure of, though the fact didn't give him any clue about what she might be. If she belonged to one of the six elder races, the beings who'd dwelt on the little world called Earth longer than humans had, she'd disguised herself well, but other things roamed the world too, and not all of them had names.

Her nature could be left for later, he decided. Two things, though, couldn't be ignored. The first was that she clearly knew more about the reason he was in Providence than anyone should have been able to guess. The second and more important was the knowledge that her question implied.

There was a secret that not even the *Necronomicon* revealed: the reason Cthulhu slept in drowned R'lyeh, dead yet dreaming until the stars were right. None of the tomes explained it; none of the traditions of the Starry Wisdom, the Esoteric Order of Dagon, the Tcho-Tcho people, or the folk of drowned Poseidonis whispered that mystery. A few scraps of lore in the *Seven Cryptical Books of Hsan* and the *Pnakotic Manuscript* hinted at it, but it had taken careless words from the patriarch Atal in that strange dimension of being called the Dreamlands, recalling a scrap of forbidden knowledge, to set the dreamer Randolph Carter on the right track—and from Carter the knowledge had come to Miriam Akeley, and then to Owen.

There had been war between Cthulhu and the King in Yellow, the monarch of the Great Old Ones whose name was not safe for mortal lips to speak—and in that war Cthulhu had been defeated and bound by the King. That was the secret.

And if the King in Yellow meant his ancient foe to remain bound—

Owen thrust the thought from his mind, kept walking.

* * *

He found the essay by Etienne-Laurent de Marigny two days later. It was tucked away in the yellowed Autumn 1931 issue of a long-defunct occult quarterly from New Orleans, between a sloppily researched article on the Eltdown Shards and a full-page advertisement for "spiritual supplies" from the Cracker Jack Drugstore on Rampart Street. De Marigny deserved his reputation, Owen decided; he wrote learnedly about the *opus vegetabilis* or vegetable work, which produced herbal balsams that could prolong human life for a century or more; the *opus mineralis* or mineral work, which yielded the Philosopher's Stone and the Elixir of Life; and the most secret alchemy of all, the *opus animalis* or animal work Joseph Curwen and Charles Dexter Ward had practiced, which could revive the dead from their essential salts. None of it seemed to bear on Owen's quest, though, until he got to the final page of the essay and read:

A young scholar of Rhode Island, a correspondent of mine for several years, found
certain papers bearing on this last and most
arcane branch of the alchemical art in a
concealed cupboard in a house once owned by
a famous alchemist of an earlier day. Such
hiding places have seen much use over the
centuries by alchemists, as the learned Ful-
canelli hints in his admirable book on the
dwellings of the philosophers; and it is by
no means unknown for the discoverer of such
a cache to return it to its original place of
concealment, or to replace it with records
of his own discoveries, for some future student to find.

Owen copied the whole paragraph into his notebook, and sat
there thinking about it for some minutes. Etienne-Laurent de
Marigny had been a friend of Randolph Carter, the Boston
author and mystic who'd vanished in 1926; de Marigny himself disappeared in 1932, leaving behind a much-reprinted
book on the Tarot cards and the best English translation of
The Seven Cryptical Books of Hsan; he'd clearly known Charles
Dexter Ward, at least by correspondence—and Owen couldn't
shake the thought that de Marigny might have meant that passage as a hint, "for some future student to find." There was
at least one such place in Providence, the secret cupboard in
Joseph Curwen's house where the old alchemist had hidden
his own papers; was it possible that Charles Dexter Ward could
have arranged to hide the Angell papers there in turn?

He got up from the table, put the magazines he'd been
reading back on the shelves where they'd been, and headed
for the part of the stacks that contained books on US history. It took him three or four tries, but he was able to find
a book on the history of colonial Providence that gave the

address of Curwen's house as 128 Olney Court, and included a photograph. He copied down the details in his notebook, and then left the library, determined to walk past Curwen's house and try to get a sense of how best to get inside and search it.

A few minutes later he was pacing along the same street he'd found the night he attended the opening of the Enoch Bowen exhibit, with the same burger place, Howard's, just in front of him. The thought of stopping for a meal was the last thing on his mind, but he happened to glance up the street at the people coming toward him. He recognized one of them in a sudden moment of cold horror: brown buzzcut hair, angular clean-shaven face, harsh blue eyes. He ducked into Howard's, let the greeter lead him to a small table on the back wall under one of the plastic glow-in-the-dark octopuses, and hoped he hadn't been spotted.

The front door, opening maybe two minutes later, told him otherwise. He glanced quickly around, noted the lack of convenient exits. Stupid, he thought, to be caught so easily. Voices wove near the door, the greeter's alto crossing a baritone Owen thought he remembered, and then footfalls crossed the room to his table. He did not let himself look up.

"Owen Merrill," the half-familiar voice said. Owen glanced up then. It was Dyson, of course, still in nondescript civilian clothes, gesturing at the empty seat. "May I?"

Owen nodded. "You have the advantage of me," he said, "Mr. Dyson."

"Michael Dyson," the other said, sitting.

Another nod acknowledged the name. "I was wondering if you were looking for me."

"Not at all. I was surprised to see you at the museum—the last I heard, you were still in Dunwich—and just as surprised to see you now."

"I visit other places now and again."

"So I see." Dyson considered him. "If I were to ask why you're here, would you tell me?"

"Yes," Owen said. "Doing some research for a friend in the libraries here." Then, meeting the other man's gaze: "If I were to ask the same question, would you tell me?"

"No."

"Fair enough."

Unexpectedly, Dyson laughed. "Good," he said. "Good. Can I pick up lunch?"

"Sure," Owen said, hiding his surprise.

"Thank you. I'm off duty and unmonitored at the moment, and it's not often that we get a chance to talk to someone from your side without guns in the way." A fractional smile creased his face. "Or tentacles. I'll tell you this much: I was doing research in one of the libraries here, too, and decided to go find a place to eat. A chance encounter, if you believe in chance."

"That depends," said Owen, "on what you mean by chance."

* * *

The waitress came over a moment later and asked if they were ready to order. "What are the specialty sandwiches?" Owen asked.

She gave him a bright smile. "The Cthulhu Burger's a fish sandwich with guacamole on top. The Burger in Yellow's a double cheeseburger with curry sauce. The Yig Burger's a chicken breast fillet Southwestern style, with pepper jack and jalapenos to give it bite. The Nyarlathotep Burger's a double hamburger with flame-broiled red bell peppers and Egyptian onions, and the Shub Sandwich is blackened chicken, bacon, lettuce, and tomato, with goat cheese, on toast."

"And the Yog-Sothoth Burger?" Owen asked then.

"One with everything," the waitress said without missing a beat.

Owen settled on the Shub Sandwich and a bottle of the local porter, Dyson on a plain hamburger, fries, and a light beer. The waitress went away. "They don't have a clue," said Dyson then. "About the beings you serve, I mean."

Owen gave him a wry look. "Your side's worked overtime to make sure the only things they know about the Great Old Ones come out of H.P. Lovecraft stories. I've wondered more than once if your people back then put him up to that."

A quick shake of Dyson's head denied it. "If our analysts had anticipated how popular his stories were going to be, he'd have been poisoned years sooner."

Owen took that in, and neither of them said anything until the waitress brought back their orders, made a little conversation, and left.

"There are two things I'd like to ask you," Dyson said then. Owen motioned with his sandwich, inviting the questions, and he went on. "First of all—the business at Chorazin. Your people had the drop on my men and me. You could have just taken us out. Instead, you let us go, and you didn't have anything ugly waiting to jump us on the road back to our base near Buffalo. That's not your side's standard procedure, and I'd like to know why you did it."

"We don't have a standard procedure," said Owen.

Dyson snorted. "I know what happened to the negation teams that went to Dunwich—and what's happened way too often since then to teams of ours that get caught out in wild country."

"That's Yhoundeh's doing. She has a grudge against your organization, you know."

"And you don't?"

Owen glanced at him. "No. I'm not sure why, but I don't. I wish you'd go away and leave the rest of us alone—but if all of you went to Mars and built your rationalist Utopia there, I'd say good riddance and wish you the best of luck."

"That was tried," Dyson said.

Owen gave him a dubious look. "Seriously?"

"Seriously. It didn't work out."

"Sounds like there's a flaw in your theories, then."

Dyson shook his head again. "It wasn't a problem on our side. There are—things on Mars, at least as bad as the ones here on Earth. Nobody who went came back."

Owen pondered that, went on after a moment. "At Chorazin, I wanted you and your men gone, and I didn't want any more casualties on my side than I could help. That was all. It didn't matter to me at all whether you or your team lived or died, as long as you left—and it was less trouble and risk for our people just to let you go."

Dyson nodded slowly after a moment, said nothing. Owen applied himself to his sandwich, which turned out to be considerably tastier than the Cthulhu Burger.

"Fair enough," Dyson said then. "The other question is this." He downed a swallow of his light beer. "I looked you up in our databases after the Chorazin business. You had a good military record, honorable discharge, solid grades at Purdue and Miskatonic—and then you threw all that away, and became an enemy of reason and progress. I want to know why."

Owen took another bite of his sandwich, chewed and swallowed. "You talk about reason and progress as though those words still mean something," he said, "as though they justify all the people your side has killed, all the lives you've ruined, everything that's happened since your goon squads hacked an old man to pieces before the moon mirror of Irem and splashed it with his blood. I bet you expect me to talk about something just as abstract—but I don't have any abstractions to offer. The choice I made was a matter of who I love, who befriended me, who gave me help and protection when I desperately needed it—and who tried to turn me into an empty husk of a human being, the way your people at Miskatonic did to Shelby Adams."

"That program's purely experimental," said Dyson. "And probably going to be discontinued. The results aren't stable."

"Will you discontinue Clark Noyes while you're at it?"

Dyson leaned forward. "What would you say if I told you that Dr. Noyes, and the others like him, are the next stage of human evolution?"

Owen met his gaze. "I'd say that you're entitled to your opinion."

It was not the answer Dyson had apparently been expecting. "It's not just my opinion."

"Yes, it is." He raised the bottle of porter, drank. "I didn't take a lot of biology classes at Purdue, but I took enough to know that when someone talks about evolution the way you've just done, they're shoveling smoke. The next stage of human evolution is however we adapt to the next set of changes the planet throws at us, if we do adapt and don't die out instead, and that's all it is. What you've said amounts to propaganda for what your side wants, what you think human beings ought to be turned into—and there again, you're entitled to your opinion."

"And you'd rather trust the monstrosities you call the Great Old Ones to do whatever they want with the future of our species?"

"All things considered," said Owen, "they've done a much better job of things so far than your side has—so yes, I would."

Dyson gave him a long hard look, began to say something else, thought better of it, and finished off his burger instead. Time passed; Owen finished his sandwich and the porter. Finally, after downing the rest of his beer, Dyson said, "Okay. I don't pretend to understand, but—" He shrugged. "I suppose that's inevitable."

Owen nodded, said nothing.

Dyson paused, and then went on in a low voice. "Still, you let my men and me go when you could have dropped us. I owe you something for that, so I'm going to take a risk. Go ahead and finish your research, but don't take too long—and when you're done, get out of Providence. Things are going to happen here, and if you're identified by the people in charge, they'll have you negated as fast as they can. Understood?"

Owen nodded. "Understood—and thank you."

Dyson considered him for another moment, then got up, and walked away from the table without another word. He glanced back while paying their tab, then headed out the door.

The waitress came by to ask Owen if he wanted another beer, and he shook his head. A few minutes later he got up and left the restaurant. There might well be a negation team waiting outside, he realized, but if so, they'd have guns trained on every possible exit. He went out into the summer light with his head up.

Nothing happened. A few pedestrians strolled along the sidewalk, a battered car drove by: that was all. A crisp breeze was blowing in from the east, and it seemed to carry an immense stillness with it—a silence that suddenly made him think of the poem about Merry Mount, and the long and bitter history that had been sitting there at the table with him and Dyson.

The thought of going on to the Curwen house occurred to him then, but he decided against it. The encounter with Dyson had left him shaken, and he might need all his wits about him to find a way into the house. After a moment, he turned and headed west toward downtown.

* * *

He got back to Federal Hill before the afternoon was half over and climbed the long narrow stair to his apartment. Once he was inside and the door was locked, he let out a long ragged breath, took off his backpack, and slumped into one of the chairs. He stared at nothing in particular for a long while, thinking about Dyson's words and his own, and about the long war between the Radiance and the Great Old Ones: between those who saw as humanity as the lords of creation, the conquerors of nature, the measure of all things, and those who knew better.

Of all the things that Dyson had said, his words about the Radiant colony on Mars set Owen's mind spinning the most. He knew as well as any other initiate that Mars had its native races and its Great Old Ones, and knew as well what to make of the odd way that so many space probes sent from Earth to Mars never reached their destination or broke down as soon as they got there. For the Radiance to ignore that, and try to colonize a world where Great Old Ones ruled unhindered: that suggested even more arrogance on their part than he'd imagined.

Arrogance, he thought. Or, just maybe, something else.

He got up, made some tea, tried to distract himself with a book. That did no noticeable good, and eventually he left the apartment for Sancipriani's. It was early yet, well before the usual dinner rush, but he decided that a good meal and an early bed were good preparations for what might be a long and difficult day ahead.

The back room at the restaurant wasn't quite empty when he got there, though. Ellen Chernak was sitting alone at one of the big tables, with a plate of spaghetti alla puttanesca and a glass of red wine in front of her. She glanced up when he came in, considered him for a moment, and then made a little gesture at the chair across from hers: you can sit here if you want.

He crossed the room and sat down. They made the ordinary pleasant noises, and by then Julie Olmert had come out with a menu in hand, which Owen didn't need, and a robust Italian beer, which he did. Once Julie was out of the room, Ellen said, "How's the research going?"

"Mixed," Owen admitted. "Found some interesting things, but not what I'm looking for."

"That happens," said Ellen. She downed some of the wine. "Speaking of interesting things, did you go to that museum exhibit about Enoch Bowen?" Owen nodded, and she went on. "So did I—but I don't think anybody else from the congregation did, and I don't recommend discussing it with them." In response to his questioning look; "Certain people get bent out of shape if anybody shows too much curiosity about Bowen, the Mother Church—or the things that used to be in the Church before it got torn down. Just a helpful hint."

Clatter of the door warned of Julie's return with bread and salad. She made a little conversation and headed off again.

Owen considered the woman across from him for a long moment. From her expression, he wasn't at all sure how much further to push that line of discussion, and instead asked, "Do you mind if I ask a personal question?" She gestured, inviting it, and he went on. "Every other congregation I know, seventh degree members are on the council of elders automatically, and you get fifth and sixth degree people in there too. Is it different here?"

She gave him an assessing look. "How do other congregations choose their elders?"

"One or more of the elders propose a new elder, and if nobody objects, they're in."

"Same here," Ellen said. "And the four we've got haven't proposed a new elder in more than twenty years now. The Watcher can raise as many people to the higher degrees as it wants; the elders don't have to care."

"There are ways to force them to act," said Owen, baffled.

She gave him another long assessing look. "There are reasons those don't get used."

Julie came in again with Owen's entree, a pizza Margherita sized for one person, then ducked back in and returned with a second beer for Owen and another glass of wine for Ellen. Once she was gone, Owen asked, "Have you considered going somewhere else?"

"Often." She raised her glass in a mocking salute, and he grinned and tapped his beer bottle against it. "But I don't like to back down; I'm enough younger than our elders that I'll pretty likely still be here when they're gone; and there's the family thing."

Owen thought he understood. "Being descended from founding members."

"Not just that. Ever heard of a place called Merry Mount?"

He gave her a startled glance, then nodded. "Yeah. Thomas Morton's place."

That got the first broad smile he'd seen on her face yet. "That's the one. My mom's people are descended from an

Indian woman who got away safe from there with Morton's own daughter three months along in her belly. Somehow that makes me a little less willing to put up with certain kinds of nonsense—and somebody's got to be here to pick up the pieces when the four of them aren't there any more."

Owen was about to ask her more when the door to the alley opened and a half dozen of the regulars came in. They gave perfunctory greetings and sat on the other side of the room, but Ellen gave him a warning look, and he nodded fractionally. They found other things to talk about while the room gradually filled, and they finished their meals and left.

It was only an hour or so after he'd left his apartment that Owen climbed the long stair again, but when he opened the door he found a sheet of paper on the floor, with typing on it. He turned on the lights and picked it up. It read:

```
    its not safe to pry into things that arent
    your business
    mazzini knows youre making eyes at his wife
    so does everybody else
    why dont you just go back where you came from
```

Owen considered it for a long moment. If it had been hand-written, or handled more than incidentally, he might have been able to sense the author's traces in the voor that pooled in the paper; that was difficult work for a third degree initiate, but he'd managed the trick a few times. As it was, he took it and placed it in an unused drawer of the bedroom dresser, then got the kettle heating for a cup of tea and sat by the table, thinking.

There was, he guessed, one person he could ask about the notes and get a straight answer, but that would have to wait until morning. In the meantime—

Just then he felt an odd feeling, not quite familiar, as though someone was looking at him from behind. He turned quickly, to find a blank wall and nothing else. The sense remained for a little while, and then slowly faded out.

CHAPTER 5

THE CASE OF CHARLES DEXTER WARD

The next morning, when Owen left the apartment, he turned away from College Hill and headed for the co-op grocery that Sam Mazzini managed. Unlicensed and unadvertised, like most of the businesses that catered solely to the Starry Wisdom community, it was tucked away in a basement under a secondhand shop cluttered with yellowing paperbacks and assorted trinkets from the stray corners of Providence's past. The way there led past a fenced back yard that he knew belonged to a Starry Wisdom family, and as he passed he heard half a dozen girl's voices rising in a singsong chant:

> "The King is in Carcosa,
> The Goat is on the hills,
> And there and back the One in Black
> Goes wand'ring where he wills.
> But down below the ocean,
> The Dreaming Lord's asleep,
> Until the night the stars are right
> And call him from the deep.
> He waits for one year, two years, three years ..."

It was a rhyme for jumping rope, one Owen had heard Asenath repeating more times than he could easily remember.

They would count the years until one of the jumpers made a misstep. He slowed, listening, and suddenly thought of Asenath back in Arkham. He clenched his hands, missing her, missing Laura and Barnabas, and only when the chant dissolved in laughter—they'd made it to the count of ten before that happened—did he head onward at his usual pace toward Sam's concealed grocery.

The shop door creaked alarmingly as Owen entered, and the gnomish old man behind the counter, whom he'd met at Sancipriani's, gave him a nod and an unreadable look, and went back to work straightening items on the shelves.

Owen waited while an elderly couple, outsiders by their look, moved forward out of sight of the door in back marked NO ADMITTANCE. Once they were gone, Owen ducked through it and descended the groaning wooden stairway on the other side into Sam's store.

Despite the difference in setting, it looked enough like the general store Jemmy Coles kept in Dunwich to shake loose a cascade of wistful memories from the decade just past. There were shelves of fresh produce and barrels of grains and dry beans, rows of glass canning jars full of last autumn's harvest, a big wheezing refrigerator case salvaged from some defunct corner grocery with milk and cream in glass bottles, round cheeses sealed in wax, an assortment of meats, and the day's catch up from Westerly, where the Esoteric Order of Dagon had a lodge and traded with the Deep Ones who dwelt on the sea floor off Brenton Point. That stirred other memories, tinged with the salt scent of Innsmouth, but Owen pushed them aside.

"Owen!" Sam said, coming out from the store office at the sound of footsteps on the stair. "Good to see you. What can I get for you?"

"Hi, Sam. It's not about groceries this time. Is there someplace private we can talk?"

"Sure." He gave Owen an uneasy look, but motioned to the office and led the way into the cramped little room. "What's up?"

Owen waited until Sam had closed the door, and then said, "A couple of really unpleasant notes somebody typed and pushed under my door."

Sam's face went gray. He stared at Owen for a long moment and then, in a low voice, said, "Oh crap. I didn't think they'd do that—not when you're from another congregation."

"Who are 'they'?" Owen asked at once.

"Nobody knows. It just happens every so often. You don't talk about it or ugly things start happening." He met Owen's startled gaze, drew in an unsteady breath, went on. "Don't breathe a word of this to anyone else, okay? The thing is, they find out stuff. Nobody knows how, but if you've got something to hide, they dig it up. There are things I've only ever told Char, and those showed up in one of those notes—I don't know if they blackmailed her into talking, or what." A drop of sweat beaded on his forehead, and then another. "And there's stupid stuff I did when I was young that I haven't told anybody about, and they know about that, too. I've gotten two notes over the years telling me they'd tell Char everything if I did this or didn't do that—and she'd wring my neck if she found out." He pulled a handkerchief out of his shirt pocket, wiped his forehead. "What did they tell you to do?"

"Go home," said Owen.

"You might want to think about doing that."

Owen shook his head. "Not until I've finished the work I came here to do."

Sam regarded him with a worried look. "It could get ugly. We had a couple of folks driven to suicide, and others who left town and nobody knows what happened to them."

"I'll take the risk," Owen said. Then, a moment later: "One of the notes claimed that I was making eyes at Charlene, by the way."

Sam winced. "I got a note last night saying that she was making eyes at you."

"You know that's not true."

"Yeah," said Sam. "But that says they've got it in for you. As I said, it could get ugly."

Owen could think of little more to say. He thanked Sam for the information, watched the way the man blanched and sweated, made the usual noises and left. The door at the top of the stairs had a peephole, so he could make sure nobody was in sight, and he paused longer than he had to before going out through the secondhand shop.

Outside in the alley, he shook his head, went back the way he'd come. The other Starry Wisdom congregations he'd known had their share of gossip, petty politics, and quarrels that stretched out over years until everyone involved was dead, but nothing like this.

If it gets ugly, he thought, I'll deal—but first things first.

He passed the Starry Wisdom church and the narrow little alley that led to his apartment, and kept going. Ahead of him, downtown's skyscrapers loomed up; beyond them College Hill rose dark into the morning sky, and north of that—

The house where Joseph Curwen had hidden his lore, and where Charles Dexter Ward might have done the same thing. His pace quickened in anticipation.

* * *

The Curwen house was in no better shape than he'd expected. Pallid and sagging in the light of midmorning, it loomed above the sidewalk, two and a half stories tall, with white clapboard sides, a plain peaked roof, a big central chimney, and a once-elegant doorway with a rayed fanlight above it and Doric pilasters to either side. Drawn curtains, old but not quite shabby, hid whatever was within.

Owen considered his options. To one side of the Curwen house was another of similar style with a FOR LEASE sign in one window, to the other side was a brick apartment building of 1950s vintage with rental information posted hopefully beside the door. The whole Stampers Hill neighborhood was shabby-genteel and an easy walk from two colleges; it was probably rented to students, he guessed, and that meant it might well be empty until the runup to fall semester.

He crossed the street, and then went through the gap between Curwen's house and the empty house next to it. The view from behind gave him no more clues than he had before, except that there was no car in the backyard parking space, and the houses on the far side of the fence looked just as untenanted as the ones on Olney Court. The kitchen door in back was almost certainly locked, he knew. Still, there was a chance …

He went to the door. It had a window in its upper half, and though there was a curtain behind it, it gapped in the middle. Through the gap he could see an ordinary kitchen with decades-old fixtures. The sink and the dishrack alike were empty, and those of the shelves he could see were bare. Worth the risk, then. He reached for the knob, tested it, found that it turned.

An instant later something thick and flexible as a ship's cable looped around his neck, yanked him backwards. He tried to twist away, struck backwards reflexively with one fist. The blow connected with something that felt like a body, but the thing around his neck tightened sharply, and other loops caught his arms and pinned them. His vision blurred and swam as whatever it was dragged him back, spun him around, and then hauled him in through the suddenly open kitchen door.

The door slammed behind him. A few moments later he was in a room further inside the house, and whatever had him in its grip forced him down onto a wooden chair. The pressure on his throat let in barely enough air to keep him conscious, and so it took a long moment before he recognized the shape in front of him. It was the young black woman he'd encountered so many times at the John Hay Library.

"If you give me any trouble," she said, "or don't answer my questions, Pierre will tear your head off. I mean that quite literally. Who are you?"

Owen tried to speak, but didn't have enough air in his lungs to manage it. The woman realized that, and nodded once to whatever held Owen pinned. The pressure on his neck let up just enough to allow him to breathe freely, and he drew in a ragged breath, another. "My name's Owen Merrill," he said.

"Why were you snooping around this house?"

"I'm doing research for a friend," he said. "This house used to belong to an alchemist named Joseph Curwen. My friend—"

He'd meant to say "my friend is a historian," but the words froze in his mouth. The young woman smiled, said nothing.

"My friend's a sorceress," Owen said then. "So are you, I'm guessing."

"Me? No."

"A witch, then."

"Not the kind you have here in America." With a peremptory gesture: "But you were telling me about your friend."

Owen considered her. She was using sorcery on him, that was clear—he'd read, in the *Necronomicon* and elsewhere, of spells that made it impossible to tell a lie—and the shapes that wrapped around his throat and arms were tentacles, he was sure of that much. That told him he was at least potentially among allies, and suggested one risky but workable way to put that to the test. "You're worried that I'm with the Radiance," he said. "I'm not."

Her eyebrows went up, and after a moment she nodded again to whatever it was that held him pinned. The last of the pressure on Owen's neck went away, and that tentacle slid off him; the others that pinned his arms remained.

"Fair enough," she said. "Again, though, you were telling me about your friend."

"There's not much more I can tell," Owen said then. "Not without knowing who you are and where you stand. If that gets my head torn off, so be it."

She nodded after a moment. "This research you're doing for your friend," she said then. "It has to do with Joseph Curwen?"

"Potentially, yes."

"And with Charles Dexter Ward?"

"Indirectly," he said after a moment. Then, taking another risk: "He may have inherited papers from Dr. Angell of Brown University. My friend needs those papers, or copies of them."

Her eyebrows went up again, further. "I know about the papers," she said.

"Do you know where they are?" She shook her head, and he went on. "One possibility is that they're in the hiding place that Joseph Curwen used for his papers. I came here to see if I could find a way into the house and look for that."

"I've already looked there, and there's nothing inside." She considered him, then nodded again to the creature that held Owen captive. The tentacles that bound his hands behind him released them. "I gather," she said then, "that we're more or less on the same side of this business. If I'm wrong, Pierre is very quick. He can follow your scent through space and time, and he's killed rather more than once."

"Pierre?" Owen asked. Only after he'd repeated the name did he remember the odd, slumped child who'd ridden to Providence with the woman in front of him.

She laughed, and gestured to the thing behind him. It came out from behind the chair with the same curious shuffling gait he'd noticed on the bus and the downtown sidewalk, but it wasn't a child. He couldn't tell what it was, for it wore a loose shapeless hooded garment like a monk's robe, but the ends of two tentacles poked out of the end of each sleeve. The feet that slipped out from under the hem of the robe as it walked were both webbed and clawed, and there seemed to be more than two of them. The creature's face was a blunt cone, with a taut lipless mouth running from one side to the other and an identical seam running vertically. From each of the four quarters of the face, a single expressionless black eye regarded Owen.

"Smile for us, Pierre," the woman said.

In response, the creature's face split open along the mouth-lines into four wedges, and gaped open. Each of its four jaws had its own arc of hooked teeth, and a long barbed tongue played briefly in the air. Then its face closed up again, and the four eyes contemplated Owen.

"We're definitely on the same side," the woman said then. She had been watching Owen the whole time. "Most people carry on like anything if they see Pierre."

"I'm used to tentacles," Owen said.

That got him an amused glance. "Are they common around here?"

He smiled unwillingly. "Where I come from, yes, actually, they are—but I have to admit I've never seen anything quite like Pierre."

"That's not surprising," she told him. "I don't believe there's another in the world, nor has been for quite a few years." She gestured. "But we can go to the library, if you like. I don't imagine that chair's very comfortable."

Owen got up, flexed his arms. "Thank you," he said. "Ms.—?"

"Ward," she said. "Hannah Ward."

"Any relation?" he asked.

He'd meant it as a joke, but she burst into a broad smile. "Why, yes," she said. "That's why I'm here. I'm Charles Dexter Ward's great-granddaughter."

* * *

"It's a common enough story," said Hannah Ward. "Boy meets girl—is there anything more old-fashioned these days? But that's how it was, and it began right here."

The ground-floor library had seen many better days. Little remained of the fine wainscoting and bolection molding that graced it when it was built in 1761; cheap wallpaper covered the walls, and though a scroll-and-urn overmantel still stood

above the fireplace, it had been battered and worn by more
than two and a half centuries of domestic incident. The fireplace itself had a manufactured stove insert filling it, and up
above the fireplace, another discordant note, was a framed
poster from a Grateful Dead concert many decades past. Still,
faint echoes of past elegance lingered here and there, and not
all of them dated from the time of Joseph Curwen.

Owen let himself settle back into the couch. On the other
end, Pierre waited silently. His alien four-eyed face regarded
Owen from beneath the hood, its expression unreadable.
Hannah sat in an armchair close by; the lamp overhead cast a
pool of light down onto the three of them.

"Lovecraft mentioned a couple named Asa and Hannah
who lived here," Owen ventured.

Her lip curled. "Yes, he did—and of course he turned them
into domestic drudges in his story, which was a flat lie. Dr. Asa
Frederic Tibbets was the professor of French language and literature at Bannister College—have you heard of it?"

"Isn't that Bannister University now?" Owen asked. "Just
north of here?"

"That's the one. What's the term? A historically black college. Back then, not so historically." That called up another
smile. "My great-great-grandfather taught there, as I said. His
wife Hannah, a Crandall originally, was the music teacher at a
school for young black ladies here in town, before she and Asa
met, fell in love, and got married. You might be interested to
know that Theodore Ward, Charles' father, attended the wedding; he was a tolerant man by the standards of the time, and
donated a good deal of money to the Bannister College scholarship fund, which is more than most white businessmen here
ever did.

"Dr. and Mrs. Tibbets had one child, a daughter, and her
name was Lydia. As you can imagine, with parents like hers,
she got as good an education as any child in Providence; she
was intelligent, literate, talented, spoke French as easily as

English, read the Latin and Greek classics, and sang like a nightingale. Oh, and she was quite remarkably pretty, too. Let me show you."

She reached into her purse, pulled out an old leather photo case, and handed it to Owen, who opened it. Inside were a pair of century-old black and white photos, only slightly faded. The one on the left showed a young white man with a thin face, blond hair, and a curious intent look. On the left was a matching portrait of a young black woman with her hair straightened and cut short in a fashionable 1920s style, who had a strong resemblance to Hannah. She hadn't exaggerated, either; her ancestress had been a woman of rare beauty. He handed the photos back. "Lydia and Charles?"

"Their wedding pictures. We'll get to that." She put the photo case back in her purse. "She and Charles first met when he was sixteen and she was fifteen, and they both fell head over heels in love. A good bit of the time Charles' family thought he was walking around Providence, he was spending time with Lydia. Of course there was nothing to be done about it; a rich white manufacturer's son couldn't marry a Negro girl, no matter how beautiful and well-educated and talented she might be. They swore to part forever, oh, half a dozen times." She laughed. "And always broke their vows and met again. By all accounts it was really quite touching.

"But Charles, I'm told, had a keen sense of honor, and so when he turned eighteen, he made an appointment with Lydia's father, told him everything, and begged him for advice. Old Dr. Tibbets wasn't a narrow-minded man, and of course such things did happen now and then even in those days. He talked to Charles, and then he talked to Lydia, and then finally he and his wife, and Charles and Lydia, sat in this very room and talked the whole thing out. The upshot of it all was that Charles and Lydia became engaged, and Charles set out to convince his family to let him go to Europe. Once he got there, the arrangement was, Lydia and her parents would join him in Paris, where interracial marriage wasn't an issue; the marriage would happen, and after that, Charles would return to the United States only as often as was necessary to keep his parents happy. Dr. Tibbets had a degree from the Sorbonne, you see, and plenty of friends in France, and he and Hannah had already planned to settle in France once he retired.

"I never learned if Charles' parents guessed what was in the wind, but they wouldn't let him travel to Europe until he came of age. That was on the twenty-eighth of April, 1923, and Charles kept his promise. On the eighteenth of June he boarded a White Star liner in Boston, and on the first of July Lydia and her parents boarded a Cunard liner in New York—they were very careful, you see. He sailed to Liverpool, took the train to Harwich, crossed the Channel from there and then caught a train to Paris, while they sailed straight to Boulogne.

"The wedding was in Paris, on the sixteenth of August, and Lydia and Charles settled into lodgings on the Left Bank. Dr. Tibbets had a friend in London who served as a mail drop—Charles sent letters to his parents to the friend, who put British postage on them and mailed them from a box in Great Russell Street. It was all very well thought out, and when the Wards made noises about visiting him in Europe, he found other mail drops in Prague, Vienna, and some corner or other of Transylvania."

"He never actually went there?" Owen interjected.

"Transylvania? Yes, but that was later—and that was because of the other side of the story, the side that Lovecraft mentioned."

"Joseph Curwen."

"Exactly. Here's another photo you might find interesting." Another photo case appeared from her purse, and she handed it to Owen. Inside was another black and white photograph, slightly blurred, of an eighteenth-century painting: a man seated in a carved wooden chair next to a window, beyond which dim forms suggested wharves and ships. The face in the portrait was identical to the one in the wedding photo, despite the centuries that divided them.

* * *

"The story Lovecraft told was tolerably close to the truth," Hannah went on. "Of course he put his usual silly slant on things. But Joseph Curwen the alchemist did indeed raise people from the dead by way of their essential salts, though not on the wholesale basis Lovecraft claimed; he was murdered by a mob of Providence citizens, stirred up by tales told them by a jealous rival; and he worked sorceries to call down the years to Charles Ward, his great-great-great-grandson, who traveled to various parts of Europe to learn how to revive him.

"What happened here in Providence after Charles returned—that I know only from Lovecraft, and from letters in the family archives, because Lydia Ward stayed behind in Paris when Charles sailed back to the United States in 1925. They missed each other dreadfully, but he had work to do here, and she had a child by then and another on the way. He wrote her letters every week, eight, ten, twelve pages in his small neat handwriting, talking about the work he was doing and the life he wanted to make with her, once he finished and sailed back to Paris. They're heartbreaking, if you know what came after.

"And then there's a letter from Joseph Curwen, telling her what happened to Charles. You know about Dr. Angell's researches, of course."

Owen nodded. "To the extent that I can without seeing the papers."

"And you know about the people who tried to wake the Dreaming Lord in 1925? Good. Charles wasn't directly involved in that, but it was when it failed that he decided he had to go back to Providence. They knew what the Radiance planned to do: the wars, the destruction of the environment, all of it. So they took dreadful risks, trying to pry loose secrets of the cosmos that would allow them to break through to R'lyeh and awaken Cthulhu, and Charles finally took one risk too many and called up something he couldn't put down, and it tore him apart."

"So it wasn't Curwen who killed him."

"It wasn't Curwen. To judge by his letter, in fact, Curwen was heartbroken. He'd loved Charles like a grandson, and felt he owed him a vast debt for bringing him back; but he knew that the only way to finish the work was to pretend to be Charles, and try to keep the charade going long enough." She shrugged. "And he failed, and knew it. He wrote one more letter to Lydia, and then they locked him up in an asylum, and a little over a month later he was dead."

She fell silent for a while. Finally Owen asked, "And Lydia?"

Hannah glanced at him. "She had her children—Theodore and Cassilda—and she had her memories. In 1929 she moved from Paris to Vyones, an old cathedral town in central France."

"I've heard of it," said Owen. That got him a questioning look, and he said, "The friend I mentioned has family there."

"What's her family name?"

"Chaudronnier."

Her eyebrows went up sharply. After a moment: "I've heard of her."

"I imagine you have," said Owen.

"In fact," Hannah said, "we're relatives of a sort by marriage. Lydia moved to Vyones on the invitation of a friend of her father's—Marcel d'Ursuras, Comte de la Frenaie, one of those rich eccentrics the French produce now and then. He was a widower with two daughters; she started out as their governess, and became their stepmother when the Comte outraged his stuck-up relatives and married her in 1938. She was still young, but she had no more children—and she outlived the Count, and both her own children, and some of her grandchildren. When I knew her, she was very old, but still lovely in her own way."

"You knew her," said Owen.

"She's why I'm here," Hannah told him. "I was born with a heart condition that nearly killed me half a dozen times. There was an operation, but it couldn't be done until I'd finished growing. Lydia—*la vieille Comtesse*, everyone called her—she knew a great deal about healing, she used herbs and stones and incantations, and she kept me alive again and again when the doctors gave up. So I lived with her from the time I was five or so, and she told me all about Charles, the things they'd studied together, the work he'd tried to do. She died just four years ago—I know, she reached an astonishing age; I think she learned some of the same tricks that kept Curwen and his friends alive so long—and I went to India to have the operation. I was flat on my back for a year, and spent a good deal longer than that recuperating, but as soon as I was well and circumstances allowed, I came here."

"Why?" Owen asked.

She considered him for a long moment. "Lydia had a long and, all in all, a happy life," she said. "Charles didn't have that chance, and he deserved a better fate than he got. The family papers in the d'Ursuras mansion near Vyones have ever so many notes on the process Curwen used, and Charles after him, to resurrect people from their essential salts. That's what I propose to do. To find the ashes of Charles Dexter Ward, wherever they might be buried; to reduce them to their essential salts; to perform the necessary rituals—and to bring him back from the grave."

Owen stared at her, and then slowly nodded. "Risky—but I think I understand."

"Good." She smiled. "Because I'm going to need some help with that, and I think I can offer you something in exchange for that help. I don't know where Charles hid the papers he got from Dr. Angell; Lydia never told me. You're welcome to look in Curwen's hiding place if you like, but you won't find anything but dust."

"Would you mind?" said Owen. "I see no reason to doubt you, but—"

"Not at all." She motioned to the Grateful Dead poster above the fireplace. "It's behind that thing. You'll want to stand on a chair; on the left part of the bottom molding there's a bit you can push in, and once you do that, if you push up, the panel will slide up and come loose."

"Thank you," said Owen, and followed her instructions. It took him only a moment to find the hidden button in the molding; a measured push on the panel thereafter, and it slid up and came away from the wall. He set it down beside the fireplace, got back up onto the chair. The cubical recess in the bare brick gaped just as Lovecraft's story described it, but it was empty.

He put the panel back into place, hauled the chair over to where it belonged. "Okay," he said then. "You were saying you had something to offer."

"Yes. As I said, I don't know where the Angell papers are; none of the letters and papers I've seen mentioned that, and if Lydia knew the secret she never told me. There's only one person who knows where to find them, and that's Charles himself."

A moment passed, and then another. "Fair enough," said Owen then. "What kind of help are we talking about?"

"To begin with, research. I want to see if any other library in town has correspondence between Angell and Charles, and we'll want to compare notes on what we've found so far. There might be other correspondence, too; Charles wrote letters by the ream to Josef Nadeh in Prague, a couple of noblemen in Transylvania, a Dr. Léon Muñoz in New York City, and I don't know who else. After that—I don't know where Charles is buried. Lovecraft gave the wrong location in his story; I've already checked. Another thing I don't know how to find is the door by the Patuxent River that lets into Joseph Curwen's laboratory, and that's the only place I know of that I can get the books and laboratory gear I'm going to need. Can you help me with those?"

"That much," said Owen, "yes, I can do. Beyond that—we'll see."

She considered him, nodded. "We can discuss the next steps when we get there."

* * *

He got back to the little apartment on Federal Hill well after dark. Climbing the stair, he wondered whether another type-written note would be waiting for him, but the floor inside the front door was mercifully blank. He stood inside for a moment, irresolute, then shrugged and went to Sancipriani's to get a late dinner.

The back room was mostly empty when he got there, but two people he knew slightly were bent over a table, talking about Sam Mazzini in low troubled tones. He greeted them and got uncomfortable looks and uneasy greetings in return. "What's up with Sam?" he asked.

It was not a question either of them wanted to answer, but one finally said, "He and Charlene had a big fight about something he did years ago—I don't know what. She's taken the kids and gone to stay with her mother."

Neither of them would say much more, and they left as quickly as they could. Julie Olmert, who was waiting tables that night as usual, made a little talk as she took his order and brought a plate of *pasta e vongole* and a salad, and then vanished. Half-familiar voices came down the hallway from a room further forward, and Owen guessed that they'd return to the back room just as soon as he left. He mulled over the conversation he'd had with Sam Mazzini, and finished as quickly as he could. No typewritten note waited in his apartment when he got back to it, but the night had a brooding air that promised trouble.

The next morning he'd arranged to meet Hannah Ward in front of the Athenaeum on Benefit Street just before it opened, and he headed out of the apartment into the gray morning with time to spare. Providence was still mostly asleep, though coffee places stood open and a few shops were turning on their lights as he hit his stride and the sagging Doric porches and cluttered windows went past. Before long the skyscrapers loomed above him. The woman with the strange eyes was sitting on the sidewalk close to where he'd gotten off the bus, and he wondered for a moment if she'd speak to him again, but she gave him a brief glance and then turned her attention back to the clowder of cats surrounding her.

He got to the pillared front entrance of the Providence Athenaeum to find Hannah Ward already waiting. They talked a little, about irrelevancies—they weren't the only people waiting for the doors to open—and filed in and staked out a table on the lower floor once the staff let them in. Thereafter, under the genial illumination of the windows on the north wall, they began hunting down every scrap of information about George Gammell Angell, Charles Dexter Ward, and Joseph Curwen that the institution had to offer.

Working together made it easier to search, but there was a vast amount of material to cover. Joseph Curwen had contributed a great deal to the old Providence Library Company, and replaced from his own library many of the books lost when the Providence courthouse burned down in 1758; there were documents concerning him in the Athenaeum archives, and a dozen books he'd donated were still in the Founders Collection, and had to be checked for marginal notes. Then there was the Private Library collection, which turned out to have more than half of Angell's library—the Athenaeum had snapped up many of the scholar's odder titles in the auction that followed his death—and those had to be checked, too.

Owen and Hannah had completed only a little of this when evening came. Outside, in a quiet corner, they compared notes and agreed to meet there the next morning.

"You don't look too enthusiastic about going home," Hannah noted, considering him.

He gave her a startled glance, then nodded. "There are—issues."

"If you need somewhere to stay, there are spare bedrooms in the place I'm renting."

Owen thanked her and promised to keep that in mind, and they said the usual things and she went down the stair to Benefit Street and walked away.

Stars had come out overhead by the time he got back to Federal Hill. Flicker of intuition as he climbed the stairs from the alley to the cramped little apartment hinted that someone had been there before him, and sure enough, another typed note had been slipped in under the doorjamb and lay waiting on the floor when he turned on the light. He gave it a long bleak look, then picked it up and read:

```
people who gossip have nasty things happen
to them
ask sam mazzini
everyone here knows youre cheating with that
black bitch
do you want your wife to know too
```

He set it down on the counter, closed the door, and took off the backpack. Then, after a moment, he systematically crumpled the note and threw it into the wastepaper basket.

CHAPTER 6

THE DOOR IN THE RIVERBANK

The next morning he met Hannah out in front of the Athenaeum just before it opened. After they'd greeted each other, Owen said, "Yesterday you made an offer."

"About a place to stay? It's still open."

"Thank you," he said. "I'd like to take you up on it."

She considered him for a moment, then nodded. "Of course."

That evening, after a long day spent chasing scraps of data about Joseph Curwen that led nowhere, he went back up Federal Hill, stowed all his things in his duffel bag, shouldered it, and went to the back door of Sancipriani's. Half a dozen people huddled over one of the tables; they glanced up when he came in, and then looked away. Owen walked past them to the counter, where Julie Olmert was busy setting out glasses.

She glanced up as he approached, and then looked down.

"Please give this back to the elders," Owen told her, dropping the key on the counter. "I won't need it from now on."

Julie's eyes closed momentarily, and then she nodded. "I'm sorry," she said in a low voice. He nodded once, and left the restaurant.

Outside the evening was turning orange and crimson as high clouds caught the sunset light. Owen got the duffel settled comfortably on his shoulder and headed down the hill. Around him Providence settled into its after-hours rhythm;

music in a cacophony of styles blared out of bars and night spots, and sounds of a poetry slam in progress came from the open doors of a café; quieter noises made the background to both, while one after another, people staring into their smart-phones trudged up and down the sidewalk, seeing and hear-ing nothing around them, the pallid light shining up from the screens turning their faces an assortment of ghastly hues.

Under the shadows of the skyscrapers, across the river, and then up the steep slopes of College Hill at an angle, veering north: it was a familiar route by then, with most of the famil-iar sights, though the woman with strange eyes was in none of her usual places. By the time he'd reached Stampers Hill and started down Olney Court, Owen had shaken off most of the bitter mood he'd been in since the night before. Whatever else had happened, he told himself, there was still some chance he'd be able to return to Arkham with the Angell manuscripts, and that would make up for any number of awkward moments and hateful notes.

When he reached Joseph Curwen's house, he went around back and tapped quietly on the kitchen door. A moment passed, and then Hannah opened the door. "Hi," she said. "You're tim-ing's good; dinner's maybe fifteen minutes out."

"Thank you," he said, meaning it. He went inside with her, to find Pierre in his monkish robe perched on a chair by the stove, holding a wooden spoon in one tentacle and stirring a pot of something that smelled like pot à feu.

"Oh, he's very helpful," Hannah said, obviously amused by his look of surprise. "And quick to learn. Clean as a cat, too; he likes to bathe daily in salt water." Then: "The bedrooms are upstairs; mine is at the end of the hall, Pierre's is the little one next to it. You can have any of the others—they're all furnished."

He thanked her again and hauled his duffel up the stairs. The room he chose for himself, after a brief inspection, could have passed for the rented room he'd lived in when he was a student at Miskatonic University. From the cracked plaster on the walls to the mismatched furniture—bed, dresser, book-shelf, desk, and desk chair—that had clearly been handed down from decades of university students and would just as clearly be handed down to decades more, it seemed achingly familiar.

It took him only a few minutes to get his things stowed. There-after he went to the bathroom, washed up, and headed down the stairs. Over dinner, which was impressively good—Hannah had put an upbringing in provincial France to good use—they talked about the work ahead of them. Then, in a break in the con-versation, Owen said, "There are two things I need to tell you. The first is that the Radiance has people here in Providence—probably a full negation team, maybe more than that."

"How do you know?" Hannah asked him point-blank.

"I got into a scrap with them in upstate New York eight years ago. I've seen one of the guys I faced there—an officer of theirs, name of Michael Dyson—on College Hill twice now. Yes, I'm sure it's the same person."

"Okay," Hannah said. "That's not good, but we can deal. What's the second thing?"

"They're not the only ones here. Do you know who April Castaigne is?"

She gave him a sudden sharp look, nodded.

"I met her in the Maine mountains ten years back—and I saw her again downtown a couple of weeks ago. Maybe it's just a coincidence, but I doubt it."

Hannah said nothing for a long moment. "Thank you," she said finally. "There are some protections I can put in place, but—" She shook her head slowly. "The Yellow Sign. I won't say I know all that much about them, but what I know scares me silly."

"I won't argue," said Owen.

She gave him a quick glance, then smiled, refilled their wineglasses.

* * *

Owen wondered more than once, during his first few days staying in Joseph Curwen's house, whether living under the same roof with an attractive younger woman would become awkward for either of them. As it turned out, that was never an issue. Hannah used her charms methodically, like every other instrument at her disposal; twice, he watched her flirt with library clerks in order to get access to documents she needed, to the point of making assignations she then ignored; if she'd decided that seducing him would further her mission, Owen guessed, she'd have set out to do it without a second thought—and how effectively he'd have been able to refuse her was, he admitted to himself, a question he didn't want to put to the test.

It never came up, though. They had work to do together, and that was all. The look of weary relief he'd seen on Hannah's face when they finished at the Athenaeum, and she could finally shake off the more persistent of her admirers on the staff, told Owen how little she liked the games she'd had to play. Pondering that, he made a point of avoiding any word or action even remotely suggestive. They never discussed the matter, but as the days passed a certain guardedness in her manner toward him faded.

They quickly found a rhythm in their work together. Hannah was a capable researcher, focused and methodical, though there were tricks he'd learned in college that she didn't know, especially when it came to using computers. "Lydia wouldn't have them in the house," Hannah explained apologetically, "and with the heart problem, I didn't get out much." With a little shrug: "One can't know everything."

The work they shared wasn't limited to research, though it felt that way at times. Pierre did much of the housework, but the two of them split the rest between them, much the same way he and Laura had done in Dunwich. The funds for the venture came from Hannah's side—she had access to plenty of money, Owen gathered, and visited a bank downtown at intervals—and she drove to a grocery store on the far side of College Hill once a week to keep the kitchen cupboards filled.

There were other preparations to be made, too. The evening after he took up residence in the Curwen house, Hannah led him down the narrow stair into the cellar, and pulled the cord that turned on an ancient light fixture with a single bare bulb. The cellar was a single room the size of the ground floor, paved with flagstones, with the brick mass of the chimney filling the center and outworn junk of various eras heaped against the walls. A well-aged furnace and water heater huddled up against the chimney, with rusted iron stovepipes leading into the brick. On the side furthest from the stair, a long workbench of colonial date extended from wall to wall, sturdily built from mortared stone with a smooth slate top. Laboratory gear dotted it—glassware, a heating plate, a sensitive balance—and a long row of jars and bottles lined the back edge. Their labels named scores of chemicals, some common, some exotic. Over to one side, a short distance from the chemicals, sat an odd little jar made of thin red stoneware. It looked, Owen thought, older than anything else in the cellar, including the cellar itself.

"Here's where I plan on doing the work," Hannah said then, unnecessarily. "I've already picked up all the equipment I could get from ordinary suppliers."

"This dates from Curwen's time, doesn't it?" Owen asked.

"The cellar? That's what Lydia told me. I'm pretty sure there used to be alchemical furnaces down here at one time—look at the patched-up openings in the chimney there and there; those are the wrong shape and position for anything else. The drain over there was put in around 1900, I think, so the cellar has pretty much everything that an alchemical laboratory needs, once we get the junk cleared away."

"We can start that any time you like," Owen said.

That got him a smile. "Lydia used to say that there's no time like the present."

For the next few days, with Pierre's patient help, they spent each evening hauling broken garden tools, corroded iron bedsprings, mop buckets with their bottoms rusted out, and much more of the same sort up the cellar stairs and out into the back-yard, where they were finally picked up by a hauling company Hannah called. Each day went into chasing down leads in the stacks of the Athenaeum. When that venerable institution finally failed them, the Rhode Island Historical Society a block and a half away was their next hope. The only documents the Society had on George Gammell Angell or Charles Dexter Ward themselves, as distinct from Lovecraft's tales about them, were articles in local history journals, and those led nowhere quickly enough, but Joseph Curwen was another matter.

The old Shepley Library, whose holdings had long since passed into the Historical Society's collections, had a mass of Curwen material that included the accounts and invoices from the old alchemist's maritime business. More to the point, though, Lovecraft's belated fame in the second half of the twentieth century sent a flurry of fans chasing after records concerning colonial Providence's most famous alchemist, and several of their books and papers gave enough information on Curwen's farm in Pawtuxet that Owen and Hannah were able to narrow down its location to within a quarter mile or so. From there, working from a topographic map and records of colonial landholdings, they chased down every reference they could find to the part of the river upstream from Rhodes-on-the-Pawtuxet that was close enough to the old Curwen farm that an underground tunnel to the riverbank would be possible.

It took them more than a week of searching, but finally Hannah drew in a sharp breath, glanced at Owen, and motioned for him to come and look. Over her shoulder, he read:

```
his diary entry for March 24, 1911, men-
tions finding the upper surface of a stone
arch protruding from the riverbank close
to the Ward-Collins dye works in Pawtuxet.
Whether this was, as he insisted, a relic
```

> of Joseph Curwen's legendary alchemical
> laboratory or some other piece of colonial
> stonework cannot now be determined, as the
> rains that apparently uncovered the arch
> were followed by more rains and a series
> of landslips that seem to have hidden it
> again. No further trace of the arch has
> been found since that time.

"The Ward-Collins dye works," Owen said. "Do we know where those were?"

"We can find out," said Hannah, with a sudden smile.

It took them only a short time to find the factory's location in an old city directory and pinpoint that on the map. Once that was done, they hurried back to the house on Olney Street.

"I'll get the car," she said as they climbed the hill. "We need to find the kind of sporting goods store that has camping supplies, and go pick those up today if we can."

"Are you planning on camping?" Owen asked her.

That got an amused look. "No. We'll need folding shovels we can carry with us without being too conspicuous, and something to haul what we need back to the car."

"Fair enough," said Owen.

* * *

As Hannah took the battered freeway through Providence toward Cranston early the next morning, Owen wondered what they would do if the door turned out to be in a crowded neighborhood. Once they left the freeway and got onto surface streets going away from the lively little neighborhood of Pawtuxet Village, though, it became clear that those worries were a waste of time. Providence suburbs had grown out that way well before Charles Dexter Ward's time, but industry and commerce had come after them, with urban blight and economic contraction following close on their heels. The road they followed was cracked and potholed, with an abandoned red brick factory building on the left and a battered guardrail above the river to their right, by the time Hannah slowed.

A cluster of derelict outbuildings alongside the former dye works offered concealment for the car. Hannah parked and they got out, put on rucksacks, picked up a pair of folding camp shovels, crossed the street and looked down the bank toward the Pawtuxet River. It took them a little searching, but they soon found a trail down the slope—crumpled beer cans of cheap national brands in various corners showed them who had made it and why—and clambered down out of sight of the road to a flat area a little back from the river's edge.

"Okay," Hannah said when she'd checked the map she'd copied from the papers at the Athenaeum. "It should be somewhere not far from here."

Owen gave her a dubious look. No trace of stonework showed anywhere on the overgrown bank. "Do we just start digging?"

She laughed. "Saint Toad, no. Trust me to manage things better than that." She took a little jar, of the sort that holds salves, out of her purse. "Close your eyes."

Owen did so, and a moment later felt her fingers dab something on each eyelid. "Once I tell you to open your eyes you'll need to move fast," she told him. "This won't work for more than a few seconds." She paused, then: "Open your eyes."

He opened them, and blinked in amazement.

The riverbank before him was a vague brown mist, the trees and shrubs insubstantial as ghosts. Through them he could see the buried entrance of a stone tunnel fifty yards or so further upriver. Deeper in the hill, dim shapes spoke of other tunnels and rooms lined with stone. Remembering what Hannah had said, he broke into a run, dodged among the vague forms of trees and shrubbery, and stood looking straight down the tunnel for a moment—and then the mist thickened and he was staring at a muddy bank overgrown with weeds, and screened by foliage from every side.

"Nicely done," Hannah said, catching up to him. "The tunnel's straight ahead?"

"Yeah." He considered the bank in front of him, tried to recall as much as possible of what he'd seen. "The top of the tunnel's closest to the surface ..." He clambered up the slope, took his shovel, and thrust it into the ground. "Somewhere right around here."

The two of them went to work at once, digging downward and inward. The hole was not much more than a foot deep when Hannah's shovel grated on stone. A few more minutes and they'd cleared the upper surface of an arch. That gave them better guidance, and not long thereafter they found the front edge and began clearing the doorway.

It took them better than two hours of hard work to get it clear, but finally it stood before them much the way it had been in Curwen's time, an arched portal of stone blocks well mortared together, with a wooden door bound with wrought iron fittings filling the portal. "I thought they hacked through the door in Curwen's time," said Owen.

"They did. This one's a replacement—according to one of the letters, Charles put it in after he and Curwen reopened the laboratory."

"I'm surprised it hasn't rotted and rusted out by now."

"That's no ordinary iron," Hannah replied, "and the wood's saturated with strange salts. Curwen was a very capable alchemist, remember, and Charles learned a lot from him."

"Fair enough," said Owen. "How do we get in?"

Hannah smiled, reached into her purse, and brought out a wrought iron key of antique pattern. "Curwen sent this to Lydia in Paris when he knew there was no hope left, and she gave it to me. With any luck, the lock won't be too full of dirt."

The keyhole was clear. Hannah put the key in, and strained at it without effect. Owen gestured—may I?—and she gave him a grateful look and stepped aside. He took hold of the great foliated end in both hands, braced himself, leaned carefully into the movement, and felt the lock strain, yield, and slowly turn with a deep unsteady creak.

Once the bolt had clicked home into the body of the lock, Owen handed the key back to Hannah and put his shoulder to the door. The old hinges groaned their complaint, but they gave way, and the door slowly pivoted inwards.

Inside was a darkness that made every night Owen had ever witnessed seem pale, and cold air that smelled of dust. Hannah pulled two small flashlights out of her purse, handed Owen one. They clicked on the lights at the same moment, shone them down the tunnel, glanced at each other. Then, warily, they went in, and Hannah pushed the door shut behind them.

* * *

The tunnel was no mere hole in the ground. Great gray flag-stones streaked with long-dried mud paved the floor, and rough blocks of stone dressed in colonial fashion formed the walls and the vaulted ceiling a dozen feet overhead. Ten feet wide or more, the way ran straight back into the riverbank, going further than the pallid glow from their flashlights could reach.

It took close to a quarter mile of walking, through utter blackness and a silence broken only by the whispering echoes of their footfalls, before the tunnel finally ended. Beyond it lay a large round room, maybe thirty feet across, with plain stone pillars supporting the ceiling. A big stone altar stood in the center, and doors opened at various places along the walls.

"This is a lot smaller than Lovecraft said it was," said Owen then. "And what about the pits with the stone grates, and the things in them?"

Hannah snorted. "He made those up. According to Lydia, if you didn't have enough of the essential salts to revive some-one, and didn't have the wit to make up the difference with the archaeus of blood and the magistery of bone, what you'd call up wouldn't live for more than a few minutes at most. I grant Lovecraft's version made for more goosebumps."

"You know his stories, then."

That got him an amused look. "Of course. Lydia used to read them aloud to me on winter nights when I was sick, and then tell me everything he'd gotten wrong."

They searched the room, found nothing, and started looking into the doors to the left of the tunnel through which they'd entered. The first few opened onto empty storerooms, but the one after that led onto a long corridor with doors on either side, some of them blocked by the warped and rotted remains of colonial-era six-paneled doors, some gaping open. Most of these were also storerooms, Owen guessed, for some of them contained moldering chests and clothespresses of eighteenth-century style, while others had cheaply made wooden shelving and an assortment of canned goods with labels that appeared to date from the 1920s. Evidently Ward and Curwen had laid in provisions for a long stay in case of emergency. The corridor ended in a mound of earth— evidently the exit from the underground rooms had been blocked, deliberately or by some accident, in the years since Curwen's time.

"Did Lydia say anything," Owen asked then, "about the part of Lovecraft's story where Dr. Willet repeated the spell and revived someone down here?"

Hannah glanced at him. "That Lovecraft didn't know as much about paleography as he thought he did. The note Willett said he found in his pocket wasn't written in Saxon minuscules, it was from two or three centuries earlier—what in Lydia's time they called sub-Roman Britain."

"I wonder who they could have gotten from back then."

"Oh, I can think of one person—and there's something in one of Charles' letters about remains they got from a hill near Carmarthen in Wales, in a really odd cave where the walls and ceiling were covered in crystals."

Owen turned to face her in astonishment, recalling the Latin inscription he'd found among Angell's papers. "You're talking about Merlin."

"I wouldn't put it past them," Hannah said. "They wanted anyone and anything who could tell them how to awaken the Dreaming Lord. They'd have revived Haon-Dor if they'd known where to find his body. If it was Merlin, though, nobody's seen him since."

They kept searching, and found storeroom after storeroom. Finally, though, one of the doors opened onto a long rectangular room lined with bookshelves. Inside, an oaken table filled the center of the room, and a pair of desks stood side by side at the far end. An oil lamp of antique pattern sat at the center of the table, with what looked like a full reservoir of oil.

"I doubt that still works," said Owen, indicating the lamp. "Pity; we could use the light."

"Give it a try," Hannah told him. He gave her a skeptical look but got a matchbook out of one pocket, lit a match, and held it to the wicking. For a long moment nothing happened but a low hiss, and then all at once the wick caught and a clear white light spread through the room.

"That's no ordinary oil," said Hannah then. "The *oleum sapientiae*—the Oil of the Wise—it's what the old alchemists used for light."

"I've read of it," said Owen. "Von Junzt said a pint would keep a lamp lit for a century."

"An understatement." She glanced at him. "A while back— this was before I was born—the cathedral in Vyones had to have parts of its foundations rebuilt, and in the process some of the tombs in the crypt had to be emptied of their inhabitants for a while. One of those belonged to a famous local wizard named Gaspard du Nord, who died in 1336. When his tomb was opened, the workmen found a lamp burning by his head. It was put back, still burning, when they reinterred his remains a year later."

By the light of the lamp, they searched the room, pulling out each of the books and opening the desk drawers. Curwen's library included nearly all the alchemical classics from Zosimus and Geber straight through to Sendivogius and the *Aurea Catena Homeri*, and a great many volumes of older and stranger lore besides. Owen noticed a large volume with the words *Qanoon-ê-Islam* printed on the spine; he pulled it down, guessing at its actual contents, and found as he'd expected that it was Curwen's copy of the Latin edition of the *Necronomicon*.

He had just returned that to the shelf, and was reaching for a volume of Borellus, when Hannah let out a low cry. He turned, to find her lifting a crude thick copybook, a stack of papers, and a composition book of early twentieth-century style from a drawer in one of the desks.

"What is it?"

"Joseph Curwen's papers," she said. "And there's something else—in Charles' hand." She set the stack on the table, opened the composition book. "It's his laboratory notebook. I'm guessing—" She turned more pages. "Yes. It's got detailed notes on the processes he used. With this, Borellus, and Curwen's copy of the *Necronomicon*, we should have all the lore we need."

"Here you go." Owen pulled out the Borellus, saw notes in a crabbed eighteenth-century hand inside, then got the *Necronomicon* as well and carried them over to the table. Hannah put them and the papers and books she'd found into her knapsack. "All we need now is the laboratory gear," she said, "and that ought to be down the corridor on the other side."

They went back into the great central hall, checked the other rooms around the outside—more empty storerooms, it turned out—and then found a short corridor lined with storerooms and a door beyond it. As they stepped through the doorway, their flashlight beams shone on dusty glassware of archaic design. The room was of some size, and had two doors leading to storerooms along one wall and another on the far end. They glanced into the storerooms and saw a great deal of rotted wood, looked through the door at the far end to see an assortment of plain leaden jars, and then turned back to the laboratory.

Hannah seemed to know exactly what she needed. She and Owen hauled retorts, alembics, cucurbits, and aludels out to the central hall, and then she started examining the jars of reagents on long wooden shelves above the laboratory bench. "I've already got most of what I need," she told Owen, "and most of the chemicals will be spoiled by now anyway, but there are a few things we can use." She pulled down one jar after another and started making a collection of bottles on the bench as Owen hauled the rest of the glassware.

Finally, she considered four bulky stoneware shapes that sat on the floor in a row, beneath what had clearly once been a chimney hood. "This one," she said finally. "It's going to be heavy, but it ought to be easier to move than any of the others."

"What is it?"

"An athanor, an alchemical furnace. Put charcoal there in the bottom, set your vessel on top, and those vents let you control the fire."

Owen nodded, took a wide stance, and lifted it. It was heavy but not too heavy, and he got it out into the central hall. By then Hannah had sorted through the glass jars of chemicals on shelves behind the workbench, and was carrying an armload of them out to join the glassware.

"That's going to be quite a load," Owen said, surveying the final collection.

"I know," said Hannah. "I'm sorry—but this is what it takes to practice alchemy."

"I'm not arguing," Owen replied, and hefted the athanor again.

* * *

It took them hours of hauling and three trips in the car to get all of the equipment, books, and chemicals back to the house on Olney Court, and then all of it had to be carried down into the cellar and set up on the stone workbench or the flagstoned floor. Owen pried loose the patching on one of the holes in the central chimney with a stray screwdriver from a drawer upstairs, and got spare pieces of stovepipe set up to carry smoke from the alchemical furnace out of the cellar, while Hannah got the chemicals and glassware arranged with Pierre's deft help.

"That will definitely do," she said then, regarding the stovepipe with a smile. "A well-equipped alchemical laboratory. Now all we need—" Her smile faltered, and she fell silent.

"The raw material."

"Yes." Looking away: "Charles' ashes." A moment later, with a visible effort, she smiled again. "But before we worry about that, I owe you a really good lunch. Do you like Portuguese?"

Owen did, and half an hour later they were settling into chairs at a little place called Henrique's just off Main Street, near what had been the old waterfront in colonial times. The wharves and the ship-chandleries were long gone, along with most of the alleys with glamorous names from colonial days—Bullion, Guilder, Doubloon, Sovereign, and the rest—leaving a sleepy neighborhood of old houses, little shops, and vacant lots.

"I can recommend the *galinha dem molho de alho*," said Hannah, "or the *misto de marisco* if seafood sounds better."

Seafood sounded too much like Arkham for Owen's mood, so he settled on the former, which turned out to be chicken in a garlic sauce over rice. That and a bottle of crisp vinho verde made for a fine lunch, and over it they discussed the next step in low voices.

"If he'd been given a regular burial there'd be no trouble," Hannah said. "But it was done secretly—my guess, though it's only a guess, is that Lovecraft had the details right, and Dr. Willett did the burying himself at night."

"You're sure that it wasn't in the Ward plot in the North Burial Ground," said Owen.

"Yes. There are—ways to tell—and I spent a day there a while back. The problem is that I can't simply go over the whole cemetery one square foot after another, not in any reasonable amount of time—and I don't know for a fact that they're even in that cemetery."

"True," Owen allowed. "There was supposedly a newspaper article."

"Good." She pulled a notebook out of her purse, wrote something in it. "That's one angle to try. Any other ideas?"

He speared a piece of chicken with his fork, contemplated it. "I wonder what happened to the Ward family papers. Charles was an only child, wasn't he?"

"He had an older sister," said Hannah. "But she died when Charles was six. That's what Lydia told me, at least."

Owen nodded. "If his family never knew about Lydia, his father might have willed the family papers to a college or the historical society."

She wrote that in the notebook, too. "Also good. Both of those are long shots, but I think they're worth trying."

The conversation drifted elsewhere, and then for a while Hannah stared at nothing in particular, obviously deep in thought, while Owen looked out through the window at the passersby. A spry old brown-skinned Portuguese man in a neatly pressed dove-gray suit came strolling along the sidewalk just then, paused outside the door to Henrique's, and came inside. He was a regular, Owen guessed; the greeter welcomed him effusively as "Mr. Gomes" and took him straight to a small table across the main room from Owen and Hannah. There he sat back, glanced incuriously around the restaurant, saw Hannah, and stared in evident surprise. An instant later he shook his head, smiled as though at some private folly, and turned his attention to the menu. More than once, though, as Hannah and Owen finished their lunch, the old man glanced at her again with a wondering expression on his face, then looked away.

CHAPTER 7

THE GREAT CONJURATION

As it turned out, it wasn't the newspaper article or the Ward family papers that gave them the clue they needed. It was a black and white photograph on a wall in the Bannister University library, and Owen found it by sheer dumb luck.

It wasn't much more than chance that brought them to Bannister University, for that matter. The newspaper article had eluded them, and neither the historical society nor any of the libraries in town had records of any bequest of papers from the elder Theodore Ward. It was only Lydia Ward's reminiscences, recalled by Hannah, that suggested that he'd made financial donations to Bannister College and might have left it something in his will.

They were waiting at the doors of Merritt Library on the Bannister University campus one morning before opening time. "I'd like to take a moment to see if they've got any of Angell's papers," Owen said. "Just in case."

"Sensible," said Hannah. "Me, I'm going to be less practical for just a bit and see what they've got on Lydia's parents. Call it genealogical nostalgia." She laughed, and so did Owen.

Doors opened and they went into the familiar library hush. A half hour later, Owen was sure that the only things with George Gammell Angell's name on it in the collection were an even dozen of his books on Semitic languages, and he got to work chasing down the Ward family papers. The search string "Theodore Ward" brought up dozens of hits, and it took Owen a fair amount of sorting before he was sure that one of them was a set of documents in the library's special collections that probably came from the right Theodore Ward.

By then Hannah was already sitting at a table by the special collections desk, leafing through the contents of a document box. "Anything?" Owen asked her in a low voice.

She shook her head. "Not of any importance. Have a look."

The papers in front of her were handwritten letters on yellowed stationery, written in neat old-fashioned penmanship in ruler-straight lines, with long curving tails above and below.

"Anyone I should know about?" he asked.

"Lydia Ward," said Hannah. "She still wrote just like this when I knew her. These are letters she wrote to her father when he was overseas with the army during the First World War." She shook her head, laughed quietly. "I know, I have better things to do. Any luck?"

"Maybe," Owen said. "We'll see."

He went to the desk, handed over a slip of paper with the right numbers on it, waited while the woman behind the desk went to get the papers. While she was gone, he glanced around the room, noted the framed black and white photographs on the walls. From the clothing and the cars in some of them, Owen guessed they were from the 1930s and 1940s.

"Yes, exactly," the librarian said when she came back with a disappointingly small box, and he asked about the photos. "There were three African-American newspapers in Rhode Island back then, and all of them had really first-rate photographers. We've got examples of their work on exhibit all over this floor."

He thanked her, took the box, and went to a table a short distance from the one where Hannah was sitting—she had papers spread all over the table and was reading something with an ambivalent look that didn't suggest she'd welcome an interruption. The box he'd gotten turned out to contain letters

Theodore Ward had written to Bannister College to accompany his regular donations to the scholarship fund, and nothing else. Finishing it, he let out a frustrated sigh, and sat back in the chair, trying to think of other options.

Just above the table was one of the photographs, a picture of a cemetery with the graves all decorated with flowers—a Memorial Day image, Owen guessed. His mind was busy enough that it took close to a minute for him to notice two odd details, but when he did, his eyes snapped suddenly wide.

Lydia was gathering up the papers on her table by then. Owen turned to her, caught her eye, and motioned with his head. She got up, came over, and asked, "What's up?"

"Do you notice anything odd about that picture?" he said, indicating the photo.

She stared at it for a few moments, shook her head. "No."

"Why are there flowers over on the left, where there's no grave?" As soon as that registered, he went on. "Now look at the name on the headstones."

She did, and her hands flew up to her mouth. A moment later: "Bicknell. Of course."

"Yeah. I'm willing to bet that Marinus Bicknell Willett buried Charles' ashes in his mother's family plot, and the Wards knew where it was and put flowers there on Memorial Day and Charles' birthday. All we have to do is find out which cemetery that's in."

"The North Burial Ground," said Hannah at once. "The Bicknells aren't that far from the Wards—I spotted their plot when I was there, just after I got to Providence. That's good news, too; some of the cemeteries still have night watchmen but the North Burial Ground hasn't had one for years." She shrugged. "Budget cuts, as usual."

"Fair enough," said Owen. "Worth a try?"

She glanced up at him with a tremendous intensity in her eyes. "Oh, yes."

* * *

Night lay heavy over the North Burial Ground as Owen hauled himself to the top of the wrought iron fence and dropped to the other side, then reached both arms through and helped Hannah up and over. Nearby, traffic muttered down a badly rutted highway, and the wind hissed in the trees as they hurried, low to the ground, toward the Bicknell plot.

They'd chosen a neglected part of the fence by Cemetery Street to make their way in, and Hannah had cast a spell over them both to keep them unseen—a gesture, a few lines of medieval Latin, and a pinch of pallid dust flung into the air above them—but Owen's nerves were taut. It wasn't just the ordinary risks of neighbors or the police that had him watching every shadow uneasily. If the Radiance or the Yellow Sign had guessed their goal, the grave of Charles Dexter Ward would be the logical place to set guards or lay a trap.

Nothing moved, though, as they passed silently among the tombstones to a tree, and stopped for a moment in its deeper shadows. Owen could just see the Bicknell name on a few of the tombstones. He waited, watching, while Hannah checked one grave after another by the faint glow of a little flashlight and the occasional gleam of headlights from the highway.

"Over here," Hannah hissed. Close by was the grave of Esther M. Bicknell, the marble headstone stained by more than a century of city soot. A tape measure made its appearance, and while Owen held one end, Hannah measured ten feet due east—their best estimate of the distance shown in the photo— and paused, traced patterns with her fingers in the air, paused again, then went a few feet further and made a mark in the grass there with her shoe. "There," she said.

Owen released the tape measure, took the folding shovel he'd brought, and went to work. A few quick thrusts and a slicing movement allowed him to peel back the sod; that done, he began to dig straight down. Willett wouldn't have been able to get too deep; the question that mattered was what kind of condition Ward's remains would be in. If Willett had simply poured them into a hastily made hole, they might well have returned entirely to earth after so many years, and even if things were otherwise—

The shovel's point caught in something that wasn't soil.

Owen set the shovel aside, got the flashlight from Hannah, and crouched down. Rotten waxy fabric bunched at the bottom of the hole—the remains of an oilcloth raincoat, he guessed from the tattered shapes. Carefully, holding the shovel right behind the blade, he scraped away the dirt, then used his hands to tear the cloth.

Inside was one edge of an old tin coffee canister, still apparently intact.

It took only a few more minutes of careful labor to free the canister and lift it from the hole. Yes, it was intact. Hannah gestured for him to open the canister, and he lifted the lid just enough to shine the flashlight in and show a gray mass of ashes strewn with bits of pale bone.

Hannah drew in a sharp breath, then bowed her head. Owen closed the canister and went to work filling in the hole as well as he could. By the time he put the sod back in place she had mastered herself, and had the canister wrapped in plastic and tucked into a canvas shopping bag. He folded the shovel and glanced at her. She nodded, and they hurried away from the grave.

The way back to Hannah's car was no less a strain on Owen's nerves, with the cars on the highway rattling past and their headlights casting unwelcome gleams on the monuments. Still, they got over the fence without incident, reached the car, and drove off. Back at the house on Olney Court, Hannah locked and barred the kitchen door once they'd entered, set Pierre to stand guard in the kitchen, and took her grisly prize down to the cellar at once. The overhead lamp went on, and by its light Hannah unwrapped the coffee canister and opened it.

Whatever emotions had stirred her in the graveyard had returned to hiding. She prodded at the ashes with a tempered glass rod, then said, "Incomplete combustion. Lovecraft must have gotten the story from someone who knew the details; this was burnt in a fireplace, not a crematorium. First thing tomorrow, we can calcine the remains, and then ..."

"The essential salts?"

"Eventually. Extracting them isn't the simplest thing in the world."

Owen nodded, said nothing.

She glanced at him, smiled. "No need to worry, though. I've done the thing several times already. I told you that the family papers in Vyones have whole notebooks Charles filled with notes on Curwen's process, but there was only one way to be sure I understood it. I extracted the essential salts of a dog, to begin with, and then an old servant who'd been buried in the family chapel. I know how to do it, and I also know how to make the archaeus of blood."

He gave her a puzzled look. "I don't think Lovecraft mentioned that."

"No, that's something Curwen didn't know about. You can use that in place of fresh blood once you've revived someone—a lot easier to get and, these days, there are too many bloodborne pathogens out there to risk drinking some random stranger's blood. So I prepared enough of it for the three months it'll be needed."

"Whose blood did you use?"

"My own, of course." She smiled. "It took me a year to get enough of it. So everything's ready. It's just the last step I haven't done."

"The last step," Owen said. "The sorcery?"

"The Great Conjuration." Her voice had gone low. "That's dangerous enough that I didn't want to try it until I knew it was worth the risk. Now—" Glancing at him again: "Once the salts are prepared, it'll be time for that."

* * *

Calcining the ashes was only the beginning, and it had to be done three times before all that was left of of Charles Dexter Ward had been wholly reduced to powder and the next stage of the work could begin. One calcination might have been enough, but the furnace they'd gotten from Curwen's laboratory was temperamental, and it took them repeated tries to figure out how to get a steady heat out of it. "They demanded more of themselves than of their equipment," Hannah said disconsolately after the second calcination, when a prodding glass rod discovered pieces of bone and masses not yet reduced to white ash. "The old alchemists. That's what Charles wrote, at any rate."

The third time, though, Owen managed to get the air vents set just right, and the furnace surprised them with a low hollow rushing sound and a blast of heat so intense they both had to stand well back until the charcoal burned down and the ashes in the vessel on top of the furnace cooled from incandescent red to pallid white. After that they took turns grinding the ashes with a mortar and pestle—metal grinders couldn't be used, Curwen's manuscript insisted, for the smallest bit of iron mixed in with the ashes after the calcination would doom their efforts. Once it was reduced to a powder so fine a fingertip couldn't feel individual grains, it went into a sealed alembic, and they got to work on the next stage the manuscript described.

The weeks that followed were among the strangest in Owen Merrill's life. The modern world seemed to have faded away, and except for a few appliances and the electric lamps that lit the house at night, he and Hannah might have been two alchemists laboring in some cellar under a narrow-fronted house in Vyones during the Middle Ages. Now and again, when the work needed only one pair of hands, with or without the assistance of Pierre's tentacles, Hannah drove to the store and came back with groceries and sacks of charcoal for the furnace. Owen, recalling the warning he'd gotten from Michael Dyson, stayed safely indoors. Most nights they slept by turns as the work permitted. Only now and then, when some substance had to go through obscure changes without interference, was there time to sit quietly in the parlor, talk across the kitchen table, or get an unbroken night's sleep.

One such time, they had dinner close to midnight. All the previous day and most of the evening had gone into preparing a substance Curwen's manuscripts called the Blood of the Green Lion, the last of half a dozen fluids that had to be used to prepare the ashes so that the essential salts could be extracted from them. It was a delicate process, requiring careful regulation of the heat, and only when the liquid in the alembic turned the proper shimmering green color at the end could they be sure that the day's work had not been wasted. The fluid had to be left for at least twelve hours before it could be used, so Owen closed up the furnace vents to extinguish the coals, Hannah put the alembic on the great stone counter and wrapped it in cloths so that it would not cool too fast, and the two of them trudged up the cellar stairs to the kitchen.

Dinner was a chicken ragout, a cheese soup with plenty of onion in it, and thick slices of *pain de campagne*, the coarse rich-flavored bread of the French provinces. "How on earth did you survive before your marriage?" Hannah asked Owen, as he sliced onions, Pierre tended the broth, and she got the chicken browning; they had been talking about recipes he'd learned from Laura and her relatives. "You can't have eaten at restaurants every day."

"Not on a student's budget," Owen said. "I cooked for myself, of course—but you probably don't want to know what."

"Try me."

"Cooked ramen noodles with some frozen vegetables and a sliced hot dog stirred into them—that was a pretty common dinner."

Hannah gave him a horrified look. "You're right," she admitted. "I didn't want to know that." They both laughed.

Later, when the meal was finished, the dishes went into the sink, and Pierre got them soaking and clambered upstairs. "We can sleep in." Hannah said. "The solvent won't be ready before tomorrow afternoon. For now, another glass of wine, I think. You?"

"Please," said Owen. "I think I could use it."

The bottle tipped, splashed a good three inches of golden liquid into each glass. "I think we both could," Hannah agreed. "I hope to Saint Toad that I don't have to try the Great Conjuration on this kind of short sleep."

Owen sipped the wine. "I've noticed that you haven't been doing rituals every night, the way Charles Dexter Ward did."

"I don't need to. He had to teach himself sorcery. Me, I was taught."

"Lydia?"

She nodded. After a moment: "I don't think she knew much of anything about sorcery before she and Charles got married. Oh, she grew up with the sort of simple charms that most black folk did back then—burning red onion peels in the stove for good luck, sprinkling pepper inside your shoes to keep from getting goofered, looking your dreams up in Kansas City Kitty's Dream Book, that sort of thing. She learned a little more when she and Charles studied the old lore in Paris, I think, but it was after she moved to Averoigne that she really started learning things. There are witches in Averoigne."

"There are witches here," Owen said. Remembering something she'd said when they'd first met: "But I'm guessing they're not the same."

"Not the same at all." She drank more of her wine. "Your witches here, they're capable enough. I've met British witches who knew their craft inside and out, and the witchcraft here comes from Britain, mostly from the English West Country and from Wales—you have to go to Pennsylvania before you find the German lineages, and south to Maryland and beyond to get the old strong lore that came out of Africa with the slaves. But Averoigne is another matter. Things go back a very long ways there. The Romans called it the province of Avaronia and the Druids before them called it Avallaune, after their word for the sunken land to the west. Even in their time it had rites and ruins and traditions that were ancient beyond measuring, things that came across the sea from Poseidonis before it drowned."

"What kinds of things?" Owen asked. "If you don't mind saying."

She considered that. "The Wine of the Fauns, for one. Do you know about that?"

"Von Junzt wrote about it."

"That's right, you've studied *Unaussprechlichen Kulten*. Yes, the Wine of the Fauns, the Wine of the Sabbat. Do you know what it does?"

"Only what von Junzt said—that it was used for shapeshifting, or something of the sort."

"Something of the sort," Hannah repeated, smiling. "That's a gentle way of putting it. There are various forms and they cause various changes; I've seen people turn into wolves, of course—practically anybody can do that—and there are other changes that are quite a bit more interesting, if you've got the right things to put in the Red Jar that Avallaunius made and are brave enough to drink the results.

"But Lydia knew how to make them all. The folk of Averoigne are very old-fashioned, you see. It didn't matter to them that she was born in America, or that she had brown skin. She was the Comtesse de la Frenaie, and that meant she had an honored place in the circles that met on the high moors if she chose to go there on certain nights—and of course she did, over and over again." With a shrug: "She wasn't the first. One Comte de la Frenaie came back from the Third Crusade with a Saracen bride, another came back in the nineteenth century from southeast Asia with a wife from one of the hill tribes there—the Tcho-Tchos, I think it was—and the village folk welcomed them both the same way."

"And they welcomed you," Owen guessed.

That got him a sudden wary glance, and then a smile. "Yes," she said. "Lydia took me there when I was twelve, on Walpurgis eve, to meet the Old Goddess and the Young Goddess. I won't tell you what we did there—any more than you'd tell me what the Starry Wisdom church does at its meetings—but that's a good bit of why I don't have to spend my nights learning sorcery the way Charles did."

Abruptly she finished her wine, stood up. "What I need to do, this night at least, is get some sleep. You have a good night, now."

Owen said something appropriate, listened to her footsteps whisper up the stairs, and then sat at the table for what seemed like a long while.

* * *

The work continued, day after day, and the fine powder they worked with slowly changed in color, becoming first pale gray, then dark gray, then black as midnight and oddly heavy into the bargain. "Good," Hannah said, as the black color deepened. "The Nigredo, the black phase—Curwen calls it *Caput Corvi*, the Head of the Crow. It's almost ready to give up the salts."

"Almost," though, meant days of further labor, keeping the furnace at a steady heat while the ashes went through strange transformations. Now and then, as the work proceeded, Hannah looked up suddenly at the low ceiling of the cellar, as though she'd heard a disquieting sound.

"Something wrong?" Owen asked the third time that happened. He'd felt an odd, half-familiar feeling, too, as though someone had been looking at the back of his head.

"Somebody's trying to use a spell to spy on us." She glanced at the work, then at him. "Not for the first time, either. I've been keeping them out with ordinary incantations, but I think this needs more than that. Do you think you can keep things going for a half hour or so?"

Owen checked the furnace, then made sure he had enough charcoal within reach. "Shouldn't be a problem."

"Good. I'll be back." She left the cellar, heading up the stairs with an expression on her face that promised nothing good to anyone who got in her way. The door at the top of the stairs opened and then closed, leaving Owen alone with the furnace.

He adjusted one vent slightly, checked the flame, watched the fluid in the alembic rise and fall, wondered what was happening outside the house: in Providence, in Arkham, in the rest of the world. That was a waste of time, he knew, and turned his attention back to the work.

A sudden shuddering jolt shot through him then. An instant passed before he realized it was nothing physical. Something Owen didn't recognize sent shockwaves through the voor that surrounded the house. A moment later it happened again, and then a third time—and then the voor twisted, hard enough that the floor seemed to lurch.

He glanced up, wondering. He'd seen witches at work, witnessed the Starry Wisdom and the Esoteric Order of Dagon at their rites, watched Jenny wield the powers of a sorceress, beheld deeds of several of the Great Old Ones, and what he sensed now, moving through the voor of the world, felt like none of those. In a single momentary glimpse, he saw great dark wheels spinning one inside another, and something small and bright tumbling through space into an outstretched hand. The glimpse vanished, and he crouched by the furnace, waiting for the next shock.

None came.

Footsteps sounded on the floor above, crossing from one side of the house to the other, paused for several minutes and then returned. Not long thereafter the door at the top of the stair opened, and Hannah came back down, smiling broadly.

In response to Owen's questioning glance, she said, "That's taken care of. I don't know who it was—probably not the Radiance, certainly not the Yellow Sign, but in any case, whoever it was won't be trying anything of the sort again."

"You were right," he said.

"Oh?"

"About the witchcraft of Averoigne. It isn't like anything else I've ever sensed."

She gave him an amused look and nodded, and they went back to work.

As the black ashes finished the last of their transformations under Owen's watchful eye, Hannah brewed the alkahest— the solvent that alone could extract the essential salts from the properly prepared ashes. Curiously scented vapors billowed up from the laboratory bench as she worked, and all the while Owen kept the heat steady and waited for the sign that would tell him the ashes were ready for the extraction.

Even so, the burst of pale light from the alembic that announced the Albedo, the white stage of the work, took him by surprise. His sudden low exclamation made Hannah turn, and they both watched as the fluid in the alembic turned from black to clear, with the ashes a pale sediment at the bottom of the vessel.

That was one of the nights they both slept long and late. The alkahest was ready, and the ashes had to dry at room temperature until all the solvent had evaporated. The next afternoon, they went down into the cellar. Owen checked the ashes, which had become oddly nonadhesive— he could pour them from one side of the drying pan to the other, and not a single grain stayed behind. Meanwhile Hannah got the alkahest and poured it into an open vessel. It shimmered and glowed as though moonlight had been caught in it.

"Ready?" Owen asked. Hannah nodded, and he slowly poured the ashes into the vessel.

They both watched in silence as the powder spread across the surface of the alkahest and dissolved into it. The powder vanished, and the liquid took on a pale milky color: that was all.

"Dissolve and coagulate until the peacock's tail appears," Hannah said then, her face set. "That's what Curwen wrote."

Owen, without a word, went to the cabinet and brought out the largest of the retorts.

* * *

In the end, they had to repeat the process more than twenty times—how many more, Owen never knew, for he gave up keeping count when the weight of apparent failure became too heavy to bear. Day after day and night after night, they distilled off the alkahest at low heat, dissolved the thick mass remaining in pure water, distilled away most of that just as slowly, and then poured the remainder into an evaporation pan to dry. The powder changed color slightly with each repetition, losing a bit of its pallid milky color and becoming a little more transparent, with a faint bottle-green hue. Each dissolution and crystallization left it as nonadhesive as before: once it had dried, it could be poured into the alembic without losing a single grain.

The first of August, the ancient festival of Lammas, dawned still and sultry. Heavy gray clouds piled up in the west, promising rain. Owen washed up, dressed, and went through his morning routine, then clattered down the rickety stairs into the cellar to check the powder.

"Dry?" Hannah asked. She was at the top of the stair by the time he reached the pan.

He tipped the evaporation pan slightly, watched the powder flow and shift, touched it with one finger. "Good to go," he said.

She came down the stairs at once. Neither of them spoke, or needed to. She got the sealed flask with the alkahest glowing faintly inside it, he brought over the alembic, the liquid went into the latter, and then the pale greenish powder followed it. It was routine, almost mechanical, until the first flicker of opalescent color danced across the surface of the alkahest.

Hannah saw it first, and her sharp indrawn breath alerted Owen. As they stared, the shimmering blur of color appeared again, more brightly than before. It faded, and then all at once light of a hundred colors flared out from the vessel, flooding the basement laboratory and casting stark shadows on the brick walls. For more than a minute it blazed, and then slowly faded, leaving the alkahest in the vessel perfectly transparent.

"You saw that." Hannah's gaze had not moved from the alembic.

"Yeah."

"Good." She shook herself. "We've seen the peacock's tail. Now …" She crossed the room to the table where Ward's notebook waited, leafed through it. "Now we've gotten to the Rubedo, the red phase. The alkahest has to evaporate off at blood heat, and then the essential salts are ready. After that there's just one more step."

"The Great Conjuration," said Owen.

"That's the one." She put the evaporation pan back on the heater, got the dial set to the right temperature, and then very carefully poured the alkahest into the pan. Within moments a sharp aromatic odor filled the basement.

They went back up the stairs and left the process to complete itself. Cooking and eating breakfast offered some distraction, but after that there was nothing left to do but wait. Owen settled on the couch and tried to think about anything other than the Conjuration, without much success. Pierre sat hunched in the far corner, looking at nothing in particular with his unreadable eyes. Hannah went to her room upstairs and paced the floor, back and forth, back and forth, descending every half hour by the clock to return to the basement and check on the drying of the essential salts. They didn't even bother with lunch.

It was four-thirty in the afternoon, and clouds massed thick above Providence, when the salts were finally dry. Hannah made sure they were ready, then went upstairs and returned with a set of men's clothing—slacks, polo shirt, underclothes, shoes. Owen gave them a startled look and then realized what she had in mind. "For Charles?"

That got a smile from Hannah. "The spell won't reconstitute his clothes, you know."

She went to the lab bench, then, and picked up the curious jar of red stoneware and handed it to Owen. "Here," she said. "If things go really wrong, and I don't survive the Conjuration—" She found a piece of paper, wrote something on it, folded it and gave it to Owen as well. "You're to mail it to this address." A moment later she caught herself, allowed a rueful smile. "Please."

Owen laughed, but nodded and said, "I hope it doesn't come to that—but yes."

"Thank you." She drew herself up. "Now for the Conjuration. That's my job; yours is to keep anybody or anything from interrupting me—it's possible someone will make an attempt, and I'm not sure that Pierre will be able to stop it by himself if it's serious enough. One way or another, it won't be safe to stay here once the ritual's over." She opened her purse, took out an automatic pistol, handed it to him. "Use this if you have to. In the meantime, you might want to get your things packed."

"I already have," said Owen.

"Good." She managed an uncertain smile. "Just keep the rest of the world outside that door—" She indicated the door at the top of the cellar stairs with a quick motion of her head. "—and with any kind of luck I'll be back up here in a couple hours."

Owen considered her, nodded, and then said, "Say hi to Charles for me."

Her smile broadened. "I'll surely do that—and I'll look forward to introducing you."

With that, she followed him up the cellar stairs, waited until he went through into the kitchen, and then closed and locked the door and descended. Owen stood for a moment in the kitchen, and glanced at Pierre. Four enigmatic onyx eyes returned the glance. Then Owen went to make sure every door and window was bolted and locked. He came back and sat at the kitchen table, gun in hand, waiting, while Pierre settled into a corner, tentacles folded into his sleeves, motionless as a statue.

A few minutes passed. Hannah would be tracing the triple circle, Owen knew, and writing words of power on the stones of the cellar floor. Shortly thereafter a pungent scent began to seep through the cracks around the door. Owen nodded, recognizing the resins she was burning over charcoal, to summon the dread being Almousin-Metatron who alone could complete the work and grant the power to raise the dead to life. A moment later her voice, muffled by the door, rose in the ancient Latin chant:

> Per Adonai Eloïm, Adonai Jehova,
> Adonai Sabaoth, Metraton On Agla Mathon,
> verbum pythonicum, mysterium salamandrae,
> conventus sylvarum, antra gnomorum,
> daemonia Coeli Gad, Almousin, Gibor, Jehosua,
> Evam, Zariatnatmik, veni, veni, veni!

Over and over again the Great Conjuration rang out and the pungent scent filled the house. Owen sat still, forcing his outer and inner senses alike away from the incantation and the rising tide of voor that answered it, toward the least sign that anyone—the neighbors, the police, the Yellow Sign, the Radiance—might be about to force a door or a window and interrupt the ceremony. Hannah's voice grew hoarse and the air seemed to swim with the fumes. The kitchen clock showed five, five-thirty, six, and still the rite went on.

Suddenly dogs began to howl all over the Stampers Hill neighborhood, and a tremendous wind rattled the window sashes. An instant later the scent of the resins Hannah had burnt was blotted out by a terrible and pervasive stench. Another instant, and light blazed outside the windows, sudden and sharp as lightning. What came afterwards, though, was not thunder but a voice: tremendous and echoing, deep as the Great Abyss, shaking the house to its foundations as it intoned the terrible words that open the portal between the living and the dead: "DIES MIES JESCHET BOENE DOESEF DOUVEMA ENITEMAUS."

As the voice fell silent, the daylight that showed through the windows darkened, and another odor as indescribable and unbearable as the first briefly filled the kitchen. From the cellar below, Hannah's voice rose up in a final unsteady crescendo: "*Y'ai ' ng'ngah Yog-Sothoth h'ee-l'geb f'ai throdog Uaaah!*"

A heartbeat later a terrible shriek rang up the stairs. Owen was on his feet in an instant, but there was nothing he could do, and he knew it. He stood beside the table, waiting, while the shriek descended into a long wail, then into sobs, and then into silence.

It was only then that Owen realized that the voice that had shrieked was not Hannah's.

Thereafter, silence gripped the house. Twice Owen thought he heard what might have been low voices from the cellar beneath, one slow and dazed, one quick and brimming with delight, but he could not be sure. Then, finally, footsteps sounded on the stair, and after what seemed like a long interval, the key turned in the lock and the cellar door opened.

Through it came a young man in his twenties, slight and blond-haired, looking somehow out of place in the slacks and polo shirt Hannah had prepared for him. Behind him was Hannah, her face lined with exhaustion but beaming. She tried to speak, but seemed unable to find words.

Owen smiled, put the pistol aside, and stepped forward. "Mr. Ward," he said. "It's good to meet you."

CHAPTER 8

A TIME OF UNRAVELING

"Oh, for heaven's sake," Hannah said then, finding her voice. "Owen, this is Charles; Charles, Owen. There. No more of that 'Mr. Ward' nonsense."

Owen laughed, and so did Charles Dexter Ward. "I'm pleased to meet you as well," Charles said. "Hannah's spoken of all the help you've given her." He reached out his hand, and Owen shook it. It felt cold and dry, with a curiously coarse texture.

"We need to get out of here now," Hannah said then. "I've got protective spells set up, but those won't hold the Radiance or the Yellow Sign forever—not after the working I've just done. That much voor in motion will draw them like flies. Owen, can you grab my bag when you get yours? It's right in front of the door of my room."

"Sure thing," said Owen, and bounded up the stairs. By the time he came back down, his duffel in one hand and a soft-sided suitcase in the other, Charles had been introduced to Pierre, Pierre had clambered into sweats and shoes, Hannah had reclaimed the red stoneware vessel and the pistol, and all three of them stood by the kitchen door.

"Okay, good." Hannah stowed the red jar in her suitcase and then opened her purse, pulled out a little glass jar of strangely colored dust, and threw a pinch of it in the air above them all;

the gesture and the words completed the spell of concealment. "Let's go. I've got a hiding place rented and ready a few blocks from here."

Outside evening was drawing on, and heavy sultry clouds hung low over the roofs. Hannah led the way through a gap in the fence behind the house, and then between two rundown houses and across a little-frequented street. After that they ducked through another yard into the paved space behind a ramshackle house. Finally she walked up to what looked, at first glance, like a plain clapboard wall. Only when Owen got right up next to it did he see the ghostly outlines of a door, hidden from human sight by sorcery.

Inside a narrow stair climbed steeply up into darkness. At the top, Hannah turned on a light, revealing a cramped little attic apartment. "We'll be safe here," she said, "and in a little while, once the hunt's passed us by and I'm sure it's safe, we can head for a restaurant—it'll help for us to keep moving." With a little diffident smile: "I didn't think to stock the kitchen here with food. In the meantime, tea?"

"I won't argue," said Owen.

She grinned and busied herself in the cramped little kitchen, while Owen and Charles settled on a couch that had seen many better days. Owen considered the revenant sitting next to him, and wondered what would be the best way to broach the subject of his quest.

Unexpectedly, Charles forestalled him. "Hannah tells me that you know what Joseph and I were trying to do." Owen nodded, and Charles went on. "I'll caution you up front that nothing we found was enough by itself to waken the Dreaming One. The rituals I got from Dr. Angell are a good part of the puzzle, but not all of it. There's one way I know of that will certainly work, but that would take three things that might not even exist in the world any more—the Ring of Eibon, the Blade of Uoht, and the *Ghorl Nigral*, the Book of Night. Unless you have those—" He shrugged. "There's no certainty of success."

By the time he finished, Owen was regarding him with wide eyes. "If you don't mind my asking," he said, "where did you learn that, about the Three Treasures of Poseidonis?"

That got him an equally startled look in response. "I gather you're versed in some very unusual lore," Charles said.

"A good friend of mine comes from an old Kingsport family," Owen admitted.

Charles nodded, after a moment. "Well. Yes, that would explain it. But the knowledge I mentioned—I got that in a place I hope I never have to recall, and I hope you never have to go. Joseph had done a good deal more in his first time on Earth than the mere waking of the dead. He knew about forms of sleep that open onto vaster universes than this one, and we used those to try to get glimpses of a certain very old lore— older than this world."

"Carved on tablets of star-quarried stone," said Owen, guessing.

Charles blanched. A long moment passed, and then he said, "Yes. You know the *Book of Eibon* rather well, I see."

Owen nodded. "Did the lore you found say what to do with the Three Treasures?"

"Just a little. There are incantations in the *Ghorl Nigral* that can be used, together with the Ring and the Blade, to accomplish the thing."

"Fair enough," said Owen. "I'd still like to get access to Dr. Angell's papers—to borrow them, if that's a possibility, or at least make a copy of them."

Hannah came back from the kitchen, set down a teapot and cups. "Here we are." A glance passed between her and Charles, and then she busied herself filling the cups. Owen and Charles both thanked her, and she sat on a nearby chair.

"I have no objection to lending them to you," Charles said then. "It's not work I plan on taking up again, and I feel I owe you rather a great deal, you know."

"Don't worry about that," said Owen.

Charles shrugged. "It's my way. You and Hannah went out to the site of Joseph's farm, didn't you? If you'd searched the library underground thoroughly enough, you'd have found them there—if nobody's disturbed them. That's where I kept them, locked in a desk drawer."

"I didn't see anything in Dr. Angell's handwriting," Hannah said then, "but I didn't search all of both desks. Once I found Joseph's papers and your notebook, that was enough for me."

"Understandably," Charles said with a smile. "Still, once you think it's safe, we can go there again and see about finding them."

"Tomorrow, maybe," Hannah said then. "We shouldn't wait long."

Owen nodded again. "That should be fine. Thank you, both of you."

"Any time," said Hannah.

* * *

An hour passed, maybe, before Hannah got up for the third time, poured water into a shallow bowl, murmured words over it, and stared into it for a long while. "Okay, we should be safe," she said. "Both the Radiance and the Yellow Sign have gotten to the house, forced their way in, and found some false clues I left—I made it look as though we were heading down to Brooklyn, to stay with friends in the Red Hook neighborhood. There's a drone hovering near the house—no, it's headed east now. So we're good."

"Glad to hear it," Owen said. Hannah laughed and replied, "Oh, I know. Tea's pretty thin rations after the kind of effort we put in."

They settled on the little Portuguese restaurant off Main Street, and went back onto the streets, leaving Pierre to keep watch in the apartment. Night had fallen, but there was still enough light for Owen to see Hannah's face when she looked at Charles, and it was the face of a woman in love. Charles' face was less expressive and more diffident, but Owen thought a hint of the same thing showed in his eyes rather more than once. It's their business and no one else's, Owen thought with a mental shrug, and kept his surprise off his face.

That wasn't the only thing that caught Owen's attention, though. The city seemed more hushed than usual, and the few passersby hurried by with hunched shoulders and bowed heads. Businesses that had been open when Owen and Hannah had walked through the neighboorhood before were dark and empty, with handwritten signs in the windows that read CLOSED UNTIL FURTHER NOTICE.

"I wonder what on earth has happened," said Hannah.

They passed a bar that was still open, and then an Indian restaurant, also open. Both of them had handlettered signs saying CASH OR TRADE ONLY, and the restaurant, which had a menu posted in a convenient window, had a piece of paper covering the prices and a note saying ASK SERVER FOR PRICES. Charles stared at the last of these for a long moment.

"This reminds me of something rather troubling," he said as they started walking again. "In the fall of '23, I needed some documents from a private library in Munich, and caught the train out there. Germany was in quite the financial mess just then, and the Reichsmark wasn't worth the paper it was printed on—people took their pay home in wheel-barrows, it was that bad. But every restaurant either had a sign like that, or a chalkboard on the wall where the prices were written—and got rewritten upwards, sometimes several times in one night. I wonder if something of the sort could have happened."

"I have no idea," Hannah admitted. "Since we got started on—our little project—I only left the house to pick up grocer-ies, and I don't think Owen's been out at all." She frowned. "Though the last time I was out, the groceries cost quite a bit more than I expected."

A few minutes later they got to Henrique's. It was open but almost empty, with just one waitress who begged their pardon from across the room and vanished into the kitchen. The same CASH OR TRADE ONLY sign they'd seen in other open businesses was in the window, and the menu and prices had been written in marker on a white board above the cash register. Owen read it and blinked in astonishment; the chicken and garlic dish he'd had on their previous visit now cost well over a thousand dollars a plate.

Hannah looked at the board, too, and said quietly to Charles, "I don't have anything like enough money with me." Then, when he didn't respond: "Charles?"

He was staring across the room at a spry old man Owen recognized, the one who'd come there for lunch that earlier time. Just then the man looked up from his appetizer and saw Charles. His eyes went round and his mouth fell open.

"Great heavens," Charles said, dumbfounded. "Tony?"

The old man bounded out of his chair and crossed the room. "Mister Charles! It *is* you!" He seized Charles' hands in his own, and beamed. "I always thought you would find some way back. And here you are. And your friends—"

"Hannah Ward," Charles said, "and Owen Merrill. They're most of the reason why I'm here tonight."

"Why, then, they are friends of mine already."

"Hannah, Owen," said Charles, "this is Antonio Gomes. He used to work for me back when Joseph and I lived in Pawtuxet."

Hands were shaken. "You will let me treat you all to dinner, I hope?" said Gomes. "With things as they are, it can't be an easy thing to pay for a meal of any quality."

"Will it be a problem for you, Tony?" Charles asked him directly.

Gomes smiled. "Oh, no. I put my time to very good use."

The waitress came out from the kitchen, then, and Gomes turned to her. "Maria, I hope you won't mind if I move to a larger table. These are good friends I haven't seen in too long— and you'll put their dinners on my check, please."

"Of course, Mr. Gomes," said the waitress, and got them settled with menus and water in a booth toward the back.

"You're looking very well-preserved, Tony," said Charles then, smiling.

"Of course. Mister Joseph taught me a great deal, and I didn't stop studying when he died, no, not at all. The elixir and the stone—oh, the labor they cost me! But I live comfortably. I have gone away from Providence twice now, and come back with the same name but a different date of birth, without the least trouble. Nobody asks hard questions of an old man whose English is only as good as he needs it to be. Even with the coming of these latest troubles, bad as they are, it is not too difficult for me to get by."

The waitress came, took their orders, returned at once with a bottle of wine, went away again. Gomes began to fill glasses. "If you don't mind my asking, Mr. Gomes," Owen began.

"Please! We are all friends, are we not? Tony."

"Tony, then," Owen said with a smile. "We've spent weeks cooped up in a basement. The troubles you mentioned—could you fill us in?"

His eyebrows went up. "Ah, you have not heard, then? It has been quite the spectacle. I do not claim to understand more than a little of it—alchemy is complicated enough for me." He chuckled. "But the government, it has been playing games with its debt for many years now, you know, and now it is all up. The country has had to default, they say. Stock markets, bond markets, everything—oh, they have not been good for a long time, but now, it is all very bad. Everything is coming unraveled, like an old sweater worn too long. Here and overseas both, politicians and bankers run about clucking like hens, and make no more sense."

Charles and Hannah looked at each other. "We'll manage," Hannah said.

"If any of you need help," Gomes said, "why, you must come talk to me. Here." He extracted a card from an old-fashioned gilt card case, gave it to Charles. "And this, perhaps, will also be of help." He pulled out something that glinted yellow in the lamplight, placed it in Charles' palm. Owen got a brief glimpse of it: a gold coin.

"I make a little gold from time to time, and exchange it for gold already minted," said Gomes. "It keeps suspicions at bay. There is much more if you need it."

The waitress came out from the kitchen with their meals, and Charles slipped the coin surreptitiously into a pocket.

* * *

There were two bedrooms in the little apartment off the alley, with one bed each. Earlier, Owen had wondered how those would be divided among the three of them, and decided that he'd offer to spend the night on the couch, but long before dinner was over he'd seen enough of the body language between Hannah and Charles to guess that the offer wouldn't be needed. Sure enough, he ended up in one of the bedrooms, and the faint sounds that came from the other told him he'd been right in his guess. He considered the subject, then made the mental equivalent of a shrug again—it was hardly any concern of his—and settled down to sleep.

The next morning they breakfasted on those leftovers from the restaurant that hadn't fed Pierre, and then Hannah went to get her car. When she pulled up to the curb, Charles gave the thing a baffled glance. "Do all cars nowadays look like this?" he asked Owen.

"No," Owen said, "but they're all just about as ugly."

Charles laughed. "I wasn't about to say it. Still—" He suppressed a shudder.

They clambered in and drove off. Hannah had used a scrying spell to look for Radiance negation teams or Yellow Sign heptads, and spotted nothing, but driving out to Pawtuxet meant taking a serious risk, and Owen knew it. Even so, what filled his mind as Hannah drove was the Angell documents, the goal that had brought him to Providence. The papers hovered before his mind's eye as though he already held them in his hands. He knew Angell's penmanship well enough to imagine how the old scholar would have printed out the many-angled Aklo letters, spelling words of power no living loremaster knew.

It might not be there, he reminded himself. The thought twisted away as he considered it, but he forced his mind back to it. It might not be there.

They reached the abandoned factory next to the Pawtuxet River without incident, and climbed out of the car. Charles looked somber, and shook his head slowly. "The changes?" Owen asked him.

"Partly that," Charles said. "Those new buildings down-town have got to be among the most hideous pieces of archi-tectural rubbish I think I've ever seen. Partly, though—my father owned this factory, and I visited it as a boy, when it first opened. To see it empty and crumbling like this …" He shook his head again.

No one else was in sight, and so they crossed the street, climbed over the guardrail and picked their way down the trail past the piles of crumpled beer cans to the edge of the river. A short distance upstream, hidden behind its screen of foliage, the hole they'd excavated still gaped open, though much of the loose dirt had washed away in summer rains and weeds and grass were colonizing the bare edges. Hannah handed Owen the key, and he unlocked it with an effort and pushed the door open.

His heart was thudding as Charles closed the door behind them and they headed into the heart of the riverbank. The same overwhelming darkness as before, barely touched by Hannah's flashlight, filled the tunnel like a solid mass. The great square pillars that held up the ceiling in the central hall loomed out of the blackness like gray sentinels.

Then they reached the door to the library, and opened it. Clear light from the lantern spilled out into the hall. Charles let out a little cry, hurried over to one of the bookshelves and then to another. Turning around with an apologetic look: "I'm sorry. It's just—these were such treasures to me, back before."

"I understand," said Owen.

"I imagine you do." Then he turned to the desks. "My desk is the one on the right. Unless Joseph moved the papers, they'll be in the bottom drawer on the right hand side."

Owen crossed to the desk, tried the handle of the drawer. It yielded a little, then jammed. Stilling his impatience with an effort, he worked the thing loose, finally got it to slide open.

The drawer was empty.

He looked up, to find Charles looking over his shoulder. "Gone? Joseph may have moved them, as I said. Let's see what we can find." He went to the other desk, and started opening drawers. Owen began searching the desk in front of him.

It was no use. They searched the entire library, the laboratory, and the storerooms for good measure, but Dr. Angell's papers were gone.

"I'm so sorry," Hannah said at last. They were standing in the central hall again, with the old oil lamp blazing improbably away on the floor nearby. "After all the help you gave me, all the work you did—it hardly seems fair that things should end up this way."

Owen met her gaze, nodded. "I knew it was a gamble when I came here."

"I know, but—" Her voice faltered.

"What do you think the odds are that Joseph took them up into the bungalow?" Owen asked Charles then.

"Fairly high, I'm afraid. We both used to do that—especially in the cold weather, when it got pretty miserable down here."

"So they're likely in the hands of the Radiance."

"I hope not. If Joseph had enough time before he was taken to the asylum, he might have burnt them. Either way—"

Charles made a little helpless shrug. "I'm at least as sorry as Hannah. As I said, I feel I owe you a great deal. If you think there's any point in searching again—"

Owen shook his head again. "No. Thank you, but I think we've done what we can."

* * *

Two hours later they were back at the little attic apartment, and Owen was shouldering his duffel. "You're sure you'll be okay," Hannah asked in a worried tone.

Owen nodded. "I'll be fine." He could have stayed longer, he knew that, but with the disappearance of the papers, the last point to remaining in Providence had gone away for good, and he wanted nothing more just then than to go back to his home and his family.

"Well," said Charles, "I hope we see you again."

"I don't know if you're ever likely to get up to Arkham," Owen said, "but if you do, don't be strangers. 638 South Powder Mill Street—it's a block off Peabody Avenue."

Hannah wrote down the address. Charles assured him they'd stop in when they traveled north, and then pressed something into Owen's hand, saying, "You may need this. Please." It was the gold coin he'd been given by old Tony Gomes. Owen nearly refused it, for he knew the Sargent bus would carry him whether he had money or not, but Charles' troubled look made him decide otherwise.

He thanked them both again. Hands got shaken and polite empty words said, and then Owen headed down the narrow stair and went out into the alley. The door closed behind him and vanished into illusory clapboards. He glanced at it, sighed, and started walking.

It took him a little wandering to find his way back to a street he recognized, but not long thereafter he began to see familiar buildings, and maybe twenty minutes after that, he was pacing along the route he'd taken so many times from the John Hay Library through downtown Providence to Federal Hill. That was painful enough, and the low shape of Federal Hill ahead of him added to the discomfort. He wondered briefly how Sam and Charlene Mazzini and their kids were doing, whether they'd patched things up again, and what had become of some of the other people in the Starry Wisdom Church, but that stirred too many unpleasant memories. He thrust the thought away, made himself concentrate on the old cracked sidewalk ahead of him.

Across the river and into downtown: it was all familiar, or should have been, but more than half the businesses he passed were closed, and those that still had lights on and people inside them had the ubiquitous CASH OR TRADE ONLY signs in their windows and some arrangement to deal with prices that rose with each passing day. Most of the pedestrians he passed had the same hunched shoulders and bowed heads he'd seen the evening before on the way to the restaurant, there were even fewer cars on the streets than before, and what music spilled out of the few open doors jarred and jangled against a spreading silence. The vending boxes for the *Providence Journal* were empty—Owen guessed that a whole pocketful of quarters wouldn't buy a paper any more—but a copy hanging in a convenience store window, with a handlettered sign next to it saying ASK FOR PRICE, had one headline about emergency meetings in New York and Washington, and another saying that the goverrnor of Rhode Island was begging residents to keep calm and stay at their jobs until things could be sorted out.

He wondered, as he neared the bus stop, if he'd see the woman with the strange eyes before he left. She wasn't in any of her usual spots, but not far from the monument where the Sargent bus stopped, there she was, sitting on the pavement of the transit mall with four cats around her like guardian statues. "Where are you going?" she asked him in her silken voice.

He glanced at her, wondered again who and what she was. "Home to Arkham."

"Why?"

Owen let out a ragged breath. "The thing I came here to do didn't work out, and so there's no reason for me to stay."

The woman considered him for a long moment, and then nodded slowly and returned her attention to the cats. Owen waited another moment, then went the rest of the way to the Civil War monument.

A few more passengers gathered over the half hour or so that followed: an old black woman and her twenty-something grandson, a middle-aged white couple, and the same young man Owen had seen on the way down to Providence well over a month before, the one with the Aztec face who'd noticed the Lovecraft novel Owen had been reading. All of them looked uneasy, and the couple huddled together and counted the money they had.

The bus pulled up finally, and old Edith Sargent clumped down the stairs and faced them. "Before you come on board," she said, "I probably ought to tell you all that this'll be the last run I make 'til things get straightened out with the economy and all. I had to borrow the diesel to get down here, and—" She shrugged. "I'm not gonna try to figure out the ticket price. Just pay me what you can, and remember there's no round trip back."

The middle-aged couple gave her a horrified look, and went away. The others filed onto the bus, Owen at the end of the line. He'd decided long since what he would do with the coin that Charles Dexter Ward had given him, and pressed it into the old woman's hand with a wink. She blinked in surprise, then nodded appreciatively and closed the door.

The bus roared to life and lurched down the cracked street.

* * *

Leaving Providence was a relief, but the highway northward stretched on and on. Owen tried to read one of the books he'd brought with him, but put it away after a while, for his mind kept straying back to the outcome of the trip he'd begun with so much hope. The towns up to North Attleboro seemed to be weathering the troubles well, and the greenery of the state forests was comforting—was it his imagination, or did the trees and undergrowth he passed seem a little wilder, a little less overawed by the passing cars, than they had when he'd passed by in June?

Beyond that, though, lay Boston's southern suburbs, and those had been hit hard by the crisis. There were still businesses open and lights on, but fewer than he'd seen in Providence and its environs. The bus passed one dark and silent mall after another, sped by clusters of office buildings where every sign of life and light had vanished. Off to the east, where Merry Mount slept beneath the houses of suburban Quincy, he could see little, and the last lines of Justin Geoffrey's poem whispered in his mind:

```
For what danced joyfully 'neath olden skies
Shall waken, and in dreadful wrath shall
rise.
```

Maybe they won't rise in wrath at all, Owen thought then. Maybe they're already rising, cold and patient, taking everything apart a little at a time. Antonio Gomes had used the right word, Owen decided: the towns he passed seemed to be unraveling as he watched.

He wondered then whether there was more to the crisis than the ordinary turbulence of a troubled time. The papers had been full of bad economic news since before he'd first come to Arkham, and what he'd seen of the outside world once he and Laura settled in Dunwich seemed to point the same direction—but was it just that? If the Radiance wanted to crash the economy, he knew, they had the money and influence to do it; the Great Old Ones, bound as they were, could doubtless find subtle ways to do the same thing; and there were other powers in the Earth, on it, and around it who might have taken action. The fragility of the human world, drifting like a bubble on the surface of dark unplumbed waters, had rarely felt so clear to him.

Downtown Boston itself still clung to shreds of its old vitality, and half a dozen people waited for the bus outside the big silent hulk of South Station, where the trains used to come. Beyond that, though, were more suburbs, more empty buildings, and a growing sense of desolation. Finally, as the sun swung over to the west, the bus left the northern suburbs of Boston behind and headed up the old highway to Salem and Beverly, where hard times had arrived years before and their traces weren't so intrusive.

From there, the coast road ran to Kingsport, where the soaring sea cliffs rose like a wall between the little seaport and the mouth of the Miskatonic River. That brought a first tentative smile back to Owen's face. He'd spent eight summers in Kingsport with Laura and the children, heading down from Dunwich when the school year ended. Every detail of the old town, from the big mansions on the central hill to the stark masts and yards of the *Miskatonic* at its berth alongside the old harbor, was an anchor for pleasant memories, and those helped.

As the road left Kingsport and began to climb into the hills south of Arkham, the slanting summer light streamed across landscapes he knew well. More than a dozen of the old farms outside Kingsport had tenants in them now, and so did a few of the houses the bus passed along Old Kingsport Road as it rose up into woodland. Further on a tall hill came into sight, a crown of standing stones upon its crest. The sight raised Owen's spirits further, made the cascading failures of his trip to Providence a little easier to bear.

Then the bus broke from the trees and started down the long slope toward Arkham and the Miskatonic River, passing the half-collapsed ruins of the abandoned Fair Isles Mall and a scattering of tumbledown farmhouses before reaching the outskirts of the city. There were only three people on the bus by the time it headed down Peabody Avenue, and so Owen shouldered his duffel, went up to the front of the bus as buildings he recognized began to roll by, and asked the driver, "Could you let me off at the corner of Pickman?"

"Sure," she said, and three blocks later brought the bus to a wheezing stop. Owen thanked her as the door lurched open, went down to the sidewalk, stood there while the bus growled into motion again and headed on toward the bus station.

As the engine noise faded, Arkham's subtler sounds wrapped around him. The wind was blowing in from the sea, tinged somehow with a sharper edge than Providence's breezes. Faint voices came from the middle distance, and from the old Knights of Pythias hall that loomed above the sidewalk where he stood seemed to come a faint subterranean rhythm, half-heard and half-sensed, as someone hammered nails into place in one of the schoolrooms on the ground floor. He drew in a deep unsteady breath, then got his duffel settled on his shoulder and started down Pickman Street. One pleasant clapboarded house after another passed, and then he turned a corner onto Powder Mill Street, passed three more doors, and stopped outside the one he knew best. It was twilight, and Owen Merrill had come home.

CHAPTER 9

THE CLOSING OF THE CIRCLE

He'd barely gotten the door closed behind him when Asenath came pelting out of the parlor into the entry and threw her arms around him. "Dad! I'm so glad you're back. I missed you so much."

He scooped her up, kissed her, set her back down. "I missed you too, Sennie." He was about to ask her where Laura was, when a familiar voice called out from the parlor: "Oh Father Dagon—Owen?"

Words seemed unnecessary. He dropped the duffel and went into the parlor as she surged up from the couch, sending a spiral notebook toppling onto the floor. An instant later she was clinging to him, her face buried in his shoulder, as he held her close. Then she glanced up at him, with just a bit of hesitation in the motion. He knew right then that something was wrong.

He let it pass, settled onto the couch with her. Asenath crossed the parlor, scooped up the fallen notebook, and handed it to her mother, then flopped onto her belly on the rug. "I want to hear all about Providence," she announced.

"First of all, dear," Laura said, "can you get down another jar of stock from the freezer, and put another package of cod to thaw?"

"Sure thing, Mom." She scrambled to her feet, headed out into the kitchen.

As the freezer door opened and jars rattled, Laura asked him, "The papers?"

He let out a ragged sigh, shook his head. "No luck," he said. "Honestly, I'm sorry I went. It was a pretty dismal experience."

Another glance upward at him, another hint of hesitation. "I'm sorry."

"So am I." He bent, kissed her cheek. "I'd have been a lot happier here."

She looked away, nodded. To fill the sudden silence, he asked, "Why the notebook?"

"Oh, that." Laura glanced back at him again, with a sudden smile. "Do you remember the letter you wrote me about the children who'd read *A Princess of Y'ha-nthlei*?"

"The Mazzini kids," he said. "Yeah."

"Sennie and I got to talking about that, and she reminded me that none of the old stories from Innsmouth ever got written down. Everybody just learned them growing up and then told them to their own children. But now that Innsmouth's gone ..." She let the sentence trickle away.

"You're writing them down."

"Yes—the ones I remember first. Later on I'll talk to people who know more of them than I do. Martha Gilman, for one—I honestly think she could tell a story every night for a year and not repeat one of them. But I've got four of them written down so far. I'm thinking of putting in other things, too—the way people in Innsmouth used to chant and clap for dances when we were too poor to have musical instruments, the songs for mending nets and oyster shucking and all the rest of it. There was so much, and somebody needs to save it."

"That's really good to hear," said Owen. "You're a good writer, you know."

Once again, he got the quick glance, the hint of hesitation. "Thank you. I wish I still had a typewriter like the one I used for *Princess*, though. Silly, I know, but that's how I like to write."

Just then Asenath came back from the kitchen, with a drowsy-looking kyrrmi perched on her shoulder. "All done," she said. "Okay, now—"

"Hi, Dad," said Barnabas, who had just come down the stairs, with a book under his arm.

"Hi, Barney."

"Dad—"

Owen glanced at the clock, guessed the timing of dinner. "At seven-thirty," he said, "you can tell me all about what you've been reading."

That got him a grin. "Thanks." He crossed the room to one of the armchairs, climbed up into it, settled down to read.

"Now?" said Asenath, with a rebellious look. Owen laughed, and started talking about Providence: the hills and rivers and the long sweep of Narragansett Bay, the buildings like and yet unlike those in Arkham, the Starry Wisdom church and the alleys around it. He left out the typewriter with the broken letter O, the house on Olney Street, the stone chambers under Joseph Curwen's old farm, the terrible voice booming out from the darkened skies over Stampers Hill, and made a light entertaining story out of it all.

Then and later, as he listened to Barnabas recounting what he'd read, helped make dinner and then helped eat it, sat in the living room with his family while Laura's pen darted across the pages of her notebook and Asenath taught Barnabas how to play Chinese checkers, and wished Barnabas a good night and received a hug and kiss from him: the sudden uncertain glance from Laura, the hesitant look. He thought he could guess why.

* * *

Night deepened. Asenath gave her parents the canonical hug and kiss, and went upstairs to bed with Rachel the kyrrmi perched on her shoulder. Doors opened and shut, the house's ancient drains gurgled, and a little later silence settled over the upper part of the house. It wasn't until then that Owen turned to Laura and said, "There's something wrong, isn't there?"

Her glance—toward him, then away, hard—told him the answer. "I got a couple of letters from Providence while you were gone," she said.

Cold certainty settled in his gut. "Typed," he said, "on an old-fashioned typewriter with a broken letter O."

"Yes." A moment passed. "I'm curious how you knew."

"Notes and letters typed on that machine have been terrorizing everybody in the Providence congregation for decades. I got three of them." He let the silence settle back into place, then: "What did the ones you got say?"

She swallowed, made herself go on. "That you were having an affair with a younger woman named Hannah Ward. That you left the apartment they lent you to move in with her. That I shouldn't waste my time expecting to see you again—and if I did, it wouldn't be for long. They also said some things about me that—that I don't really want to talk about."

He closed his eyes, opened them, let out a slow ragged breath. "Laura," he said then.

She looked back at him, a dozen conflicting emotions in her eyes.

"That's not what happened."

"I didn't want to believe any of it," she told him. "But the letters mentioned—some very intimate details."

"I bet they did," Owen replied at once. "I talked to a guy in Providence, Sam Mazzini—the only person who would say a word to me about any of this—and he got letters with things in them he'd never told to another living person. He didn't know how the writer got the details, and neither do I, but there it is."

She nodded, slowly.

"Do you want to hear what actually happened?"

"Please." Before he could begin: "Is there a woman named Hannah Ward in Providence?"

"Yes. She's Charles Dexter Ward's great-granddaughter, and some kind of relative of Jenny's family by marriage—and she's an alchemist."

That startled her. "Seriously? A competent one?"

"You could say that. She raised her great-grandfather from the dead, the way he raised Joseph Curwen." She gave him an astonished look and he nodded. "Can I tell you the whole story, with everything I didn't tell Sennie? It might be easier that way."

"Please," she said, and he started from the beginning— the trip down to Providence, the welcome he'd gotten from the congregation there at first, and the way that every door on Federal Hill had slowly closed in his face thereafter; his encounters with Hannah Ward, the work they'd done together, the triumph of Charles Dexter Ward's resurrection and the final bitter failure of the whole project the next day.

"And so I came home," he said. Then: "Laura?"

She looked up at him again. Her eyes were wet and her lower lip trembled.

"I didn't have sex with her," he said then. "I wouldn't— and even if I'd wanted to, as far as Hannah Ward's concerned, there's only one man on Earth." In response to her questioning look: "Her great-grandfather."

Laura blinked. "That seems kind of ..." Her voice trickled away.

"I know," he said. "But—" He shrugged. "She looks a lot like her great-grandmother, and for all practical purposes he's still twenty-six years old. I figured it was their business."

She tried to say something, but started crying instead. He reached for her, drew her against him, stroked her hair as she clung to him.

"The letters also s—said that you wanted a normal woman," she said sometime later, her voice indistinct. "Not a cripple, or a—a monster."

He kept his hands from clenching into fists by an act of will. "I hope I never have to go back to Providence," he said after a time, in a measured tone. "If I do, and I ever find out who wrote that to you, I'm going to hurt them. Really, seriously hurt them."

One red-rimmed eye glanced up at him. "Don't."

He met her gaze with his own, said nothing, and after a moment she closed the eye and crumpled against him. When another moment had passed: "The thing is, Owen, I know I'm becoming a burden to you in some ways—and it's going to get worse."

"I knew that would happen before I married you," he reminded her. "Besides, I'm not exactly the dashing young idiot I was ten years ago, either."

She started laughing then. "Owen, I don't deserve you."

"No, probably not," he allowed. "But I'm sorry to say you're stuck with me anyway."

She slid one tentacle past him, twisted around in a way no human being could move, until she'd settled on her back on the couch. Then, still laughing, she drew him down to her.

* * *

The next day Miriam Akeley came to lunch. She lived just a few blocks away, in an old apartment building that had seen many better days, and she and Laura had taken to meeting over lunch during Owen's absence. "She knows an astonishing amount about the old lore," Laura explained as she and Owen assembled a pair of sack lunches for the children, who would be going to the playground south of Saltonstall Street with a dozen other Innsmouth children and two sturdy grandmothers. "Even more than I'd realized. But it's all theory and no practice, except for dreamwork—she's better at that than anyone I've ever met."

"I wonder why," he said drily, and she gave him an amused look.

He handed her the cutting board with the tomatoes he'd sliced, and she got them arranged on the sandwiches, put the top slices of bread on, and started wrapping them up in waxed cloth.

"So you two usually talk shop?" Owen said then. "I can get lost, if you like."

"Not a chance. She'll want to hear everything you learned about Angell and Ward."

They finished preparing the sack lunches, and Owen glanced at the clock on the kitchen wall. "Does she ever mention Martin?"

That got a sudden laugh. "Only when she slips, and that's not often."

Owen laughed as well. It was an open secret that Dr. Akeley and Jenny's uncle Martin had some kind of relationship going, but what that entailed was anyone's guess. Was it just that both of them were intensely private people, or was there more to it? Owen knew that he'd find out when Miriam and Martin were good and ready to say something, and not a moment before.

A quarter hour later, Asenath and Barnabas went trotting out the back door, canvas lunch bags in hand, to meet the other children and their chaperones. A half hour after that, a quick trio of knocks sounded at the door, and Owen went to answer it.

"Owen!" Miriam said, as he opened the door. "I'm glad you're back."

"Me too," Owen replied. "Hi, Miriam."

They said the usual things, and the door clicked shut behind her. As they crossed the living room, she asked him, "Any luck finding Angell's papers?" He shook his head, and she nodded, as though she'd expected that. "Well, I'm sorry to hear that. Hi, Laura."

They got settled at the table, and lunch made its appearance: green salad, a clam soup, fresh bread, and the sliced raw fish that had so ubiquitous a place in Innsmouth cooking, with half a dozen dipping sauces. Two pitchers of water, one fresh for Owen and Miriam, one salt for Laura, rounded out the meal. The conversation ranged from the usual polite topics to Owen's journey, the things he'd learned about George Angell and Charles Dexter Ward, and Miriam's work on the *Seven Cryptical Books of Hsan*. Then, in a lull in the conversation, Owen asked, "Should I ask about how Miskatonic's weathering the economic mess?"

Miriam gave him a bleak look. "The short version is that it isn't. Even before this latest business, the university was in deep trouble, and now the securities that used to be our endowment fund are worthless and all our other sources of funding are gone. Word from the state assembly is that they're going to try somehow to find the money to bail out Harvard and MIT, and maybe keep the doors of the community colleges open, but that's all." She shrugged. "I can't fault them for that; it's a reasonable decision. But Miskatonic University is bankrupt. We don't have the funds to cover payroll, much less anything else, and creditors are circling like sharks, hoping to snap up the real estate while their money's still worth something."

Owen gave her a horrified look. "I'm so sorry," Laura said. "Are you going to be okay?"

"Oh, I'll be fine." She speared a piece of raw fish with a little two-tined fork, dipped it in a spicy red sauce. "I'm still not sure how I survived all these years without this," she said with a sudden smile, gesturing with the fish. "I grew up eating sashimi, but this is so much better."

Owen and Laura both took the hint and steered the conversation elsewhere. Later, though, when the three of them had settled in the living room, Miriam said, "I envy the two of you, you know. It must be really pleasant not to have to depend on the money economy."

"If things get tight for you," said Laura, "we could find room for you, you know."

That got her a surprised look. "I'm not sure what I'd do that your people would value."

"Classes in Aklo," said Owen. "Classes in the *Necronomicon* and the other tomes."

"You've got your own educational system," Miriam pointed out.

"Yes," Laura said, "but it's got its limits. You know plenty of things about the old lore that I've never heard of—things I'm not sure anybody in the order or the church has heard of."

Miriam took that in, then started laughing. "I can see it now," she said. "History of Ideas 496, Special Topics in the *Pnakotic Manuscript*."

"Don't laugh," said Owen. "If you offered that, you'd fill a good-sized seminar room just with initiates who are already here in Arkham. Seriously, if you're willing and we can find you a space, I know people who would really be interested in that."

After a moment, Miriam began nodding slowly. "There might be a space," she said. "You remember Phil, Michael Peaslee's husband?"

"I heard of him," Owen said. "I haven't had the chance to meet him. He's a stockbroker, isn't he? He's got to be having a rough time, with everything that's going on."

"No, he had the good sense to retire and cash out all his investments two years ago—he said at the time he thought there was something very fishy going on between the government and the big banks, and he didn't want to get caught in the mess if it blew up." With a little laugh: "As it has. But he went into real estate after that—here in Arkham, south to Kingsport, north and west along the Miskatonic valley, buying up abandoned farms and renting them out to people who want to get into farming and don't have the capital. He and Martin are thick as thieves these days; they both understand money. No, let me correct that: they both understand wealth, which isn't the same thing at all."

"You don't have to convince us of that," Laura said with a smile.

"Granted—and you're lucky to know that. But Phil's been working on a special project for a while now. With all the financial trouble the university's had, some of us started thinking a good while back about what to do if things fold completely, and Michael's part of that—and of course that means Phil is in on it as well. He's setting up a three-way real estate swap with the university, some of its creditors, and a holding corporation he and Martin cooked up. They're pretty close to signing; once it goes through, a chunk of Miskatonic's debt is going to be cleared, and the old campus downtown will be sold to the corporation and leased for a dollar a year to a nonprofit, of which I happen to be the president."

Owen's mouth fell open. "Seriously? That's pretty clever."

"Oh, the idea wasn't mine." Miriam sat back in the chair. "I met Nyarlathotep in the Dreamlands, what was it? Three years ago, I think. He outlined the plan and asked me to do it, and I agreed. I didn't know why until a few weeks ago. Now I do."

* * *

Over the days that followed, Owen tried to settle back into the half-familiar routines of the house on Powder Mill Street and the crumbling old town around it. The garden out in back duly took shape, with the little stone altar to Shub-Ne'hurrath in its proper place between the seedbed and the wood-slatted compost bin, and another house in the block started being cleaned out, repaired, and painted for Laura's parents, who would be moving down from Dunwich toward the beginning of autumn.

Meanwhile the downstairs rooms in the old Knights of Pythias hall that would house the parochial school—there would be only one school, drawing children from the Starry Wisdom and the Esoteric Order of Dagon alike, another breach in old barriers—got fitted out for their future purpose, with blackboards up front and rows of wooden chairs and desks facing them. Those all had to be extracted from the long-abandoned East High School a few blocks away on High Street, along with a white marble bust of a former principal named Joel Manton that everyone thought added a nice touch to the main classroom.

One afternoon he took Asenath and Barnabas to see the carousel at Upton Park, just past Boundary Street under the pleasant green shade of Hangman's Hill. The Arkham carousel had been built by the famous Looff firm back in 1909, and refurbished in 1976; there was still a faded sign with the old Bicentennial logo on it. In the years since it had seen little maintenance, though, and spent most of a decade padlocked for lack of funds. Now it was being put back into working order and repainted in bright colors. The great wooden tentacles that rayed out across the carousel's ceiling were a deep sea green again, with gilded suckers, and a few of the sea creatures it had in place of ponies—squid, porpoises, sea serpents, krakens, whales, and more—had been restored and put back in their places. Owen sat down on a nearby bench while the children joined half a dozen others with their faces pressed against the chainlink fence, watching in awe as two artists applied gilding to the saddle and reins of a seahorse. He watched and smiled, and tried to convince himself that he was happy.

Meanwhile the Starry Wisdom church four blocks north settled into its routine of services and initiations, and familiar faces and comfortable conversations there helped wash away some part of the bitterness Owen brought back from Providence. Laura donned the elaborate golden tiara of a priestess to celebrate the high rituals of the Esoteric Order of Dagon, and their children trotted off to Sunday school in their black hooded robes, while he drew up lesson plans for the upcoming school year, and spent evenings wrestling with the arcane lore that would eventually prepare him to advance to the Starry Wisdom's fourth degree. It was the life he'd planned ever since he and Laura first heard the talk about a new community in old Arkham, the Innsmouth folk dreaming of salt air and seashores again, folk from Dunwich and Chorazin imagining new prospects away from villages that were beginning to feel just a little crowded and overfamiliar.

Why, then, he wondered, did everything around him feel somehow out of place? His prayers and his meditations brought no answers.

A few days after Miriam's visit, he set out for the north end of town with a bulging canvas bag in hand. The morning was already hot, and haze veiled the standing stones on distant hills. As he left the house he could hear Asenath's voice from in back, mingled with those of half a dozen of her friends, chanting a familiar rhyme:

> "The King is in Carcosa,
> The Goat is on the hills …"

He smiled and kept walking, and the voices faded to silence behind him.

Two more businesses had opened in little narrow storefronts on Peabody Avenue, a used bookstore and a secondhand shop; both had cash registers up front on the off chance that the economy got straightened out, but Owen knew that both had entrances in back for the people of the Great Old Ones. A little further down the hill, another space was being refitted for use as a fish market, by young men and women who grinned at Owen and greeted him as he passed. Scores of other storefronts stood empty around them, bleak stigmata of the ancient town, poised between a lingering death and a fragile and crepuscular rebirth.

The college district north of the river looked even more dilapidated than it had when he'd passed through it in June— no surprises there. The Lovecraft Museum on the north side of Derby Street, in the old Arkham Sanitarium building, had no lights on and the CLOSED sign behind the glass door was already yellowing with age. Out in front stood the great bronze statue of Cthulhu, rising up as though from the sea, one mighty hand raised to grasp at nothing. Offerings rested on the pedestal and the sidewalk in front of the statue: silver coins, seashells, plaited chaplets of seaweed of the sort children in abandoned Innsmouth used to make. Owen added a carefully chosen shell to the collection, and went on through the narrow passage between the flat brick planes of Armitage Union and the ornate Gothic spires of Orne Library to the once-familiar quad.

The state of the campus appalled him. Fully a third of the windows in the great brick mass of Morgan Hall were boarded up with sheets of plywood, and most of those, from their color, had been there for at least one winter. The delirious spires and rugose bulges of Wilmarth Hall next to it had sheltered its windows more effectively, but the signs of decay were still painfully evident. The quad itself hadn't been mowed in weeks, and tall weeds rose above the luxuriant grass. Owen shook his head slowly, and took the long way around.

The mechanical doors at the main entrance to Wilmarth Hall had been taken out some years back—a good idea, since they'd relied on some kind of innovative technology and so only worked now and then—and replaced with a pair of plain glass doors, which opened without difficulty. Once inside, Owen made his way to the central stairway that wound up through the heart of the building. The power had evidently been shut off, and the only illumination came from the landings, where doors had been taken off their hinges. By that uncertain light Owen made his way up to the seventh floor, followed the subtle windings of the hallway to the seventh door, and knocked on it.

"Please come in," said Miriam Akeley's voice, stirring old and painful memories.

The office inside had changed only a little. The slightly trapezoidal window at the far end still let in views of the West Campus Parking Garage and the green whaleback shape of Meadow Hill beyond it; the bookshelves, none of them quite straight or parallel to the others, groaned beneath scholarly literature. The computer screen on Miriam's desk was black, though, and she set down a pen and a spiral-bound notebook as she rose to greet him.

They said the usual comfortable things, he settled into a convenient chair, and then glanced around the room with an ambivalent look.

"It's been a long time," Miriam said then.

He allowed a sharp laugh. "That's one way of putting it."

Her laugh, gentler, joined his. "When you knocked I was just thinking about—well, all the changes since you were here ten years ago. It's been a rough road for all of us."

"True enough." Owen pulled a bundle wrapped in waxed cloth, a bottle, and a pair of sturdy glasses out of the canvas bag. "First things first," he said. "Here's our lunch, and I've also got something for the librarians. Are you sure Dr. Whipple doesn't want anything?"

Miriam shook her head. "Some of us have offered rather more than once." With a smile: "But you're going to make yourself very popular on campus, you know."

He served out the meal—robust fish sandwiches on home-baked bread, with a tart white wine—and they busied themselves with that for a few minutes, while they talked about her plans to keep some semblance of Miskatonic going despite the financial crisis. "I don't imagine that things have gotten any better with the university finances," he said then.

He was surprised to see amusement crease her face. "That depends on your definition of 'better.' We still don't have money, but one of our biggest and most useless expenses has gone away." In response to his questioning look: "President Phillips resigned two days ago, and he's already left town. You're now looking at the president pro tem of what's left of Miskatonic."

Owen congratulated her, and then asked, "There used to be some odd stories about the university's charter."

"Some of them are apparently true," Miriam replied. "The Board of Overseers gave me the lead box this morning, and read out the traditional warning not to open it."

"Were you tempted?" Owen asked, smiling.

"Of course—but not enough to risk what happened to President Greeley back in 1842." She shook her head. "But we had a little party last night once Phillips resigned. His departure doesn't solve our problems, but it's some consolation after that ugly business five years ago."

"Clark Noyes' project."

"Exactly," Miriam said.

"Any word of Noyes recently?"

"In a manner of speaking." She sipped her wine. "He's still at that place in Oklahoma—Binger State University."

"Do you know if they've still got funding?" Owen asked.

"I have no idea," admitted Miriam, "and I wish I did." With a sidelong glance at him: "You're wondering if the other side has something to do with the crisis."

"That's occurred to me."

"You're not the only one." Owen nodded, and she went on. "I haven't been able to find anybody who's willing to talk about what's going on at Binger State—but a friend of a friend got a visiting professorship for a year at a university in the Midwest. I promised not to mention where, so let's just say it was another place the noology people went when they left here."

"Fair enough," said Owen.

"They wanted her out there to teach an upper-division course on Lomarian."

Owen stared at her for a long moment. "That seems—"

"Odd? That was what I thought, too. Then I remembered that all the places they went had strong liberal arts and language programs."

"I remember," Owen admitted. "We talked about that."

"Exactly. They were quite evasive about why they wanted a Lomarian specialist, but of course they had to let my friend's friend know what vocabulary they needed, and what period of the language they had in mind—so it's pretty clear they're studying the *Pnakotic Manuscript*."

"I'd wondered if that was it."

"Maybe that's the only part of the old lore they're studying," Miriam said then, "but I doubt it. There was another thing, too. My friend's friend said that the way they were fixated on specific details was really quite odd." She sipped her wine. "She told me there was something about it all that smacked of desperation."

* * *

An hour later, Miriam showed him the one unlocked door into Orne Library and introduced him to the three librarians who still labored there without benefit of pay, and he handed over a big pot of seafood chowder and three loaves of fresh bread and accepted their thanks. Thereafter, he crossed the main floor of the library to an inconspicuous door over to one side, and clicked on the flashlight the librarians had lent him. The stair, the corridor, and the little bare room at the far end hadn't changed at all in ten years. He went to the sturdy metal door on the far side of the room, rapped on it in the curious rhythm Miriam had taught him.

The door opened fractionally, admitting the gaze of one startlingly blue eye. "Who is it?"

"Owen Merrill."

"Ah, yes. Miriam told me you were back." The door opened wide, and Abelard Whipple, Orne Library's restricted-collections librarian, waved him inside. "Come in, come in."

Owen glanced around as the old man locked the door behind them. The fluorescent lights on the ceiling were dark, and the only illumination came from a green-shaded oil lamp on Whipple's desk. Steel shelves marched into shadow, lined with Miskatonic's world-famous collection of rare books on mysticism, occultism, and archaic religions. Many of the books, Owen saw, had been wrapped neatly in paper, labeled, and tied in small bundles.

"Yes, the collection's about to find a new home," said Whipple, following Owen's gaze. "Did Miriam mention the arrangement she's worked out with the old campus downtown? That's been settled now. The library building there is still in quite decent shape, and it doesn't depend on electricity anything like as much as this one does. With no power for the dehumidifiers, this is a shockingly bad place to keep books, you know. But I'm told that Miriam and some of the other professors are also talking about teaching classes there this autumn."

"That sounds like a good idea," said Owen.

"Oh, agreed, agreed." The bright blue eyes considered him. "It's good to see you again."

"Thank you, and likewise." With a sudden grin: "It's good to be seen."

The old man laughed, as though at a joke. "I'm sure it is. Well. Now Miriam mentioned that you had something you wanted to ask me about, something about the old lore."

"Yes, though it's—" He fumbled for a word. "Peripheral, maybe."

Whipple waved him to a seat at the nearest of the big steel tables, fetched the lantern, and sat down on the other side, placing the lantern between them so that it made a pool of light on the tabletop. "By all means. What do you have in mind?"

"This," Owen said, pulling a piece of note paper out of a pocket and handing it across the table. "I found it in George Gammell Angell's papers in Providence."

Pencilled letters on the paper spelled out names in Babylonian and Greek. Whipple glanced at it and looked up sharply at Owen, the look of amiable distraction gone utterly from his wrinkled face. He glanced at the paper again. "Not peripheral at all," he said. "Do you know what the words mean?"

"*Dumu-ne Zalaga*, the Children of Light," said Owen. "*Hetairia Photis*, the Society of Light. I can put another name to the same organization, if you like."

"I'm sure you could," said the old man. "As can I." He nodded slowly. "So Angell got that much of the secret. I admit I'd wondered."

"What do the other names mean?"

Whipple considered him for a moment, as if deciding how much to say, and then went on. "I'd have to look up Altberg-Ehrenstein—I seem to recall him as a German archeologist before the First World War, an aristocrat who dabbled in archeology while on leave from the Imperial German Navy, but that's a guess. The tablet from Irem, that I would have to look up too, but I'd be willing to bet good money that it includes a reference to the destruction of the Moon Temple."

"And the Weird of Hali?" Owen ventured.

That got him an amused look in response. "I imagine you know better than that." He considered the paper again. "The others? What they look like. Shamash-Nazir was an astronomer-priest in Babylon, a founding member of the *Dumu-ne Zalaga* and its first head. Agathocles of Megara was one of the philosophers who guided Alexander in his wars of conquest, and he wasn't present at the desecration of the holy places, so he was still alive when they knew for certain that their great gamble had succeeded. He became head of the reorganized order, the *Hetairia Photis*. There have been reorganizations since then, of course."

Owen took that in. "You know quite a bit about them."

The blue eyes met his briefly, intent but also amused. "It's necessary lore—as I believe you have good reason to know."

"Granted, but I admit I wonder how you found all that out."

"We have certain mutual friends, shall we say, who pass on details from time to time. I've also been researching the subject on my own for quite a while. Carefully, of course." Indicating the paper: "That knowledge may have been the cause of Angell's death, you know."

"I haven't shown this to anyone besides you and Miriam," Owen assured him.

"That's wise." Whipple picked up the note paper, glanced at it, handed it back. "They still cling to secrecy, just as we do," he said, "but the time's coming when they'll abandon it. We'll need to be ready for that." Then, as if he'd put on a mask, the hard clarity left his eyes and he sat back, again the elderly and slightly bemused scholar. "Anything else I can help you with? No? Well, by all means drop in another time."

CHAPTER 10

AN OFFERING IN ARKHAM

By the time he got back home from Orne Library it was in the middle of the afternoon. Barnabas was asleep—he never fussed about his afternoon nap, so long as it happened at exactly the same time every day, and was preceded by the same snack of milk and homebaked crackers and the same centuries-old Innsmouth story told by his mother—and Laura was curled up on the couch, a distracted look on her face and a pen in her hand marching line by line across the pages of her notebook. She roused herself from the writing long enough to give him a kiss, but he knew better than to start a conversation.

He went into the kitchen, where Asenath sat at the table cutting potatoes for dinner, and Rachel perched nearby, nibbling meditatively on a spare potato slice and watching the whole process with evident interest. A hug and kiss from his daughter, a friendly chirr from the kyrrmi, and a beer from the refrigerator later, he headed upstairs to his study, sat sipping the beer and looking moodily out over the gardens in back. Most of the plots were green and growing, and people he knew—members of two different Waite families, three assorted Gilmans, and a stray Eliot or two—were industriously pulling weeds and training beans up poles. I should be out there too, he told himself, but sat there in silence anyway, nursing his beer, wondering why everything around him still seemed out of place.

Or was he the one that didn't quite fit?

Finally, when the bottle was empty and solitude pressed too close around him, he picked up Miriam Akeley's translation of the Pnakotic Manuscript and went back downstairs. Laura gave him a smile and returned to her writing, and he settled on the other end of the couch, stared at the manuscript in his hands, and tried to make the opening lines make sense: *When from the places to anthward and ulthward, hand no longer joined hand, and the great concord was broken, and a way stood open to those from the cold places outside …*

He sighed in frustration. Anth and ulth, those were the two spatial directions human beings couldn't perceive, off in the fourth dimension at right angles to north, south, east, and west, but the joining of hands, the great concord, and the ones from the cold places—he should know exactly what those meant, he'd encountered all the necessary lore already, but the knowledge remained just out of reach.

He was still wrestling with the words when a knock sounded at the door.

Owen glanced at Laura, who looked up, startled. An instant later he was on his feet, and handed her the manuscript, which she concealed under her notebook. As she adjusted her tentacles to make the shapes beneath her skirt look like legs, he went to the door and opened it.

Outside stood the cat-eyed woman he'd seen so many times in Providence, uncombed and disheveled as ever, but looking up at him with a terrible intensity in her eyes.

He stared at her, and she said in her silken voice, "May I come in?"

"Please," he said, and stepped out of the way.

She went past him as though the house was her own, walked into the living room. Laura gave her a startled look, and then her eyes went round. "Good," said the woman. "You know." To Owen: "Sit." She gestured to the couch, and before he could think of a response he found himself returning to the place where he'd been seated a moment before.

"Who are you?" Owen finally managed to say.

"She knows," said the woman, glancing at Laura with a smile. "But you—" The tawny eyes turned toward him as she sat in one of the armchairs. "You did a very great favor for a sister of mine, not so long ago, and she gave you three gifts in return. My presence is one of them—and your prayers might have brought me here even if that did not."

Then he understood. Across the room, he noticed Asenath; she'd come up the hallway from the kitchen and was staring at their visitor with wide eyes.

"Can we offer you something?" Laura said then. It took Owen a moment to realize that she'd used the verb in its religious sense.

The thought seemed to startle their visitor. "Yes," she said. "That would be very welcome. Milk, perhaps, or if you have it, cream?"

Laura made to get up, but Asenath said, "I'll get it, Mom."

"Bottom shelf of the fridge door, dear," said Laura.

"I know." She disappeared down the hallway, came back again with a large bowl and a glass bottle of cream. With a curtsey, she set the bowl at the woman's feet, emptied the cream into it, and backed away.

"Thank you," said the woman. "Now open a window."

"Sure," said Asenath. As she finished pushing open one of the windows, the woman gestured toward the floor by her feet. "Sit here, child." Asenath suddenly looked dazed, and without another word settled down on the floor next to the chair.

A moment later cats began leaping in through the window— lean, scrawny alley cats like the ones Owen had seen around the woman in Providence. They clustered around the bowl, lapped up its contents, purred up at their mistress, and then bounded away. Before long the bowl was empty and the last of the cats vanished through the open window.

Owen found his voice. "You're Phauz, aren't you?"

"Why, yes," the woman said. She rested a hand atop Asenath's head; the child's eyes drifted shut, and the hand began to tangle in her hair, tracing complex patterns across her scalp. "Do you know why I'm here?"

Owen shook his head.

"You left Providence too soon," she said. "The thing you wanted to find is still there. I want you to return with me and find it."

Owen stared at her for a time, and then glanced at Laura. The look in her eyes told him everything he needed to know. "When should I go?" he asked Phauz.

"Tomorrow. There's a bus station in this town."

"Right across the river."

"Exactly. Be ready to take the bus tomorrow, in the usual time and manner. I'll arrange a way to Providence."

"I'll be there," said Owen.

"Good." Phauz glanced down at Asenath, untangled her hand from the child's hair, and then stood up. "Because you welcomed me and did what's fitting, I've given this child of yours a gift. Your other child—it's not my place to give him anything; the one who watches over him will see to that. But you …"

She glanced from Owen to Laura and back again. "You've both been lied to. You—" The tawny eyes flicked back toward Laura. "—the more cruelly, you—" She turned toward Owen again. "—by those you trusted. If I can, I'll lead you through the lies to the thing you seek, but I warn you—"

She raised her hands, facing each other, and flexed the fingers. From the tips, hooked claws slid out, slender and terrible.

"You'll be going into great danger, Owen Merrill, and I—I will be going to war." The claws slid back out of sight. "Will you come?"

"As I said," Owen told her, "I'll be there. Should I bring a weapon?"

"That won't be necessary." Phauz stood, then, and without another word went to the door. Owen followed her and let her out. She glanced back at him with a smile, and then walked away, a clowder of cats bounding up to follow at her heels. Owen stared after her for a time, then turned, went back into the living room, and met Laura's shocked gaze.

* * *

Asenath blinked awake just then. "Mom, Dad," she said, "I was ..." Then she blinked again, shook herself, and stood up, looking around in bafflement. "Where ..." Then, embarrassed: "I must have gone to sleep or something. I had the weirdest dream."

"It wasn't a dream, Sennie," said Laura. "Look down."

She looked and saw the empty bowl, then gave her mother an incredulous look. Owen went to the window and closed it. A silent moment passed, and then Asenath said, "She's the cat goddess, isn't she?"

"Phauz," said Owen.

The child's face lit up. "I remember," she said. "She took me to a place where the sky was golden, and she said ..." Her voice trailed off. Then, in obvious frustration: "It's not fair. I remember and then I don't."

"I know," said Laura. "Sennie, when I was younger than you are now, your grandmother took me to stay with her now and then. When I got back I could only remember the tiniest scraps—but the memories came back when I needed them. Yours will, too." Asenath nodded uncertainly, and Laura went on: "How are those potatoes coming along, by the way?"

Asenath sighed and rolled her eyes. "Mom."

"And please take the bowl and the bottle with you, dear."

That got Laura a mutinous look. After a moment, though, Asenath gathered up the remnants of the offering and went back into the kitchen, and thereafter Owen heard her talking to Rachel and the kyrrmi responding with a chirr.

He sat down next to Laura. "I can't think of anything in the world I want to do less than go back to Providence."

"I know." She put her arms around him, drew him to her. "But it's not finished, is it?"

"I guess not," Owen admitted.

"Even before—this—I felt that. I think you did too."

He nodded after a moment. "Yeah."

And it was true, of course; he knew as much the moment she'd said the words. The feeling that had haunted him since his return, that everything was out of place, or that he was—it had been trying to tell him that he should have stayed in Providence, kept searching for the Angell papers no matter what.

You've both been lied to, Phauz had said. *You, by those you trusted.* Owen thought he could guess what that meant. And the other lies the Great Old One had mentioned …

Just then Asenath came back into the living room. "The potatoes are done," she said in a sulky voice. "What do you want me to do with them?"

"Help me make scalloped potatoes."

The sulky mood vanished. "Really? Can we have cheese on them?"

"Of course, dear." Laura leaned forward, kissed Owen, then stood in a single fluid motion and went into the kitchen with her daughter trotting behind her.

Later that evening, after dinner, he got the old Miskatonic University duffel bag he'd taken to Providence the first time and started gathering the clothes he'd need for the second trip. Once he'd gotten them out, he opened the bag, and found a folded piece of paper lying in the bottom of it. He gave it a blank look, pulled it out and unfolded it. On it, written in neat old-fashioned penmanship with long curving tails above and below the lines, was an address in the *département Haute-Isoile* in France.

Of course, he recalled after a moment. The address Hannah gave me, where the strange red jar was to be mailed if the conjuration went wrong and she died.

Why, though, did the penmanship seem so familiar?

After a moment, when nothing came to mind, he shrugged and went on with packing.

* * *

He left home early the next morning, just as he'd done that June day when he first went to Providence. The sagging gambrel roofs of Arkham hadn't changed in the interval, and the day was clear and warm, with a wind off the ocean promising some relief from the summer heat. Still, Owen shouldered his duffel and headed down Peabody Avenue without a scrap of the hopeful mood he'd felt that earlier time. He was walking into danger, and knew it.

The old downtown with its traces of renewed life seemed frail as he walked through it, and the old college neighborhood on the far side of the Miskatonic was practically a wasteland, its last businesses shuttered now that the university had closed down. Still, the bus stop on Dyer Street was open for business, and a county bus lurched into motion and rolled away from it as he walked up. The metal benches under the shelter were empty, though, with one exception: a woman with uncombed tawny hair and garments that looked slept in, who looked up at him, smiled, and motioned toward the bench beside her.

He sat down, tried to think of something to say. Phauz glanced at him and smiled again, and turned to watch the seagulls wheeling and crying in the sky above the station.

Maybe five minutes passed before anyone else showed up. Then the young man Owen had seen twice before on the bus, the one with the Aztec face who'd noticed Owen's book, walked up to the station. He looked discouraged, but spotted

Owen and came over toward him. "Hi," he said. "Do you know if the bus to Providence is running again?"

It was Phauz, though, who spoke. "The bus will be here in eleven minutes."

His face lit up. "Seriously? Thanks." Then, as the sudden hopeful look faded: "Uh—do you know how much the fare's going to be?"

"There will be no fare this time," she told him.

He stared at her, and tried to say something. She met his gaze, and then motioned to another of the benches. Without another word, still staring at her, he crossed slowly to the bench and sat down.

Exactly eleven minutes later, according to the big clock at one end of the shelter, the Sargent Bus Company bus came wheezing and rattling up to the stop. Owen got up, shouldered his duffel, and followed Phauz to the bus door, with the young man behind them.

The door clanked and hissed open as usual, but old Edith Sargent wasn't in the driver's seat. Instead, something half-shapeless slumped there. The old clothes on it clearly weren't covering a human form. Its face, if it had one, was concealed by a hoodie and a floppy broad-brimmed hat, and whatever it had instead of hands didn't quite fill the driving gloves it wore. Owen, who was used to such things, nodded amiably to the driver and followed Phauz three seats back, sitting next to her. The young man behind him stared, swallowed audibly, and then went to the very back of the bus and pressed himself into a corner.

The bus roared to life and rolled away from the stop. As it headed toward Peabody Avenue and the long road south, Owen considered the goddess next to him. She was looking at nothing in particular, but after a moment she glanced his way.

Do you mind if I ask you a question? he thought at her, guessing that she would hear that as clearly as spoken words.

Not at all, the answer came at once.

You said yesterday that this was one of your sister Yhoundeh's three gifts—and then you told me you were going to war. That seems like—more than a gift.

Does it? Her silent laughter rustled through his mind like wind in leaves. *But you are right, there is more. You seek to awaken Great Cthulhu. I want you to succeed.*

He stared at her for a time, and then nodded slowly. *Would it be okay,* he thought then, *if I asked you why?*

Yes. After a few moments: *There is much you cannot know—but you know about the strife between Cthulhu and Hastur.* Owen nodded, and she went on. *That happened long ago, as you count time—it was sixty-five million years ago, I think you would call it, when their war came close to shattering the greater Earth, and Hastur triumphed at last—and the discord between them began long ages before that, before your ancestors first crawled up out of the oceans onto the land. So I was told—for I was spawned long after all of that was over. Did you know that I am the youngest of the Great Old Ones?*

I had no idea, Owen replied.

It is so. I am scarcely nine million years old, as you count time, and in our reckoning I am little more than a hatchling.

But you still have your own ideas about what happened.

The quarrel should never have been, she replied. *If the old breach is not healed, this world will die, and I will not have that.*

Owen considered that for a long cold moment, while the half-overgrown wreckage of the Fair Isles Mall slid past outside the window. *Thank you,* he thought at her a moment later. *I appreciate that.* Then: *And I know it wouldn't be good for your cats.*

She glanced at him. *Nor for those who will come after them and from them.*

Owen hadn't intended to look at Phauz, but his head turned anyway. His gaze met hers, and for an instant he sensed the terrible vastness of the mind behind the cat's eyes. It was not the first time he'd glimpsed the mind of one of the Great Old

Ones, but in some ways this was more shattering than those earlier moments of insight. He knew instantly that she had told him the truth—that she was a child still, compared to the vaster and more ancient powers he'd encountered—and yet the gap between her mind and his was greater than the one that lay between him and the dust-mites who crawled unnoticed across his skin.

Then, all at once, that greater mind seized him and sent him falling forward through time. In a single fleeting glimpse he saw the rest of human history, its triumphs, its tragedies, and its many absurdities; then a second glimpse showed him the other intelligent species that would begin their history when humanity was a waning elder race, or later still, when humanity was no more. One of those species would rise when the sun blazed the color of aged gold in the heavens, and its history-to-be unfolded itself before Owen's stunned gaze.

He saw tall slender figures pacing intricate pavements, mounting sky-piercing towers, pondering scrolls written in elegant incomprehensible scripts, wielding savagely hooked blades, piloting strange craft through the skies. They were bipeds and mammals, but not human, not even remotely— and a hundred hints in the shapes of their heads and limbs, their soaring architecture, their solitary pride and their sudden unreasoning passions, told him that they were the distant descendants of the household cats of his day.

They are mine, Phauz said to him. *I shall guide them and they shall serve me. If this world lives, they are promised to me. Now do you wonder that I risk the wrath of Hastur? I will not abandon them or their world that will be to the consequences of a foolish quarrel.*

Abruptly the vision ended, and he stared at her. It took some minutes for the chaos of his thoughts to calm. Finally he asked, *Does every intelligent species have one of the Great Old Ones to guide it, the way you will guide—them?*

Of course. Some greater and some lesser, some younger and some older.

And ours—

Is dead yet dreaming. Why do you think your species wanders in such confusion?

Owen thought about that all the way to Providence.

* * *

The bus wheezed and rattled as it rolled to a stop. Owen got to his feet at once, and stepped out of the way as Phauz unfolded herself from the seat with feline grace and headed to the door. Behind them, the young man with the Aztec face got up, glanced nervously at the shapeless driver, and then followed them down onto the street and hurried away.

The downtown district of Providence hadn't changed much, though there were fewer people around than there had been the afternoon Owen had boarded the bus to Providence, and more of the buildings were closed and dark. Phauz led the way without a moment's hesitation, toward the river and the slopes of College Hill beyond it. Owen followed, wary and unsure.

Her voice whispered in his mind as they came within sight of an unfamiliar bridge. *Over the river we will be on ground held by the enemies of the Great Old Ones. They are here, with as great a force as they have gathered in years.*

Why?

The tawny eyes glanced back at him with an expression he could not read at all. *They came to take advantage of the crisis to seize certain books, some in libraries, some in private collections— there are more books on the old lore here in Providence than in any other city on this continent. But they detected the work in which you took part, and so they are also hunting those you know.*

And we—

Are seeking those same ones also. Come.

The green roiling waters of the Providence River moved smoothly past as they crossed the bridge. On the far side nothing seemed different at first, but Owen noticed that all the businesses were closed and too many of the homes had their curtains pulled tight. No one walked the streets. Furtive movements caught his eye here and there, but they were most of two blocks up the hill, veering north toward Stampers Hill, before he realized what they were.

Cats. Every block had two or three of them at least, stalking purposefully through the yards or bounding across rooflines. At intersections Owen looked down side streets and saw more cats, scores of them, darting across the empty thoroughfares. Most of them seemed to be going the same way he and Phauz were, uphill and angling to the north, but some veered off in other directions and some perched on rooftops and tree branches, gazing in various directions.

They're keeping watch for you, he thought at Phauz. *The cats.*

Of course. Another backward glance at him, unreadable as the first. *Throughout the great world, and especially throughout this little world, whatever a cat senses, I sense.*

Owen tried to imagine what it would be like to have sights and sounds and scents from millions of cat-minds pouring through his awareness at each moment, gave up a moment later.

Somewhere in the middle distance, a car engine started, loud against the stillness. *This way*, Phauz said at once. *They are close, and one is with them whose mind I cannot confuse.*

She darted between two houses, veered left, flattened herself against a wall. Owen followed her, duplicated the motion. The car stopped again, close. He could hear the doors open, boots hit the pavement, a low voice giving orders.

They have detected my presence, Phauz told him, *as I foresaw. Remain still. I will act.*

Footfalls came closer, and then all at once a man in paramilitary gear came around the corner of the house and saw them. His face tensed. "Stop right there," he said. "You're going to come with me." He reached out to grab Phauz by the arm.

Owen saw the claws burst from her fingertips again, the quick savage movement. Then the man crumpled to the ground, his throat a red ruin. *Quickly*, Phauz told Owen, and darted out from between the houses, across the street beyond.

The others were close, Owen knew, too close. He followed the goddess, expecting to hear gunfire at any moment. A voice in the middle distance and a sudden pounding of boots told him that they had been spotted. Phauz turned suddenly, pushed him up against a clapboard wall, then stepped past him into the open and raised her arms in a sweeping motion, gesturing with claw-tipped fingers.

All at once a shrieking torrent of cats bounded past the two of them, poured out of every gap between houses, flung themselves down from porches and raised terraces, sounding the shrill war-cry of their kind. There had to be thousands of them, Owen guessed, and more followed like floodwaters before a rising tide. Over the war-cry of the cats he heard a burst of gunfire, another, and then screams that had to be human.

Phauz could see what was happening, though Owen could only see her. The look on her face was one he'd seen often in wild predators, and now and again glimpsed momentarily in his own children: at once innocent and ferocious. It chilled him to the marrow. Lines from Geoffrey's poem suddenly surfaced in his memory:

```
For what danced joyfully 'neath olden skies
Shall waken, and in dreadful wrath shall
rise.
```

No, he thought suddenly. Dreadfully, but not in wrath. We would have to be much more than we are, to earn their anger.

The screams fell silent, and so, a little later, did the cats. *It is done*, Phauz said, turning back toward him. *Now we must go, quickly. More will come soon.*

They hurried into a narrow gap between two houses, crossed the little patch of yard beyond them, found a way between the houses on the other side of the block to a street a little further up that led north. Hundreds of cats streamed past them, bounding silently away, and many of them had blood on their muzzles and their paws. The sight made him wince, but it also stirred memories. *I saw Nyarlathotep do something like that once,* he said to Phauz.

Did you? She seemed pleased. *I learned it from him. He has certain responsibilities toward the hatchlings of the Great Old Ones.*

I'm a little surprised I haven't seen him here.

He cannot be here. He is our soul as well as our mighty messenger, and where the Great Old Ones are divided in will, he does not go. In such places hatchlings such as I must fend for ourselves. A flicker of amusement, then: *There can be certain advantages to that.*

The street crested the top of a rise. Off to the right, the street offered glimpses of the Brown University campus. Half a dozen gray SUVs stood parked at the edge of sight, and another drove away, a reminder that danger was still too close for Owen's comfort.

Tell me something, Phauz said then. *The men I caused to die— they feared death, wished to flee from it. Why, when your people die so soon anyway?*

Owen considered her for a time as they walked, and then said, *We have so little life that we don't like losing any of it.*

The quick glance he got from her then, tinged with uncertainty, reminded him that she was indeed still a child. *I will consider that,* she told him, and said nothing else for a time.

* * *

The afternoon deepened around them. Not much further on, Phauz had the two of them leave the street and duck out of sight behind a convenient house. A few minutes later a car drove slowly past, and they waited until the sound of its engine had blurred into background noise before going on. They did the same thing a second time half a dozen blocks further on. The cats still accompanied them, a silent furtive presence pacing through the streets and yards of the neighborhood, lending Phauz their eyes and ears. The goddess herself moved calmly ahead as though she knew exactly where she was going.

They were well into the Stampers Hill neighborhood when Owen noticed something odd about the streets before them: a curious distortion of perspective, maybe, that led his eyes off at strange angles. He blinked and tried to focus on the streetscape ahead of them, but the effect grew stronger with each step he took, until it took some work to keep walking straight along the cracked sidewalk.

You sense it? Phauz asked him then.

Yes. What is it?

Witchcraft. She is old as your people measure time, old and very wise, and she spins a web around herself that few can break.

Owen gave her a startled glance. Before he could respond, though, she went on. *Look only at me. That alone will bring you alive and sane through the web. Look only at me.*

Then she was walking ahead. Owen managed to fix his gaze on her, and followed.

Around him, a step at a time, the world went mad.

It was almost subtle at first, a twisting of lines and shapes just too slow to track, but its effects could not be ignored. The street they followed seemed to bend back around them until it headed off into the sky at an impossible angle, while the houses flowed this way and that, folding and unfolding. The cats scattered and vanished. Phauz kept walking, apparently unconcerned.

Owen followed her, though it cost him constant effort to look only at her slender form, to keep his gaze from being caught by any of the weirdly angled shapes that lurched toward him out of the chaos or tumbled away into the unseen. A shrieking, roaring confusion of sound filled his ears, and his own body seemed stretched and twisted into unnerving forms. Illusion, he told himself, it's all illusion—but the only thing that enabled him to keep believing that was Phauz, walking ahead of him, the one thing in the universe that seemed untouched by the spell.

How far they went, Owen had no idea; it may only have been a few blocks, though it felt like much more. The shrieking and roaring in his ears rose step by step to a crescendo, and so did the twisting and lurching of the impossibly shaped things around him. Then, all at once, he broke through the spell, and he stumbled and nearly fell as the world suddenly snapped back to its usual shape.

He and Phauz were standing in back of an ordinary Providence house of eighteenth-century date, with white clapboard siding, a plain peaked roof, and a big central chimney rising up above all. It took Owen just a moment to recognize it as the Curwen house on Olney Place.

"Now," said Phauz aloud. "Follow me. They will be waiting." She went to the kitchen door and gestured. The door flew open as though shoved by an unseen hand. A more than natural darkness seemed to crouch within, and then a half-seen shape with flailing tentacles and four fanged jaws sprang forward toward Phauz. She gestured again, and some force Owen could neither see nor sense flung the shape back into the darkness. A sudden crash sounded.

"Enough," said Phauz to the darkness. "You know me, and you know the one that comes with me—and I know you also, Lydia Ward."

CHAPTER 11

THE WINE OF THE FAUNS

For a moment nothing moved. Owen stared with wide eyes at Phauz, the pieces of a puzzle he hadn't known was before him falling all at once into place. Then the voice of the woman he'd known as Hannah Ward spoke out of the darkness, heavy with weariness and grief. "Very well," she said, and spoke a word in a language Owen didn't know.

The darkness vanished instantly, and Phauz went through the kitchen into the hallway beyond. Pierre lay sprawled over a fallen kitchen chair—he'd hit it and knocked it flying when Phauz flung him aside, Owen guessed—and slowly lifted his conical head. Down the hall, past Phauz' slender form, Owen could see the door to the library hanging open, and beyond it Hannah—or was it Lydia?—and Charles in the midst of a triple circle drawn in chalk, lit by candles around the outside. She had a small book, leatherbound with hasps of iron, open in one hand, but closed it and raised her chin as she faced the goddess.

Owen went over to Pierre and in a low voice said, "Are you okay?" The creature nodded, but when it pulled itself to its webbed and clawed feet it moved as though bruised.

By then Phauz stood in the library, just outside the chalk circle, facing the two within it. "Lydia Ward," she said again. "Do you know why I'm here?"

That got a defeated sigh in answer, and then: "No. I don't suppose there's any reason to hope that you're here to rescue us, though."

The silken laugh of the goddess filled the room. "You're quite wrong—but there'll be a price, of course." She gestured at the circle. "Release that. I've set the Alala to guard this house for as long as necessary."

Lydia gave her a look full of astonishment, then nodded wordlessly and made certain gestures with her hands, murmuring phrases that sounded to Owen like a jumble of medieval Latin and some antique French dialect. The candles around the circle flared and went out. Phauz nodded once, then gestured at the couch, and Lydia and Charles sat on it side by side staring at her. The goddess settled into one of the armchairs, then glanced Owen's way and summoned him in with a motion of her head. He entered the room, sat in one of the armchairs, and let his duffel slide off his shoulder onto the floor.

Lydia glanced at him, then at the goddess. "Did you send him?"

"No—but I want him to find what he seeks." The tawny eyes glanced from Lydia to Charles and back again. "And I know the lie you told him."

Lydia closed her eyes briefly, opened them again. "You mentioned a price," she said, her voice level. "Name it."

Phauz said nothing, simply looked straight into her eyes, and a moment later Lydia's face went stark with horror. "No!" she shouted.

The goddess said nothing in answer, or nothing Owen could hear.

"After all that's happened—" Lydia started to say, and then her voice trailed away into silence and she lowered her face into her hands. Charles looked on, puzzled and aghast.

Phauz spoke then, her silken voice unyielding. "You broke oaths you took among the witches on the high moors of Averoigne, oaths made in my name and my mother's, and you took a certain precious thing you had no right to take, because you hoped you could use it. So you'll use it, in the way I've shown you, and when you've done so, you'll give this man what he seeks. I offer you no other choice."

"Damn you," Lydia whispered. Then, in a louder voice: "I'll do it."

"Good. Shall I spell out where and when?"

"No." She lifted her face from her hands. "That's plain enough."

Phauz rose to her feet in a single supple motion. "Good." she repeated. "The Alala will guard this place for one hour, while I prepare the way. Follow when the time is done. Stay longer, or go a different way, and nothing will keep the hunters from you."

"I said I'll do it," Lydia said in a flat tone.

Phauz nodded once, wordlessly, and then turned and left the room. A moment later the kitchen door opened and closed, and she was gone.

The moment the door closed Lydia Ward sprang to her feet and went into the kitchen. She came back a moment later, carrying Pierre; they apparently had some kind of wordless conversation, and she set him down on the other end of the couch, where he huddled against the cushions and watched the others.

"Where are we going?" Owen asked.

"Curwen's laboratory," she said.

Charles gave her a horrified look. "If we do that we'll be caught the way Tony was. We can bar the door—the bars ought to be there still—but those won't hold out forever."

"I know." She clenched her eyes shut. "Please—you'll have to trust me." Then, glancing at Owen: "Both of you."

"What happened to Tony?" Owen asked then.

"The Radiance got him," said Charles grimly. "Oh, they made it look like an ordinary robbery, but robbers don't throw the corpse of an old man into his own bathtub and then pour sulfuric acid over it. They also don't ransack a house for obscure books on alchemy and leave dozens of things that could have been fenced without the least difficulty." With a sharp gesture: "We went there to find out if he knew any way to get out of Providence without being spotted by the other side—and by the time we left, one of those little flying things was already tailing us."

"A drone," Lydia said. "The thing is, we're almost out of food, so we'd have had to risk leaving soon anyway." Bitterly: "The Young Goddess chose her timing well." She turned back toward the kitchen. "Owen, if you care to dine with us, I can offer bread and cheese, some cold sliced sausage, and a little wine. Not much for what might be a last meal."

* * *

"Was there ever actually a person named Hannah Ward?" Owen asked then. They were sitting around the kitchen table, sharing out the meager dinner.

Lydia gave him a quick glance, nodded after a moment. "Yes. Most of the story I told you was true. Hannah was my great-granddaughter, and she had a heart defect—but there was no surgery, no chance of a cure. I kept her alive as long as I could, but she died just before her nineteenth birthday. She's buried in the family vault in Vyones, in a tomb with my name on it."

"You switched identities."

"It was her idea originally. I told her everything: about Charles and me, about Joseph Curwen, about alchemy. We read the old books together, and when she was strong enough, she went with me to the circles on the high moors to work magic and invoke the two goddesses. When we both knew that she wasn't going to live much longer, she begged me to take her name and form and go through the charade about an experimental operation in India. Where I actually went—and this was her idea as well—was a place called Chorazin."

Owen blinked in surprise. "Not the town in upstate New York."

She managed a laugh. "No, though I've heard some strange stories about that town, too. This was the place it was named for, an old ruined city by the shores of the Dead Sea, barely even an archeological site these days. There's nothing there to speak of, unless you know the secret of the Black Pilgrimage."

"I've heard of that," said Owen. "Wasn't there something about it in von Junzt?"

"Not much more than the name, as I recall," Charles said.

"You need to have access to some very rare books to know more than that," said Lydia. "The d'Ursuras family had relatives in Sweden, I forget their family name, and one of them a few centuries back, a Count Magnus, went on the Pilgrimage. Somehow a nineteenth-century copy of his journal got into the archives in Vyones, so I knew what to do. Not everyone comes back from the Black Pilgrimage, not by a long ways, but those who survive it have a greatly extended life and the help of a very special servant thereafter."

"Pierre," Owen guessed.

"That's the one. So I went, I survived, and then I used something I got in Averoigne to give myself a younger woman's body again, so I could pass for Hannah without having to cast spells of illusion every single day—and for other reasons."

Owen let the last remark pass. "Something you got in Averoigne," he repeated. "The thing Phauz talked about?"

Lydia looked down at the last bit of wine in her glass for a moment. "Yes. I knew I was breaking oaths and running a terrible risk in doing that, but—" She glanced up at him then. "I didn't think the Great Old Ones would concern themselves with it. They care so little about us and our doings, and I wasn't going to let anything stand in my way. It wasn't the worst thing I've done, for that matter. As it was—"

Something shifted in the air around them, and Lydia glanced up sharply.

"The Alala?" Charles asked.

"Yes. It's preparing to leave—and so should we." She got up, went for her purse, returned with car keys in hand. "Owen, can you bring the car around? Thank you. Charles, dear, if you could, get the Red Vase—you know where it is. I—" Her face tensed. "I have to explain to Pierre why he can't come with us, and what he's going to have to do."

Owen went out back, hurried down the street to the little parking lot where Lydia's car waited. Around him, the afternoon was turning toward evening; a breeze blowing off the sea brought the scent of salt water with it, and gulls circled and cried.

By the time he started the car, though, a little black shape that didn't move like a bird was hovering high above the rooftops. Owen glanced up at it, drove the car to the back yard of the Curwen house, and went in. "We've already been spotted."

"I'm not surprised," said Charles, who was just coming up from the cellar with the odd little red jar in one hand. "I hope Phauz really has prepared the way for us."

* * *

Apparently she had, because they got to the ruined factory alongside the Pawtuxet River without meeting any trouble. The drone had remained behind in Providence, hovering over Stampers Hill, and no others had appeared; at the factory, a quick glance down the road to either side showed no watching eyes anywhere. Owen in the lead, the three of them ran across the road, vaulted the battered guardrail, scrambled down the muddy trail to the riverside and pushed through a quarter mile of thick foliage as quickly as they could.

The doorway was still unburied, and the door locked tight as they'd left it. Owen unlocked it and shoved, and Lydia and Charles hurried up the tunnel while he locked it again from inside, splashed the dim gleam of a flashlight around, spotted the bars Charles had mentioned. They must have weighed close to fifty pounds each, but it took Owen only a few moments to heave them into place and blockade the door. Once that was done, he turned and paced after the others.

By the time he got to the central hall with its great gray pillars, they were already in the laboratory, with the lamp full of alchemical oil hung from a hook in the ceiling. Lydia had half a dozen of the glass jars of chemicals down, and Charles was getting a fire under way in one of the alchemical furnaces. Owen went to help him, and it took them only a few moments after that to get the coal burning and a steady heat rising upwards.

"Excellent," Lydia said. "Owen, I need this distilled." She handed him a retort full of a greenish fluid that bubbled. "Charles, dear, can you make me two drams of aqua regia?"

"In my sleep," said Charles. She gave both of them grateful glances, busied herself with another set of chemicals.

Over the hours that followed, the three of them worked together like musicians in a trio. Owen knew that he was the least experienced among them, and if he'd had any question, the practiced skill with which Charles and Lydia handled glassware and chemicals, weighed this, filtered that, would have reminded him. Even so, he'd learned much as Lydia's apprentice, and lent his aid to half a dozen processes as the retort he tended bled out its product drop by drop.

He had little attention to spare for most of the work Charles and Lydia were doing, or for the quick murmured conversation that they had once their labor was finished and the red jar had been filled with a shimmering liquid and sealed with wax. He glanced their way once when Lydia chanted a low formula under her breath; to Owen's surprise, Charles was half undressed, with his shirt and undershirt pulled up and his belly bare. He looked away, only to give them another worried glance when Charles gasped in evident pain; the revenant was half doubled over, clutching his midsection, but a moment later, moving awkwardly, he straightened up and got his clothes back in place. Some moments passed before Owen realized he didn't know what had happened to the red jar.

He turned his attention back to his own work. A few moments later, as the last few drops tumbled from the spout of the retort he tended, a sudden boom came rolling down the tunnel toward the laboratory. It took Owen only an instant to realize that the door on the riverbank must have been blasted in.

"Drink this," said Lydia, grabbing the vessel with the liquid he'd just distilled and handing it to him. "Now!"

He didn't argue. It tasted bitter and acrid, but he choked it down. As he put down the receiving flask, he heard running footfalls echoing in the room outside, braced himself.

Then a blinding light and a roar filled the doorway. The shock of the flash grenade left Owen dazed for just a moment too long. By the time he'd recovered his sight and hearing, half a dozen Radiant gunmen had rushed the laboratory and stood there, handguns trained on the three of them. Others followed, and behind them a figure Owen expected to see.

Michael Dyson considered them for a moment. "You know the drill," he said. "Legs apart, hands high. Do anything stupid and you'll be headshot. Understood?"

Owen's only answer was to take a wide stance and raise his hands as he'd been told. One of the gunmen patted him down expertly while two more kept their pistols aimed at his skull.

Once the others had been searched the same way, Dyson said, "Okay. Hands down and behind your back." Owen complied, and felt a tie clamp around both wrists. He considered the man in front of him, thought of the way they'd faced each other at Chorazin and at that strange, guarded lunch at the burger place on College Hill, and met his gaze without flinching.

A moment passed, and Dyson's eyes narrowed. All at once he turned to one of the others. "Jeffries, take the prisoners and your team to the staging area. The other team will stay with me. I'm convinced there are more hostiles in these tunnels."

The man looked surprised, but said, "Yes, sir." He nodded to the other gunmen, and someone grabbed Owen's arm from behind and pushed him to the door.

Only the faintest light trickled down the tunnel from the wrecked door. Outside, a night without stars lay heavy over Pawtuxet; the damp wind promised rain. The unseen guard pushed Owen up along the trail and over the guardrail to the road beside the ruined factory, where three gray SUVs waited. One of the others opened the rear hatch of one of the vehicles.

"Lay flat and don't move," said the man behind Owen. "If you do or say anything, we're going to start shooting through the seat, and we won't stop until we run out of rounds. Got it?"

Owen nodded. That was apparently enough; the man shoved him forward, into the rear compartment. A few moments later Lydia joined him, and then Charles. The hatch closed; the SUV's engine snarled to life, and gravel sprayed audibly as it lurched onto the road.

* * *

It seemed like a long time before the SUV finally stopped. Owen heard doors open and boots hit the ground, and a moment later the rear hatch swung open. "Out you come," said one of the uniformed men, grabbed the closest limb, and hauled. Lydia tumbled out and hit the pavement, hard. Despite the wrist tie, Owen managed to push his way out himself, and landed on his feet. Two other guards leveled pistols at him and stood there, eyes narrowed, while the first guard dragged Lydia to her feet and then pulled Charles out. "That way," the officer said, motioning with his head. "Don't give me an excuse to waste you."

Thunder rumbled high overhead, muttered into silence. Around the SUV and its passengers, abandoned buildings rose up to either side of what looked like a parking lot. Ahead at the lot's far side, beyond a lamppost from which a single sodium light blazed down, a moving darkness scattered with glints of reflected light and a chill salt breeze told Owen he was beside Narragansett Bay. The negation team, Owen knew, might simply be planning to shoot them and dump their weighted bodies into the water, but something in the men's bearing denied that. They seemed tense, as though waiting for—what? He could not tell.

They were most of the way to the far side of the lot when headlights approaching from somewhere behind lit the cracked asphalt of the lot. One after another, four SUVs pulled past, turned and parked in a line near the water's edge, under the glare of the sodium lamp. The doors of three of them opened at once, and figures in urban camouflage came out, guns at the ready.

One of the newcomers, a stocky gray-haired man with a scar down one side of his face, strode across the lot to the team that held Owen and the others prisoner, glanced at the captives, and then turned to the officer in charge. "Where's Dyson?"

"At the site, sir."

"Why?"

"He thinks there are more hostiles in the tunnels, sir. He's searching for them."

The newcomer gave him a cold look. "Those weren't his orders."

"Yes, sir."

A sharp gesture told the officer to follow, and the man turned and led the way back to the fourth SUV. Its rear door swung open, and a single figure climbed out and stood waiting for them: a woman with white hair, dressed in conventional business wear. All the guards Owen could see drew themselves up straight.

"Director," said the man who'd questioned the officer. "Here they are."

"So I gather," the woman said. There was no feeling in the voice, nor any other trace of humanity; the flat sounds could as well have come from a machine. Owen met her gaze, saw the utter emptiness behind the eyes, and recognized it at once. This one was a senior adept of the Radiance, maybe—if the title of Director meant what he thought it did—the current head of the entire organization, the heir of Shamash-Nazir and Agathocles.

She considered each of the captives and then said, "You've checked identities."

"Yes, ma'am," said the officer. "Checked and confirmed. One's known: Owen Merrill. The other two aren't in my files, but we got a clear Tillinghast reading on them. They were involved in the working."

"The other two are known," said the Director. "Lydia Ward and Charles Dexter Ward. An old case that should have been closed long ago." She turned to consider Owen again, then Lydia. "These two are worth interrogating before they're negated—they'll come with me on the boat to Conanicut. They've had close contact with the other side, and there's information I want extracted from them."

"Should I report them to our allies, ma'am?" the officer asked.

That got a sudden look and a sudden silence. "No," the director said.

Something stirred in the officer's face, something brief and fugitive that might have been relief and might have been dread. In that moment Owen sensed that it hadn't been arrogance that had sent a Radiant team to try to establish a colony on Mars. Miriam's correspondent was right: they were desperate. Why? He could not tell.

"But this thing …" The director turned to Charles Dexter Ward. "This should not exist at all." To the officer: "Did you notice anything unusual about its skin?"

"No, ma'am."

"You need to work on your observation skills. The skin will have an abnormally coarse texture, and it will be morbidly cold and dry. You won't have had the chance to notice the other physiological details. Have Central Training give you access to the file on alchemical revenants in case you have to deal with them. You may. Where there's one, there are usually others."

Owen sensed Lydia's sudden tension, heard her draw in a sudden breath, and all at once guessed where the red jar was and what incantation she was about to repeat: the last words in any language she wished to say, the words that would return Charles Dexter Ward to lifeless dust. The Director forestalled her, though. "Fortunately," the old woman said, "there's a simple way to negate any such abomination." She turned to Charles, and in a raised voice said, "*Ogthrod ai'f geb'l-ee'h Yog-Sothoth 'nghah'ng ai'y Zhro!*"

The moment she began to speak, Charles turned toward Lydia, with a look of longing in his eyes. Lydia cried out wordlessly, but the spell finished its work, and Charles Dexter Ward's body unravelled layer by layer and dissolved into a cloud of greenish dust—with an ancient red stoneware jar suspended in the midst of it.

Then, in the sudden silence, the jar fell to the ground and shattered.

A vast cloud of stinging black smoke billowed up from the place where Charles had stood a moment before. Owen clenched his eyes shut, felt droplets of something that was not rain spatter against his hands and face. "Secure the area," the Director's voice said, emotionless but loud. "Get decontamination gear, and send a message to thhh … glb … ungl … ungl … rrlh … chchch …"

The change in her voice was sudden and terrible enough that Owen's eyes snapped open. What he saw made him wish that he'd kept them shut. Her face was slumping like heated wax. Holes spread in her clothing, as though someone had splashed acid on them. As he watched in horror, her skin began to bubble, and the flesh beneath flowed, dripping from her bones. A quick glance to either side showed that the same thing was happening to all the guards and officers—to every member of the Radiance within sight.

He looked down at himself, then, and saw holes opening in his own clothing.

* * *

Movement to his left drew his attention. One of the guards, with a visible effort, was trying to raise a gun with an arm that looked more liquid than solid with every passing moment. They had bound Owen's wrists but not his feet, and so he kicked up at the gun, sudden and hard. It flew away, and took half the man's arm with it. Owen fought back nausea as what was left of the guard let out a mewling sound and slumped to the asphalt.

At that moment Lydia's voice rose suddenly behind him in a shout: "*Y'ai ' ng'ngah Yog-Sothoth h'ee-l'geb f'ai throdog Uaaah!*"

He turned, to see her standing with arms outflung, her clothing already in rags from the effect of the black cloud. Before her the cloud of dust that had been Charles Dexter Ward boiled and swirled in the air, drew together into a human shape, and then began to waver and flow. Lydia took hold of Charles' half-formed hands and began chanting strange syllables unlike any of the languages of lore Owen had ever heard, jumbled up with snatches of medieval Latin he could almost understand.

Her face was taut with effort as she worked her witchcraft, and struggled with whatever terrible magic the shattering of the red jar had unleashed. Owen saw dread and desperate passion in her eyes as Charles' body wavered and slumped, struggled back to a human shape, slumped again, recovered—and then, slowly, a look of triumph showed on her face as Charles' body settled firmly into its proper shape.

"Now, Charles," she said. "With me."

Holding his hands still, she chanted three long words, and he chanted them with her.

All at once, both their bodies flowed and changed, rising far above human stature, and the shapes that took form in the stark orange light of the sodium lamp had nothing else human about them, either. Towering and many-limbed, they gazed down at Owen with great faceted eyes set in faces festooned with tentacles, while wings unfolded like uncoiling fronds behind them, pair after pair after pair. Above them, thunder rolled again, and the first fat drops of rain spattered down onto the asphalt.

"Owen," said one of the creatures, and the voice was beyond any doubt Lydia's.

He felt the wrist tie give way behind him, dissolving like his clothing, and jerked his hands forward. They were still their normal shape, the skin unblistered, the flesh solid.

The shape that had been Lydia laughed. "You'll be fine," she said. "The thing I had you drink was the antidote. Do you know what it was that I put in Charles' body?"

Owen shook his head, unable to speak. Around him, the rain began to fall more heavily.

"The Red Jar that Avallaunius made, the key to the *Vinum Sabbati*, the black wine of the Sabbat, the Wine of the Fauns. Prepare the Jar with certain chemicals, and pour wine into it and out of it, and the one who drinks it changes to another shape— that's one of the old secrets of the witchcraft of Averoigne, as I told you. But to break the jar—that unleashes its most terrible powers. Do that, knowing how to master those powers, and you can transform yourself into anything you desire. Lack that knowledge, and you dissolve into the slime from which all life originally came."

Owen found his voice. "Is there anything—"

"For them, no." The voice of the ancient woman she'd been sounded briefly through the alien mouthparts, harsh as the sodium glare. "Half an hour from now, all they are and all they might have been will have washed away in the rain. It's no better than they deserve. But you—"

The great shape bent, and one many-jointed limb held out something that glittered. "You'll need this. The clothes you've got on won't last long—and you should look behind the Grateful Dead poster in the old library, the place where poor Joseph hid his papers. There's something there that I happened to get when we were working together, and you ought to know what to do with it." The key to the house on Olney Court dropped into his hand.

"There's another thing," said the creature that had been Charles. "Phauz was right, of course. I'm bitterly ashamed to say it, but yes, we lied to you about Dr. Angell's papers."

"Why?" Owen asked him.

The towering unhuman form seemed to shrink into itself a little. "The King in Yellow," he said in a low voice. "Lydia told me that you'd seen the Fellowship of the Yellow Sign here in Providence, and hunting. The King sees far too much when he casts the bones in the wind from Yhtill. We both guessed that if he found out we'd helped you learn how to raise his ancient enemy, he would strike—and his hands have cast down planets from their orbits. We weren't willing to risk his wrath. I'm sorry, Owen."

"The King will know now," Owen said.

"I know—but that was the bargain Phauz made with us: what we wanted, in exchange for what you required. She's promised to protect us."

"The Angell papers," Owen said. "Where are they?"

"Go to 17 Wayland Lane tomorrow and say that Brother Josephus sent you. That'll get you inside. Getting the papers from their keeper—why, that's up to you."

"17 Wayland Lane," Owen repeated.

"That's the one."

"And you two?"

"To another world," Lydia's voice said. "A world just one step ulthward from ours, for a little while. A human body can't take that step. This body can—and then we can change back into our own forms, and have everything that we dreamed of having, when we used to watch the sunset from Olney Court."

"I hope you get that," he said.

The tentacles on the face that had been Lydia's rippled. "Owen, you're a sweetheart." Then: "If you find Pierre, or he finds you, please take care of him, or find someone else who will. Where I'm going, he can't follow, and he'll be lost without someone to help him find his way in the human world."

"I'll do that," Owen promised.

The great faceted eyes met his. "Owen—thank you."

Then the wings swept down all at once, the tall forms rose up into the air, and the sky tore open along a line at right angles to all three-dimensional space. Owen staggered as the wet parking lot seemed to sway and spin around him.

A moment later the sky closed again and they were gone.

He glanced this way and that, saw dim shapes in the steady rain. Little remained of the negation teams or their Director—a scattering of guns and other metal items, low heaps of clothing that had not yet finished dissolving, and a thickness in the rainwater that gurgled and splashed down a nearby grating, at which he was careful not too look too closely. Not far away, an assortment of SUVs stood empty and abandoned, with doors gaping open to the rain.

The Director had mentioned a boat to Conanicut Island, he recalled, and he knew it would not be safe to be there when it arrived. His clothing was coming apart, and he had no idea where in or near Providence he was, but he turned and walked away from the water, into the night.

CHAPTER 12

THE HAUNTER OF THE DARK

Fortunately, it didn't take him long to find his bearings. The skyscrapers of downtown Providence loomed up in the distance, and scattered streetlights showed him the long slow rise of Federal Hill to the left and the steep mass of College Hill across the river to the right. As he reached the edges of downtown he found a bridge to take him across the water, and had no trouble finding Benefit Street and following it to the foot of Stampers Hill. That was as well, because his clothes were in tatters by then, and the last scraps dissolved and washed away in the rain by the time he reached Olney Court. He was grateful that no one was wandering outdoors to remark on a naked man walking up to Joseph Curwen's house.

He was tired by the time he got there, bone-tired, but still had enough presence of mind to know that the Radiance might still have a drone there, or even a negation team lying in wait. For a long moment he waited, and then two points of light opened on the porch: a cat's eyes, mirroring back the streetlamps. The cat made sure he'd seen it, then turned, rubbed its face against the door, and bounded away. "Thank you," Owen said aloud, and unlocked the door.

Even so, he listened for a long moment before closing the door, locking it behind him, and turning on the hall light. Nothing moved in the old house. After a moment, he retrieved his duffel from the library, went upstairs, wrote down the address and password Lydia had given him on the first piece of paper he could find, climbed into the shower to wash the last of the Wine of the Fauns from his skin, toweled off very approximately, and stumbled into bed.

By the time he woke again it was on the far side of noon. He stretched, rubbed his eyes, and noticed another cat perched on the ledge outside his window, considering him. It bounded away, too, once he'd seen it. The scrap of paper with the address and the password still sat on the dresser where he'd left it. He washed, dressed, and then went to the kitchen to fix some kind of meal out of the little he could find in the cupboards and the fridge. It wasn't much—the last third or so of a baguette, two fried eggs, and a can of consommé heated up and sipped from a coffee mug—but it was enough for the moment. When he was finished, he sat thinking of Lydia and Charles, and their long strange journey through time. "An old case that should have been closed long ago," the Director had said. No, Owen thought. No, and it's not closed yet.

He heaved himself to his feet, then, and headed out into the afternoon.

Wayland Lane was well east of Stampers Hill, far enough away from the colleges that it seemed to have escaped the attentions of the Radiance, and 17 Wayland Lane was a plain clapboard-sided house with one gable facing the street and a Georgian doorway up a flight of narrow stairs. Owen paused, then climbed the stairs and, finding no doorbell, knocked.

A long silence followed, and then the lock rattled and the door opened the few inches allowed by a stout chain. "Yes?" an elderly male voice said.

"Brother Josephus sent me," Owen replied.

The door shut, the chain rattled, and then a moment later the door opened wide. "Ah. In that case, please come in."

The entry was decorated fussily, in a style more than a century old, and the man who stood there could be described in exactly the same terms. Bald except for a thin halo of white hair around three sides of his crown, he wore a ornate dressing gown of Victorian cut with a white ascot visible at the neck, and regarded Owen through glasses with thin gilt frames. "I suppose Charles was the one who actually sent you," he said. "I trust he's well."

"Very much so," said Owen. "He and Lydia left Providence last night."

"Ah," said the old man, smiling. "I see you're privy to that particular secret. Well, that's good to hear. I don't suppose he told you who I am."

"No," said Owen, "but I've seen your photo. You're Professor Angell, aren't you?"

The old man beamed. "Why, yes," he said. "Perhaps you would favor me—"

"Owen Merrill."

"Very pleased to meet you, Mr. Merrill."

They shook hands. Angell's was cold and dry, and the skin had a curious coarse texture that Owen recognized at once.

"Are you at all partial to tea, Mr. Merrill? Ah, good. Perhaps we can take some in the library. I receive few guests these days, as I'm sure you can imagine, and I'd be most pleased if you could tell me how Charles managed to get back after that unfortunate business in 1928."

* * *

"Charles resurrected me in September of 1927," the old man said. He and Owen were seated in a pleasant room lined with bookshelves, full of the enticing scents of leather bindings and old paper; two bone china teacups and a pot graced the table between them. "He always was a conscientious young man, and as soon as he had figured out the method and reopened the laboratory in Pawtuxet, why, he and Joseph and a few friends managed to get my remains from the North Burial

Ground where I was interred, extracted the essential salts, and said the words. I admit I was startled—one moment toppling to the ground on a street on College Hill, the next standing quite naked in an underground room of Colonial date with two identical copies of Charles standing in front of me—but of course they explained, and I knew enough about Charles' researches that I had no trouble at all understanding what had happened."

"Did you help them with their work?"

"To a limited extent. Mostly I translated things for them, and made sure their incantations were correct. Beyond that, no." He shook his head. "They took tremendous risks, and saw no need for me to share those, for which I admit I'm grateful. It was a desperate attempt, really, and I suppose it was never likely to end any other way."

Owen considered him. "Do you know what they were trying to do, Dr. Angell?"

"Why, of course." The old man's bright eyes met his gaze squarely. "They were trying to learn the proper way to awaken Great Cthulhu."

"I'm wondering what you think about that," Owen said.

"Whether I answer that," said Angell, "will depend a great deal on why you are asking."

Owen considered him, then nodded. "Fair enough. I want to do the same thing."

"Ah," said the old man. "I wondered if that was what brought you to me."

"That's what brought me to Providence," Owen said. "Dr. Angell, your friend Albert Wilmarth wrote in his diary that you had copies of rituals in Aklo that he'd never seen before—and you know better than I do how learned he was. A friend of mine, a sorceress from an old family in Kingsport, sent me to try to find those rituals. Lydia Ward told me that you have them now. I don't know whether you're willing to give them to me, or let me make a copy, but that's why I'm here—and you already know what my friend and I are going to try to do with those rituals, if you're willing to share them."

Angell nodded slowly, and sipped at his cup of tea before replying. "When I first found out about the Cthulhu cult, and realized that there was more to it than mere superstition, I was horrified, of course. The thought that there might actually be some primeval devil-god sleeping in the ocean was awful enough, but the thought that there were people who wanted to awaken him, to end humanity's rule over the planet and force us to share this world with beings that are older and wiser than we are—that gave me many nightmares and many sleepless nights.

"But time teaches many lessons, Mr. Merrill. Since my resurrection, while I've pursued my researches, I've also paid attention to what's happened in the world outside this comfortable study of mine, and compared it to certain rumors about a very ancient prophecy."

"The Weird of Hali," Owen ventured.

"Ah, you know about that? Excellent."

"I know a little."

Angell considered him through the gold-rimmed glasses. "I don't suppose you might know any of the text." When Owen responded in the negative: "Ah, well. It was merely a fancy. Charles believed that certain scraps of that might have survived in the records of a certain very ancient organization."

"The *Dumu-ne Zalaga*," said Owen.

"Ah." The old man sipped tea. "I see you know quite a range of recondite lore."

"I've tangled with their modern heirs more than once."

"I can well believe that," Angell said. "I believe Joseph had repeated run-ins with them in his own time." He shook his head. "But it's more than their activities, more even than the Weird of Hali. For more than a century now, I've watched humanity stumble blindly toward a terrible future—and I've become rather too aware that the organization you just named craves that terrible future, and sees it as humanity's final triumph over Nature. Now—" He shrugged. "One way or another, the time of our dominion over the earth is ending, and if that ending isn't to our taste, why, to a very great extent we've brought that on ourselves."

Owen nodded, and then remembered the fragment of the poem he'd found on the margin of one of the letters in Angell's papers, and quoted:

"For what danced joyously 'neath olden skies
Shall waken, and in dreadful wrath shall rise."

Angell's face lit up. "You're familiar with Geoffrey's poetry? Good, very good. Yes, and of course he was quite right. We really have made a mess of things, haven't we? At this point I have to think that handing the world back to Great Cthulhu really is the best idea after all."

Abruptly Angell pushed back his chair, stood up, went to a file cabinet in a corner of the library and extracted two manila folders stuffed with papers from the topmost drawer. He returned to the table, and set the first folder in front of Owen. "This is the original collection of rituals I got from poor Harley Warren before he died." The second folder joined them. "These are notes on the research I've done since then—and that's been a considerable part of the work that's occupied my time since my resurrection. You're welcome to them." With a dismissive gesture: "I have copies of the material, and plenty of other things to keep me busy."

Owen opened the first folder, leafed through the thirty or so sheets of paper, handwritten partly in English and partly in Aklo. Passages here and there reminded him of texts from the *Necronomicon* and the *Pnakotic Manuscript*, but these were of much greater length. Words of power he had never encountered before, scarcely pronounceable by a human mouth, bristled on the pages, and the structure of the ritual involved intricacies unlike anything he'd encountered in the old lore. The papers in the second folder turned out to be a closely annotated analysis of the ritual texts. Angell hadn't exaggerated about the work involved; the text spoke of decades of painstaking scholarly labors.

He looked up at the old man then. "Thank you."

"You're quite welcome. May I offer you more tea?" Owen said something agreeable, and the old man refilled both their cups.

* * *

He left the little house on Wayland Lane with the two folders of documents tucked into his backpack. The afternoon had turned sultry, with long gray clouds drifting slowly by. He found a street going west, started walking toward the corner where it joined Olney Court, and tried to figure out what his next step should be.

Common sense suggested that he should head downtown at once, find a way back to Arkham even if that meant walking the whole distance, and get the rituals into Jenny Chaudronnier's hands before anything else could happen to them. The only things that argued against that were the promise he'd given Lydia Ward to take care of Pierre if the two of them found each other, an uncomfortable feeling that he'd forgotten something having to do with the old house on Olney Court, and the cats.

There weren't many of them, just a few perched here and there on porch or a windowsill, but they all watched him with calm unreadable eyes. Did they want something from him? Not in any sense comprehensible to human minds, he guessed; they waited, or the mind that looked out through them waited, to see what choice he would make, and to act accordingly. He thought of the terrible vastness of the consciousness that had brushed against his so briefly on the bus down from Arkham, and a shiver went through him despite the warmth of the day.

By the time he reached Olney Court, he'd made his choice, and turned toward Joseph Curwen's house. The cats watched him with no sign of approval or disapproval as he reached the familiar facade, went around to the back, unlocked the kitchen door and went in.

It wasn't until he was in the kitchen, with all the memories of Lydia and the work they'd done together pressing around him, that he remembered what she'd said about the hiding place in the library. He blinked, then went down the hall, pushed open the door, stepped inside.

The floor still had traces of the triple circle of chalk marked on it and the ring of candles around the outside—Lydia hadn't taken more than a few moments to clear them away when the three of them hurried into the kitchen for that last sparse meal before the drive to Pawtuxet. Owen went to the fireplace, then hauled a chair over, climbed up on it, and found the concealed button in the molding. A firm push, and the panel behind it came loose. Owen lowered it to the floor and looked into the recess. Something gleamed there, and he reached inside, took something out, set it on the mantel below and got down.

Dim light gleamed off yellow metal: a curious box with seven sides, no two of which were the same breadth, and seven corners, no two of which were the same angle. The flat lid and the sides had strange bas-reliefs on them, showing rugose alien shapes with starfish-shaped heads rising up on great outspread wings. He stared at it uncomprehending for a moment, then realized what he was seeing, swayed, and sat down all at once on the armchair.

The box with seven differing sides and seven differing angles, fashioned—he was sure of it—by the crinoid things of Antarctica some two hundred million years back, when Cthulhu and the King in Yellow still reigned in amity in their cities of R'lyeh and Carcosa, at the ulthward and anthward poles of the greater Earth; the box that had been treasured by the serpent-folk of primeval Valusia, inherited from them by the first humans in long-drowned Yhe, and passed on to

Atlantis in the days of its power; the box that had been netted up from the deeps by a Minoan fisherman and sold by him to the servants of Nephren-Ka, the last pharaoh of the Third Dynasty of Egypt's Old Kingdom; the box that had been found in the crypts of a forgotten temple in the ruins of Heliopolis by Dr. Enoch Bowen of Brown University in the year 1842—

It could contain only one thing.

The question was how on Earth, or off it, Lydia Ward had come into possession of the most sacred relic of the Church of the Starry Wisdom, the lost Shining Trapezohedron. Owen pondered that, and thought of Lydia's words—"something there that I happened to get when we were working together"—and then he remembered the afternoon when she'd sensed someone spying on their work by means of sorcery, and had gone away and wielded strange powers to put an end to it. The brief glimpse he'd gotten then, of vast dark wheels of force and a bright shape tumbling through space to an outstretched hand, finally found a meaning.

It was a meaning that sat in his mind and his heart like ice, but it didn't make him flinch. The secrets of using the Shining Trapezohedron, of making use of its powers as a window on all time and space, had been lost after the time of Nephren-Ka and regained only through years of perilous experimentation by old Enoch Bowen and his successors. As far as Owen knew, no one outside the Starry Wisdom church knew the rediscovered lore—and since someone had been using the stone to spy on Lydia, or on him …

He sat there for something close to an hour, considering his options, remembering all that he'd learned about the Shining Trapezohedron, remembering the hieroglyphic inscription he'd seen at the museum, and making plans for the thing he would have to do. Finally, his face set, he got up, picked up the golden box, and left the house on Olney Street.

* * *

The Wednesday evening service had not quite begun when Owen reached the Starry Wisdom church atop Federal Hill. The congregation was sparse, maybe half the number he'd been used to seeing there, and silence lay over them like a blanket. All four of the elders were in their usual places in the east, under the great ankh, but they looked haggard, as though from prolonged strain. Phaedra Dexter evidently noticed Owen, and turned to murmur something to Peter O'Halloran. Owen kept his face unreadable, went to his usual pew in the section reserved for third degree members, and sat on the outside, closest to the wall.

Maybe two minutes after he'd settled into place, Alexandra Bowen got up and went to the pulpit. As she stepped into the direct light of the easternmost of the lamps, the strained look on her face was even more striking than before. She seemed only half present, as though something else held her attention fast. Still, she began the words of the opening meditation in a clear voice, and though the congregation responded in a low, sullen muttering, she did not falter.

After the opening meditation came the presentation of offerings, when those members of the congregation who wished to give something to the Great Old Ones, to fulfill a vow or ask a favor they might or might not grant, were invited to do so. The two deacons went down the central aisle with their black wooden trays, though they received little, and went to the outside aisles when they reached the western end of the hall. As one of them came near, Owen turned and indicated with a nod that he had something to offer. The man paused, giving him a startled look. Owen smiled, took the golden box from inside his jacket, and set it on the tray.

The deacon nearly dropped his tray. He stared at Owen with eyes gone suddenly round, but Owen simply nodded and turned back to face the east. After a moment, the deacon started on his way again, unsteadily. As he reached the east and carried his burden to the offering table, some of the members of the congregation saw the thing on his tray, and a low shocked murmur spread through the hall.

Owen waited until the elders had seen it as well, and then stood. "Mrs. Bowen," he said.

The old woman considered him. "Mr. Merrill."

"Please correct me if I'm wrong, but I think it's customary for those who make a special offering to explain the circumstances."

A long moment passed, then: "That's correct, Mr. Merrill."

"Thank you," said Owen. "That box, and the thing that's in it, were in the keeping of an alchemist who stayed here in Providence for a while. She left last night, and told me to take it to the proper place. As you see, I've done that.

"The alchemist only got it in July of this year, though. Someone tried to use it to spy on her, but she knows a good deal about practical sorcery, and so she was able to take it from the one who had it.

"The thing is, that wasn't the first time it's been used for spying—not at all. It's been used to spy on members of this congregation for years now, in fact, and the results have ended up on typed notes, made on a typewriter with a broken letter O."

Dead silence reigned, and then a murmur moved through the hall. Owen let his words sink in for a moment before going on. "And no one outside the Starry Wisdom church knows how to use the powers of the Shining Trapezohedron. That means at least one of the elders of this church is responsible for the spying, the notes, all of it."

Bowen simply stared at him, her face frozen. O'Halloran looked at Owen in bafflement. Phaedra Dexter glanced at Bowen, then said in her soft plaintive voice, "That's a terrible lie!"

"I'm glad to hear that, Miss Dexter," Owen replied. "You can prove your innocence to everyone right now, too. All you have to do is open the box."

Bowen found her voice. "That will happen in due time," she said.

"No." Owen took two steps to the wall, and reached for the circuit breakers. "That box is going to be opened here and now, Miss Bowen, or I'm going to turn out the lights—and we all know what's going to happen then."

The entire hall went dead quiet. "Mr. Merrill—" Bowen began.

"Open the box," Owen said, his voice hard.

In the hush that followed, a dull heavy thump sounded from somewhere above the hall. Bowen glanced up in obvious horror, and so did half the congregation.

"The box has been shut since sometime in July," Owen said then. "The Watcher's in full physical manifestation by now, and you know as well as I do that it's going to be looking for whoever misused the Trapezohedron. All it needs to find its prey is darkness. Open the box, now, or I turn off the lights."

In answer, a voice Owen recognized—Sam Mazzini's— growled from further up the hall, where the fifth degree initiates sat: "Turn 'em off, Owen. Let the Watcher sort 'em out."

Bowen clutched the podium and stared at Owen; her mouth worked, but no sound came from it. Behind her, beyond the doors to the sanctuary, a slow sliding sound came, and then another thump, close by. All at once, in response, Albert Pearse threw himself out of his chair and bolted down the steps of the dais toward the offering table.

Dexter shrieked and flung herself after him, but before she could stop him, Pearse had reached the table of offerings. He knelt, took the golden box in both hands, and opened it.

Sudden searing brilliance filled the eastern end of the hall, as though a bolt of lightning had struck. Owen turned his face away and clenched his eyes shut, but even so a minute or more passed before his vision recovered and he could see anything at all.

At first, as he turned toward the dais, he could only make out dim blurs: something dark and rectangular, and a crumpled shape on the floor before it; another slumped shape on the stairs below the dais; dark forms behind them, strangely angled, that very slowly became recognizable as chairs. He blinked, rubbed his eyes, and blinked again.

Only then could he make out the four figures. One of them—Phaedra Dexter—lay sprawled and motionless where she'd fallen on the stairs. The second and third, Bowen and O'Halloran, lay on the dais, making vague uncertain movements. The fourth, Albert Pearse, picked himself up off the floor, turned toward the dais, and then crumpled again, hiding his face in his hands.

* * *

Owen left the circuit breakers and started for the dais as soon as his vision cleared. He listened for further noises from the door to the sanctuary, but none came. He nodded to himself. *Let the one who uses it never depart from Maat*, the hieroglyphic text had said, *or the one who watches will avenge*. The Watcher had done that, and returned to its place outside space and time.

Most of the congregation had had the great good sense to dive behind the pews in front of them, and began to pick themselves up off the floor. A few pulled themselves out from behind their pews and approached Owen as he reached the foot of the dais.

"I'm sorry that was necessary," Owen said to them.

Ellen Chernak was among the first to reach the dais. "So am I," she said. "Still, it *was* necessary. Thank you, Owen."

He nodded, said nothing.

"You were right about the Watcher," said Sam Mazzini, who had gone back to make sure Charlene was unharmed and then came forward. "They had the lights on here in the church and in the rectory day and night since sometime in July, and that's not the first time there's been a sound from up above." A murmur of agreement sounded from behind him.

Ellen went to Dexter's body, and turned it over. The old woman's face was frozen into a rictus of stark terror, her eyes glassy and bulging, as though they still gazed on the light that had killed her. "Dead," Ellen said unnecessarily, and closed the staring eyes. A few more steps took her up onto the dais, where she checked the other two prostrate figures. "These two are still with us. Can I get somebody to carry them down to the fellowship hall?" Half a dozen men responded, clambering up onto the dais.

"They didn't look into the stone," said Owen.

"No," said Albert Pearse, as he rose to his feet. "No, that was Phaedra's and hers alone."

Everyone turned to face him. "So you knew all about it," said Sam Mazzini.

"All about it? No, but enough."

"Mr. Pearse," Owen said then. "Did the Radiance put you up to any of this?"

The shock in his face was too sudden to fake. "No!" He met Owen's gaze for a moment, then his gaze faltered and he bowed his head. "No. Phaedra got the thing from her grandfather, Ambrose Dexter, the man who claimed he'd thrown it into Narragansett Bay. Her mother's people were members of the church from way back, you know. But the Radiance—" He shuddered. "No. I was willing to put up with a lot, but not that."

Owen nodded slowly. It was the hard lesson of Merry Mount, then, the ease with which the persecuted could turn into the persecutor.

"You could have talked to me," Ellen said to Pearse then. "You could have told me."

He gave her a bleak look. "My dear," he said, "do you really want me to tell you what Phaedra Dexter knew about me?"

"No," said Ellen. "And I don't care. Once we finish here, you're going to let us into the rectory, we're going to find everything she wrote down, and we're going to burn it all unread."

She considered him then. "With your permission, of course. You might as well be the entire council of elders right now."

A faint smile twisted his face. "That, at least, can be remedied." He drew in a ragged breath, and said in a louder voice, "I appoint you, Ellen Chernak, to the council of elders. Anyone object? No? You're in—and I resign. If the Great Old Ones feast on whatever soul I've got left it's no more than I've earned."

"Albert," Ellen said.

He looked up.

"They don't care. You know that—or you used to. They really don't care."

Pearse stared at her, then crumpled, burying his face in his hands a second time.

"Okay," Ellen said then. "I'd like all the fifth and sixth degree initiates to come here." Sam Mazzini looked startled, but approached her. Half a dozen others joined him. "I appoint each of you—" She recited all their names. "—to the council of elders. Unless anyone objects?" No one did, though some of the new elders would have looked less stunned if she'd struck them on the head with a mallet. "Good. We've got a lot of work ahead of us, to get this church back to what it ought to be."

She turned toward Owen, then, and said, "First things first, though. Owen, the Shining Trapezohedron needs to be taken to its place in the sanctuary right now, before anything else happens. That's not usually a third degree initiate's work, but under the circumstances I'd like to ask you to do that."

"I'd be honored," Owen said.

He went to the table of offerings and lifted the golden box, taking care not to look into the crystal inside it. He bowed to the cast and to Phaedra Dexter's twisted corpse, a gesture of respect, and then carried the box and the black stone within it toward the sanctuary doors.

Ellen said something, and others went to the doors and opened them. A fetid scent hung in the air, sign of the presence of the Watcher, but no vast unhuman entity waited there, nor would wait again so long as any light reached the Shining Trapezohedron. Owen passed by the open door that led to the long dark stair up to the steeple, and passed between the tall black pylons and through the door into the sanctuary at the eastern end of the building.

There in the dimness, in the center of a circle of seven high-backed chairs of Gothic style, under the gaze of seven tall statues that resembled nothing so much as the great stone heads of Easter Island, stood an oddly angled pillar four feet high. On it was a golden box like the one Owen carried, and in that, supported by a metal band and seven queerly designed supports, was a smoky crystal from which a faint flickering glow emanated.

"We'll keep this," Ellen said, lifting the box reverently from the pillar, "and pass it on to the next new church that gets founded. It's served us well—but now the true stone is recovered." The other elders formed a circle around the pillar, and the rest of the congregation packed the doorway, parents lifting children to see a sight they would remember all their lives.

The doing of it was prosaic enough, though painters and sculptors in after years would do their best to embellish it. Owen simply put the box he carried where the other had been. Ellen stepped forward and traced a few patterns in the air over it with her hands, and stepped back. A pale shimmering glow like moonlight kindled in the heart of the Shining Trapezohedron, reflected back from the watching faces and statues and the old wooden furniture.

It was in the world of the unseen—in the kingdom of Voor, the place where the light goes when it is put out, and the water goes when the sun dries it up—that unexpected things took place. As soon as the light began to glimmer inside the stone, voor surged and swirled around it, and took on a strange and dancing quality. It filled the sanctuary, flowed along the moon paths, sent ripples of itself surging outward through Providence, New England, and the world.

* * *

"There were no spies," Owen said, "and nobody said anything to anybody they shouldn't have. It was all just one old woman misusing the Shining Trapezohedron for her own nasty ends, using it as a window on all space and time, and typing those wretched notes we all got."

He was sitting in the back room of Sancipriani's, surrounded by Starry Wisdom folk. Pizza of a dozen different varieties sat on the tables. Julie Olmert, beaming, came out as Owen paused, removed two empty pans and set three more full of assorted pizzas in the open space. All the pizzas had a subtly different scent than usual, and Owen knew why. Below in the basement, where the great brick ovens received their fuel, the contents of six filing cabinets full of typed dossiers were going in among the firewood under the watchful eyes of half a dozen church members that everyone trusted not to read a single word.

"You mentioned you got some," Sam Mazzini said.

"I got three," Owen told him. "My wife got two—one of two pages and one of four."

That got a sudden silence broken only by sharp indrawn breaths. "She must have hated your guts," said Tom Castro.

"After I read those letters," Owen said, "the feeling was mutual."

Sam threw his head back and laughed. For a moment, a shocked silence spread through the room, but then others started laughing as well. Before long everyone but Owen had joined in. He smiled, picked up a piece of pizza, and ate it, hearing the first steps toward healing in the strained and raucous sounds around him.

Charlene Mazzini stopped laughing sooner than most of the others, and glanced at Owen from across the table, obviously trying to work up the courage to say something. Owen motioned toward her, inviting. "Mr. Merrill—" she began. He gave her a wry look, and she managed a chuckle and said, "Okay. Owen. I don't want to know what was in those letters your wife got, but ..." Her voice trickled away.

"You want to know what kind of things were in them."
In response to her nod: "Some true things, some lies, some very
intimate details—the Trapezohedron's a window on all space
and time, remember, and that includes bedrooms."

Charlene turned bright red and looked away.

"And that's just it," Owen went on. "I know you were all
convinced you couldn't trust anybody, not even the people you
loved, because the most private things ended up in those notes.
I'm pretty sure that's what Dexter was after. If you could have
trusted each other, you'd have figured out what was going on
a long time ago, and put an end to it. So she went looking for
the things that would hurt the most when you thought they'd
been betrayed, and mixed them with lies that hurt even more."
He shook his head. "Laura and I got off pretty easy, all things
considered. I can't imagine what it would have been like to live
with that for years."

Charlene glanced at Sam, who met her gaze and then ten-
tatively put an arm around her shoulders. She closed her
eyes and crumpled against him. Someone else refilled her
wineglass.

Clatter of the door announced Ellen Chernak's arrival.
"Well, that's over," she said, weaving through the crowd to the
central table. She carried an old fabric-covered hard case with
rounded corners, a little over a foot wide and long and maybe
eight inches high, and set it on the table between two pans of
pizza.

"Miss Dexter?" Julie Olmert asked.

"Yep. We told the medical examiner's people she'd been
doing something with the electrical system and got careless.
They didn't argue." Ellen found a seat, slumped into it. "The
other two—I'm not sure if they'll ever be right again, but
we'll see. And I've been through the rectory. There were some
amazing things there—books I don't think any of us know the
church had, an old printing press down in the basement, all
kinds of stuff."

"Are you going to be moving in there?" Tom Castro asked her.

Ellen shook her head. "Not unless I have to." Turning to Owen: "Do the other churches you know have rectories?"

"Not in Dunwich or Chorazin or Lefferts Corners," Owen told her. "In Arkham, a rectory came with the church we bought, but nobody's going to live there. We're turning it into a community center: the church library, the clothing and tool exchange, the Sunday school for kids, the night school for adults who want to earn the higher degrees, that sort of thing."

"That," said Ellen, "sounds like a really good idea. If the other elders agree, we'll do the same thing here." She glanced some of the others, who nodded, and then at Sam, who gave her a blank look, and then blinked and said, "Oh. Yeah. Sorry. I think it's a great idea." Then: "One of these days I might be able to think the words 'Elder Sam Mazzini' without my head spinning, but that won't be any time soon."

That got a general laugh. As it faded, Owen asked, "What's in the case?"

The smile fell from Ellen's face. "A memento I'm not sure what to do with," she said, and reached for the latch. The top swung back to reveal an old manual typewriter.

"Broken letter O?" Owen asked.

Ellen nodded. "I thought about taking it out in a boat and dumping it into Narragansett Bay, the way Ambrose Dexter supposedly dumped the Trapezohedron, but—" An eloquent shrug. "I'd be happy to listen to other suggestions."

Owen considered the machine. Though it was a good deal older than anyone in the room, it looked well maintained. "I might have one," he said. "I know somebody in Arkham who could really use a typewriter."

Ellen looked relieved. "That would be great," she said. "I want it out of Providence, and if it could be put to some worthwhile use, all the better." She glanced around. "Unless anyone has a different suggestion?"

Sam had a mouthful of pizza just then, and smiled and shook his head. The others seemed happy with the plan, so Ellen motioned to Owen, and he reached over and closed the lid. It shut with a loud click.

"End of an era," said Tom Castro.

CHAPTER 13

THE THING ON THE DOORSTEP

It was a good many hours later when Owen let himself into the little apartment where he'd stayed when he first came to Providence. Nobody else was using it yet, Julie Olmert had assured him, and fished the key out of a little locked box under the counter. Half a dozen of his friends among the Providence Starry Wisdom congregation had offered him a spare room for the night, but he knew from their expressions that doing otherwise was the better choice—a great many marriages and friendships strained close to the breaking point by Phaedra Dexter's machinations needed time and privacy to begin to heal.

The cramped little space that served as kitchen, dining room, and sitting room looked bare without the books he'd brought, but that was the only change. He put his duffel onto the floor by the couch and set the typewriter on the table, then considered the flat cardboard box he'd carried up from Sancipriani's. There had been so much paper to burn that plenty of pizza remained even after everyone had eaten their fill, and boxes of random slices went home with everyone who was willing to take one. Owen's box bulged at the top, it was that full. It took some effort to get it wedged into the little refrigerator under the kitchenette's one small counter.

Evening prayers followed, and then washing up: the little rituals of the night brought back some sense of normality to the shattered rhythms of the days just past. Once those were done, he crawled into bed. Exhaustion and the tolerably large amount of wine he'd taken in did their work, and plunged him promptly into dreamless sleep.

Toward dawn, though, he woke—or was it a vivid dream? He could not tell. Someone or something else was sitting at the foot of the bed, facing him. At times it looked like a cat with a woman's breasts, at times it looked like a vast dark shape with many tentacles and many eyes, and at times it looked like a woman of indeterminate age, dressed in shabby rumpled clothing, with uncombed hair and eyes that reflected back light at him.

"Everything's happened as I desired," she was saying in her silken voice. "You have the rituals, the Shining Trapezohedron is back in its proper place, the enemies of the Great Old Ones have new reasons to fear, the Yellow Sign struck hard and has recovered the books that were stolen—and I've made my will known even on the black pavements of Carcosa."

"Do the other Great Old Ones consider you a child still?" Owen asked her.

"I am a child still," she said, with a sudden smile. "But I won't be a child forever. They know, as I know, that when I'm grown I'll be mighty among the Great Old Ones—and now they know that I won't be slow to act even if it means defying my father the King."

"That seems risky."

"Oh, it is." The woman-breasted cat laughed, the sound ringing like bells. "And he won't forget me—or you. I've arranged for you to return to Arkham in safety, so you should be ready to take the bus as usual once day comes. When you reach home, have copies made of the rituals, beware the Yellow Sign, and remember that he knows even your unborn thoughts."

A silence came and went. "And Lydia and Charles—are they okay?" Owen asked then.

"Of course. I promised them their safety if they did as I asked, and I kept my side of the bargain as they kept theirs."

With another quick smile: "Just ulthward of this place, beneath an emerald sky, an ancient golden city stands above a plain with mountains far to the east and the ocean far to the west. The beings there know little of your species, but when two humans came to the city, one with pink skin, one with brown, they received a hospitable welcome."

Owen nodded slowly. "I wish them well," he said.

"They will think of you," said Phauz. A moment passed, then: "As will I."

"Thank you," said Owen.

She paused again, and then said in a wistful tone, "If I were of age to spawn, we would mate, your wife would have another little one to raise, and you and all your descendants would carry my blessing with them in life and death." She shrugged. "But it will be millions of years yet, as you count time, before I'm of age to spawn hatchlings of my own."

Before he could think of anything at all to say in answer to that, she stood and took on her human form. "But the blessing—you'll have that anyway." She bent suddenly, and her lips brushed his forehead.

He blinked awake, and found himself alone in the cramped little bedroom. The first light of dawn trickled in through the thin curtains covering the room's one window. He stretched, shook his head, and then went into the bathroom.

The mirror above the sink was only a foot wide and not much taller, and it had seen many better days, but it showed him his face as he came through the door. Something on the skin of his forehead looked odd, and he stopped, rubbed his eyes, took a closer look.

Something showed there that hadn't been present the night before: an irregular darkening of the skin. It was subtle enough that a casual glance might miss it, but as Owen blinked and stared at it, he realized that it was shaped like the footprint of a cat.

* * *

Prayer, meditation, his usual morning workout, and a cold shower left him feeling a little less shaken, and he went into the other room with a towel wrapped around his middle to see what he could find for breakfast. The refrigerator was empty except for the box of pizza, and the kitchen cabinets held some tea, some coffee, some salt and baking powder, and not much else. Back in his college days, a box full of cold leftover pizza for breakfast would have been a welcome prospect, but he considered it with a frown and decided that it might be worth waiting for something a little less challenging to the stomach.

He went to the stove, got a kettle heating for tea, and then went back into the bedroom to dress. By the time he returned to the kitchen, more or less ready for the day, the kettle was close to boiling. A few moments later he took it off the burner, filled a cup and got a bag steeping.

It was in the quiet moment that followed that he heard the noise.

Soft and rhythmic, it came whispering up through the fabric of the old building. Owen wondered at first if a tree branch was brushing against an outside wall in the wind, but a glance out the window showed only the faintest breeze. For a moment, as a car drove by somewhere in the middle distance, he thought the noise had stopped, but heard it again once quiet returned.

He got up after a moment, went to the door of the apartment, and opened it. Yes, the noise was clearer there, and seemed to be coming up the stairs from the alley door below.

That was when he guessed what it was. He hurried down the stair and opened the door. As he'd thought, a little huddled shape in a filthy hoodie and sweat pants stood slumped on the doorstep. Its head was bowed, and something that was not a hand protruded from one sleeve.

"Pierre?" he said, and the familiar four-eyed face turned up toward his.

He motioned for the creature to come inside. Once Pierre entered, he looked at the stair, at Owen, and drew himself up as though preparing for an ordeal. What Owen could see of the creature's face had an odd pinched look he didn't remember seeing there before, but he could guess what it meant.

"May I?" he asked, and reached down. Pierre gave him an unreadable look, but nodded. Owen picked him up and got him settled in the crook of one arm, and Pierre reached out with a tentacle and clung to his back for stability. The clothes were wet as well as filthy, but the creature wasn't as heavy as he'd expected, lighter than Barnabas in fact, and it was an easy matter for Owen to carry him up the stairs and bring him into the apartment.

"I'm guessing," Owen said then, "that you haven't eaten in days." That got a slow weary shake of the creature's head, and Owen pondered briefly. "Are you okay with cold pizza?"

Pierre looked up at him again and nodded with what looked like enthusiasm, so he set him down on one of the two chairs by the little dining room table, got out the box of pizza, set it on the table and opened it. "Help yourself."

He reached a tentacle, then stopped, pulled at the filthy garments. Owen said, "Yes, you can get rid of those if you want. We'll have to find you something clean anyway."

Pierre shrugged himself out of the hoodie, dropped it onto the floor. The sweat pants and a pair of ragged shoes followed them. Uncovered, he turned out to have four muscular tentacles and four short bent legs with clawed, webbed feet. His body, more or less barrel-shaped, was covered with something that looked like pale gray fur but moved in waves like cilia, and his neck was lean and flexible. He stretched and shook his tentacles as though the hoodie had left them feeling cramped, then picked up a piece of pizza Margherita and began to eat. Owen went to get his tea, then sat down in the other chair and after a moment, with a mental shrug, picked up a slice for himself.

The creature downed three slices before Owen finished one, then made a tentative gesture toward the teacup. "Of course,"

Owen said aloud. "I'm sorry, I should have thought of that. Do you want tea? Water?" The latter got a welcoming nod, so Owen got him a glass of water, and he lapped up most of it with his barbed tongue.

Pierre ate two more slices before sitting back in the chair, decidedly rounder about the middle than he had been, and considered Owen with expressionless eyes.

"I don't know if you know this yet, but Lydia's gone," Owen said then.

The creature nodded slowly.

"She's okay, and so is Charles—but they had to go to another realm, outside this world. She told me you can't follow her there, and she asked me to take care of you." Pierre looked at him, and he went on. "I'm fine with that. If you're willing to come to Arkham with me—that's where I live—we can find you a place to stay and make sure you get the things you need."

Pierre nodded again, then slowly extended a tentacle. It took Owen a moment to realize what the creature meant to communicate, but then he reached out his hand, and the tentacle wrapped around it, gripped with surprising firmness. "Deal," Owen said.

He ate more pizza while Pierre lapped up the last of his water and sat back again in the chair, evidently sated for the moment. "We'll be leaving today," Owen said, "on the same bus that brought you and Lydia here. Before we go, though, I want to see if I can get something less ragged for you to wear."

The creature glanced down at the sweats, and Owen guessed from the way he moved that he disliked them. "I know," he said. "Those have got to be uncomfortable to walk in, but most humans can't handle seeing you, you know."

Pierre nodded dolefully.

"Once we get home you won't have to worry about that," Owen reassured him. "My sister-in-law and my best friend's son have more tentacles than you do, and nobody makes a fuss about them. You'll fit right in."

* * *

It took Owen some time to find new clothing for Pierre, and a good deal more to say his goodbyes—long enough that Pierre had time to run a saltwater bath in the cramped little tub, scrub himself clean, and finish off the leftover pizza. Long before the bus was due at the stop downtown, though, the two of them set out down Federal Hill toward the skyscrapers. Owen had his duffel over one shoulder and the typewriter in its case in the other hand. Pierre wore a child-sized Brown University hoodie and sweat pants, and walked in the same slumped posture, face down and tentacles in pockets, Owen remembered so vividly from his arrival in Providence.

Most of the businesses they passed were still closed, but here and there one that had been shut had reopened its doors, and the music of the city was picking up again. Here a fado tune spilled from the door of a Portuguese eatery, there a Bach cantata rang out from the window of an apartment well above street level. A copy of the *Providence Journal* hanging in a shop window told Owen part of the reason: the Rhode Island state government had started issuing a temporary currency to pay its employees and its bills, and that seemed to be putting some life back into the local economy. Most of the signs in the windows now said CASH SCRIP AND TRADE ONLY, and here and there cheap photocopied posters announced an upcoming WaterFire festival. All around him, he could feel Providence struggling back to life.

Then there were the cats. They sat here and there on balconies, porches, windowsills and roofs, watching Owen and Pierre with inscrutable eyes all the way down the hill into downtown Providence. The first time Owen saw one, he bowed to it, knowing who would see the gesture. The cat did not react at all, nor did Owen expect anything different.

He was not sure whether he could expect to see Phauz in one of her usual haunts among the concrete and the skyscrapers. The stray cats were there, squabbling over territory and moving in and out of shadows, but she was not. When he and Pierre got to the sidewalk where the bus stopped, though, a different though equally familiar face turned toward them with evident relief—the young man from Arkham with the Aztec face who'd ridden down with them on the bus two days before. He was standing next to a young woman and a few pieces of cheap luggage.

"Hi," he said. "Do you know if the bus is going to come today?"

"That's what I've been told," said Owen.

"Oh, good." Then, with an uneasy look: "Do you know if the driver ..."

"You shouldn't worry about the driver," the young woman told him, smiling. She had dark curling hair, slightly protuberant eyes, and a complexion just a little to the green side of olive. A faint tang of salt seemed to fill the air around her.

"She's right," Owen said. "It's just one of those things."

The young man looked uncomfortable, but nodded. "I'm John Romero, by the way. This is my girlfriend Sybil Morrow."

"Pleased to meet you," Owen said, shaking hands. "Owen Merrill."

The young woman's eyes went wide. "It's a pleasure to meet you, Mr. Merrill."

"From Westerly, by any chance?" Owen asked her, and she beamed and nodded.

John Romero was looking uneasily down at Pierre. To forestall awkward questions, Owen said, "And you're from Arkham, I know."

"Well, these days," he admitted. "I grew up in Boston, but my folks are from New Mexico. I'm going to Miskatonic—they were saying it was going to shut down for good, with the financial crisis and everything, but it turns out they're going to be offering classes in my major this fall anyway."

"That's good to hear," said Owen. "How's that going to work?"

"What I heard," John replied, "is that some programs—the ones that are staying open—are moving to the old campus downtown, and taking work-study hours in place of tuition.

It's just a temporary thing, until things get straightened out again."

Owen nodded. Just a temporary thing: that had Miriam Akeley's deft fingerprints all over it, a way to ease students and professors alike into an unfamiliar reality.

Just then the growl of a diesel engine came echoing down the street. John turned to look, sagged in evident relief as the bus came into sight. A moment later he gathered up the luggage.

"Do you need a hand with any of that?" Owen asked.

"No, I'm fine," he said. "Sybil packed light in case we had to walk."

The bus pulled up then, and the door clanked and hissed open. Whether or not it was the same shapeless thing behind the wheel, concealed beneath the baggy clothing, was not a question Owen cared to ask. He waited for Sybil and John to board, then made sure Pierre was with him and followed them up the stair into the bus.

* * *

The miles and the minutes rolled past. Pawtucket, Woonsocket, and Attleboro slipped by, and then the bus passed through state forests and green belts that looked even wilder than they had when he'd last taken the bus through them. The southern suburbs of Boston still seemed to crouch under the burden of the economic crisis, but the sun came out from behind clouds as they passed the signs pointing to Quincy. Owen looked out the window to eastward, wondering which of the distant heights had been Merry Mount. The persecuted so easily become the persecutors, he thought. All things considered, isn't that what I've done?

The sunlight on the distant trees brought him no answers. He glanced at Pierre, slumped wearily on the seat next to him; glanced back at Sybil and John, who were talking in low voices; thought of the Starry Wisdom congregation in Providence and the one in Arkham, the people he knew in each of them, one and all trying to cope with the confusions of a world that had been out of joint since the seven great temples of the Great Old Ones were destroyed and defiled by the *Dumu-ne Zalaga*; and then thought of the Great Old Ones themselves, riven by their own bitter quarrel, kept from manifesting their full power in the world by the dire rituals worked at the desecration of those temples, and thought: we're all caught up in this, driven to hard deeds by one terrible necessity or another. He remembered Phauz's face when she'd called her cats to tear a Radiance negation team to bloody shreds, and shuddered.

By late afternoon the bus came out of the hills south of Arkham beneath a clear blue sky. As the ruins of the abandoned Fair Isles Mall slid into the distance behind the bus and the outermost houses of Arkham came close, Owen went up front and asked the driver to stop at the corner of Pickman and Peabody.

Its only answer was a slight hunching that might have been a nod, but as the big brick mass of the former Knights of Pythias hall came into sight, the bus slowed to a stop.

"Here we go," Owen said to Pierre, and then turned. "Good luck with everything."

Sybil and John both thanked him, and Sybil said, "I hope we'll see you soon."

"You will," Owen replied. "Bye for now." He got his duffel down from the rack, and headed for the front with Pierre at his heels. The shapeless thing in the driver's seat extended a half-filled glove, pushed the button that opened the door. A few moments later Owen and Pierre stood on the sidewalk on Peabody Avenue as the bus pulled away in a cloud of diesel smoke, heading down the slope toward the Miskatonic River.

"Just a couple of blocks," said Owen, shouldering his duffel again. Pierre nodded without lifting his head, and followed Owen's lead around the corner onto Pickman Street. Familiar housefronts went by, and then they turned again, passed three more houses, and came to the plain white door with 638 beside it in old-fashioned metal numbers.

He was scarcely inside when Asenath came pelting into the entry to throw her arms around him. "Dad! Oh, I'm so glad you're back. I was really scared."

"I'm fine, Sennie," he said. "It's good to be back."

"Owen?" The couch in the living room creaked, and then Laura came into the entry as fast as her tentacles could carry her. Owen had just enough time to set the duffel and the type-writer case down before she flung herself into his arms.

"Oh, hi," Asenath said behind him. "Who're you?"

"His name is Pierre," said Owen over his shoulder. "He can't talk but he understands English." Then: "Pierre, you don't have to hide here."

Laura blinked, and glanced past him as the creature lifted his fourfold face. "Father Dagon," she said. "Pierre, I didn't know any of your people still existed."

That got a sudden intent look from the creature, an interested look from Asenath, and a baffled look from Owen. "You know what he is?" he asked.

"Why, yes," said Laura. "Have you read the book by Johannes Aldrovandus that Jenny's family has, the one with the chapter on kyrrmis? That and Mulder's *Secret Mysteries of Asia* both talk about the Black Pilgrimage and the familiars who come from the waters of the Dead Sea." Then, half turning toward the creature: "Pierre, would you like some salt water?"

The creature nodded enthusiastically. "I'll get it, Mom," said Asenath, and trotted into the kitchen with a bright smile.

A few minutes later Pierre was curled up in one of the arm-chairs, divested of his uncomfortable clothing, lapping up salt water from a tall glass; Asenath had gone pattering up the stairs to find a black hooded Sunday school robe she'd outgrown, for their guest to wear; and Owen and Laura were sitting on the couch. "And Dr. Angell's papers?"

"I've got them," said Owen. He got up, went out to the entry, and retrieved his duffel. Then, picking up the typewriter case: "And something else—a gift for you."

She recognized it as he brought it back into the living room. "Owen, thank you! That's so sweet of you—and when you had so much else to worry about."

"We'll have to get someone to repair the letter O," he said. "It's broken."

Laura stared at him then, her mouth open. After a moment, she started to laugh. "I really do feel sorry for your enemies," she said. "The person who wrote those letters—"

"She's dead," Owen admitted. "Partly my doing, partly her own. I can tell you the whole story in a little while, if you want."

"Please," said Laura.

Later, after dinner, they sat on the couch again. Crockery clattered and water splashed as the children washed the dishes; Pierre, exhausted from whatever adventures he'd had finding his way to Owen's apartment, had gone upstairs already and settled down to sleep on the easy chair in Owen's study with a warm blanket over him. "Of course Pierre can stay with us," Laura said. "We'll work something out, and introduce him to everybody—especially to those with tentacles. He's got to be feeling pretty thoroughly lost." Glancing at him: "I don't imagine you found time to go to the ruined city by the Dead Sea."

"No, it was Lydia Ward," said Owen. "The woman who called herself Hannah Ward."

"Charles Dexter Ward's wife."

"Yeah."

She considered that for a long moment. "I hope they're happy," she said at last.

"So do I."

Laura smiled up at him, and then nestled her face into his shoulder.

A detail he hadn't mentioned yet occurred to him then. "Have you heard anything about a young lady named Sybil Morrow, from Westerly?"

Her eyes blinked open. "Why, yes. We had a letter from the Westerly lodge a few days ago. She wants to marry someone from outside—a Miskatonic student named John Romero— and the priestesses and elders in Westerly decided they'd probably be better off here."

"Where marriages to outsiders are a little less shocking?" he said, teasing.

Laura smiled, said nothing. He bent to kiss the top of her head, drew in a lungful of the salt scent that surrounded her, kissed her again.

* * *

Sun streamed in at an angle through tall windows, splashed over two bookcases and a big comfortable desk, oaken relics of an older time. Visible through age-blurred glass, recently pruned trees half filled the old Miskatonic quad downtown, by turns hiding and revealing the sturdy brick walls and ornate windows of the building on the far side.

"I'm impressed," said Owen.

"Thank you." Miriam Akeley allowed a wistful smile. "I admit I'll miss the oddities of Wilmarth Hall, if only because they're so familiar. Still, this is nicer, no question." With a glance at Laura: "And more convenient. I hope you didn't have any trouble with the ramp."

"Not at all," said Laura. She was sitting in a wheelchair, her tentacles looped comfortably around the footplates. On the way there she'd had them folded up neatly under her skirt to suggest amputation below the knees. The deception allowed her to get around the neighborhood without attracting unwanted attention. "It's good to finally be able to visit you in your office."

"I hope I'll see you here often," Miriam said. "I—"

A quiet knock sounded on the door, and Miriam went at once to answer it. "Good afternoon, Jenny."

"Hi, Miriam." The sorceress looked tired, but brightened when she saw the others in the room. "Hi, Laura. Hi, Owen. Miriam tells me you have some good news."

"Yeah," said Owen. "Welcome back. Should I ask about your trip?"

"Oh, it was a lot better than it could have been." She found a chair, slumped into it. "I only got shot at twice, I met some really interesting witches and initiates and a couple of bona fide madmen, which was entertaining, and the economic thing didn't really hit there until I was back in Vyones—though there's more than one European country in real trouble now. But the very short version is that if the Angell papers got there at all, there aren't any surviving copies. I did find some oddities, though. Do you know if anybody on this side of the Atlantic has a copy of the original Greek version of the *Testament of Carnamagos*?"

That got sudden startled looks from the other three. "There was supposed to be one in California a century ago," said Miriam, "but I haven't heard anything of it recently."

"I've got one," Jenny said. "It's not something you want to read without serious protective amulets on hand, but it has some very useful things in it."

Someone else knocked on the door. Miriam answered it again. "Good afternoon, Abelard. I hope everything's fine upstairs?"

"Very much so." Abelard Whipple waited while Miriam locked the door behind him, then took Jenny's hand, and Owen's. "I don't believe we've met," he said to Laura.

"My wife Laura," said Owen. "A priestess in the Esoteric Order of Dagon. Laura, this is Dr. Abelard Whipple, the restricted collections librarian." He grinned. "You know, Dr. Whipple, this is the first time I've ever seen you outside Orne Library's basement."

"True enough—but the collection's here now, and so I'm here as well." He took Laura's hand. "A pleasure to meet you, Mrs. Merrill."

More chairs made their appearance. Once everyone was seated, Owen opened his backpack and pulled out stacked and stapled photocopies. "Here you go," he said, handing them out to Miriam, Jenny, and Abelard. "Courtesy of the Esoteric Order of Dagon's office copier. This is the original set of rituals Angell got, and this is the commentary he wrote later on."

"How much later?" Miriam asked, puzzled. "He died, what? Maybe a year after he got the rituals, if the diary you two found is accurate."

"Charles Dexter Ward revived him," Owen said. "He's still living in Providence."

Miriam stared at him, then: "Do you think he'd be willing to talk to visitors?"

"I don't know," Owen admitted, "but I can write to him and ask."

"Please do," said Jenny. She had been leafing through the commentary, nodding slowly. "He's got a remarkable grasp of some very unusual branches of the lore." She looked up. "Laura, you probably know the Aklo formulae better than anyone else here. Have you ever seen anything like the parallel structure in the fourth and sixth incantations Angell got?"

"There are a few passages in the Dho-Hna formula and the Aklo Sabaoth that aren't completely different," Laura said, "and the fifteenth summoning in chapter five of *The Mysteries of the Worm* might be a garbled version, but that's all I can think of."

Abelard glanced up at her. "There was a time when the Esoteric Order of Dagon had quite a reputation for scholarship," he said. "I'm glad to see that's still the case."

Laura blushed and thanked him. Thereafter, for some minutes, no one said anything; three pairs of eyes studied the Angell papers, while Laura waited calmly and Owen glanced around the room, thinking of the office in Wilmarth Hall he'd known so well ten years before.

"These are important," said Jenny finally. "Extremely important. I'm not sure they're enough to do the job all by themselves—"

"That's what Charles Dexter Ward said," Owen agreed.

She gave him a startled glance, then nodded once and went on. "But we're a big step closer, and it's just possible that if we can correlate this with the other bits of lore we've got already, we might be within reach of it."

"If there's any help I can offer," said Abelard, "why, by all means ask." Owen glanced at him, but the mask of genial distraction had not slipped in the least.

Later on, when Jenny and Abelard had gone upstairs to the new restricted stacks of the library to consult some archaic text in a language none of the others could read, Laura, Owen, and Miriam remained in the office. "I hope it won't be any kind of imposition," said Laura, "but I'd like to ask your advice about something involving—well, dreaming, and kyrrmis."

"It's not an imposition at all," Miriam assured her. "What do you have in mind?"

"It's Asenath," Laura said. "I told you about the visit we had from Phauz." Miriam nodded. "Ever since then, she's been having strange dreams. She says she goes to places where her body looks twisted and wrong, and everything goes off at odd angles."

"I know those places," said Miriam. "Some of them, at least."

Laura nodded. "But I was wondering if you could teach her—well, what she needs to know to stay out of trouble anywhere she's likely to end up."

"I'd be happy to do that," said Miriam. "Has she started studying with Martha Price yet? No? I'll talk to Martha about it anyway—we met for lunch yesterday."

"I'm glad to hear that," Owen said.

"In a certain sense, that's your doing," Miriam told him. "Yours and Laura's both, rather. The suggestion you made about classes seemed worth following up, so I talked to various people about it, and it's an understatement to say they were enthusiastic." With a smile and a slight shrug: "So there will be classes—and yes, we'll be happy to take tuition in kind."

"I'll have to talk to the elders," said Laura with an answering smile, "but I think we can keep you and the other professors well supplied with fish."

"That," said Miriam, "would be very welcome." Then: "But I'll want to talk to Sennie and learn more about what she dreams. Most children go to the Dreamlands often enough, but it's pretty much unheard of for someone to go outside the four dimensions entirely without some very specific training. If that's the gift Phauz gave her, it's a strange one."

Laura nodded. "That's not surprising, given Phauz's parentage."

Miriam gave her a puzzled look. "I thought she was Shub-Ne'hurrath's daughter."

"Yes," said Laura, "but the King in Yellow's her father."

"And she defied him to get us these papers," said Owen. His gesture indicated the photocopies.

Miriam nodded slowly. "The Great Old Ones are still divided against one another," she said after a moment. "Nor will they join hands again—that's what Atal told me when we translated the *Fourth Book of Hsan*—until the stars come round right again and Great Cthulhu wakes from his sleep. But there's another thing Atal told me in Ulthar one evening, when we'd finished work on one of the really obscure parts of the *Pnakotic Manuscript*, and Randolph had come to visit." With a smile: "A certain amount of wine was involved. Atal's teacher Barzai the Wise told him that it wouldn't be the eldest and mightiest of the Great Old Ones who would bring the Weird of Hali to its fulfillment—it would be the youngest."

"Phauz," Owen said.

The professor nodded again. "Maybe getting us these papers is the thing that will do it. Maybe the Weird of Hali will do it. Maybe it'll be something else entirely. Maybe we'll never know." She picked up her copy of Angell's papers. "But at least we have something to work with, for now."

ACKNOWLEDGMENTS

Like the previous novels in this series, this fantasia on a theme by H.P. Lovecraft depends even more than most fiction on the labors of earlier writers. Lovecraft's near-lifelong residence in Providence inspired him to set some of his most iconic stories there, and three of them—"The Call of Cthulhu," "The Haunter of the Dark," and the short novel *The Case of Charles Dexter Ward*—provided much of the raw material for my tale. I am also indebted to stories by three of the writers Lovecraft most admired, M.R. James, Arthur Machen, and Clark Ashton Smith, for important elements of plot and setting.

The geography of Providence in my tale is partly real and partly fictional. The Stampers Hill neighborhood actually existed in Lovecraft's time, but like many other minority residential and business districts in the US, it was deliberately eliminated by "urban renewal" projects after the Second World War. Bannister University is my invention; the brown alleys of Federal Hill and the site of the Mother Church were Lovecraft's.

Readers who are curious about Phauz, the woman-breasted cat-goddess of Hyperborea, may want to know that her sole original appearance was in a 1935 letter from Clark Ashton Smith to Robert H. Barlow. Whether or not Smith planned to reference her in some unwritten Hyperborean tale of his own, the joint mythos Smith shared with Lovecraft and their fellow authors has a definite goddess shortage, and this one was far too interesting to be neglected.

For the references to African-American magic in the story, I am indebted for a great deal of instruction to Catherine Yronwode, proprietress of the Lucky Mojo Curio Company and teacher of the Hoodoo Rootwork Correspondence Course, and also to Carolyn Morrow Long's lively and solidly researched book *Spiritual Merchants: Religion, Magic, and Commerce*.

My philosophical debts remain essentially what they were in earlier volumes of this series. I also owe, once again, debts to Sara Greer and Dana Driscoll, who read and critiqued the manuscript. I hope it is unnecessary to remind the reader that none of the above are responsible in any way for the use I have made of their work.

Printed in the USA
CPSIA information can be obtained
at www.ICGtesting.com
JSHW031920200524
63489JS00013B/480

9 781912 573950